Also by Pete Hautman

Hole in the Sky
Mrs. Million
Stone Cold
Ring Game
The Mortal Nuts
Mr. Was
Short Money
Drawing Dead

Rag Man

A Novel

Pete Hautman 1952

SIMON & SCHUSTER
New York · London · Toronto · Sydney · Singapore

SIMON & SCHUSTER
Rockefeller Center
1230 Avenue of the Americas
New York, NY 10020

For information regarding special discounts for bulk purchases,
please contact Simon & Schuster Special Sales:
1-800-456-6798 or business@simonandschuster.com

Designed by Lauren Simonetti

Manufactured in the United States of America

10 9 8 7 6 5 4 3 2 1

Library of Congress Cataloging-in-Publication Data
Hautman, Pete.
Rag man / Pete Hautman.
p. cm.
1. Businessmen—Fiction. 2. Business ethics—Fiction. I. Title.
PS3558.A766 R3 2001
813'.54—dc21   2001032849

ISBN 0-7432-0559-6

To Mary

There is no crime of which one cannot
imagine oneself to be the author.
—Johann W. von Goethe

Rag Man

I see his fingers slip and for a heartbeat he is balanced on the narrow rock shelf, arms wheeling, eyes immense with fear, jaw hard with effort, then he is falling backward and hope crosses his face, only for an instant, as if he expects a raft of hands to catch him and gently set him upright once again. The half smile comes and goes in less than a blink; the hands are not there for him. His mouth opens wide and his body eclipses his face and I see the bottoms of his huaraches as he does a sprawling backward midair flip and his head strikes the sharp lava shelf twenty feet below. There must be a sound, machete cleaving coconut, but the wind and surf are all I hear as his body twists and continues toward the sea. He hits another outcropping, shredding his guayabera, white fabric blooming red, and again he skids down the razor rock, and I lose sight of him but somehow I am still with him because I am falling, too.

Part One

1

Mack MacWray had quit smoking eight years ago on his thirtieth birthday. He now sat on the empty cutting table puffing on a Virginia Slim. On the concrete floor below his feet, twelve cigarette butts lay amidst scraps of cloth, bits of colored thread, and a scattering of industrial dust bunnies.

He stared through the haze of gray smoke at rows of silent black-and-silver sewing machines crouching on their tables. Frozen mechanical mosquitoes. The sour taste of burning filter forced him to drop his thirteenth cigarette. He leaned forward, looked past the edge of the table to make sure it had not fallen on something flammable. As bad as things were, he was not ready to light his own pyre.

~

The way Lars had explained it, starting a new business would be like picking cash off the ground. Just borrow a little money, buy some fabric, lease a building, order a few sewing machines, print up a couple hundred order forms. Lars would take care of the sales and marketing, and all Mack had to do was sew the stuff together.

"Hire some Hmongs," Lars had said. "The Twin Cities are full of Hmongs, sew like demons, every one. You run out of Hmongs you get yourself some Laotians. You run out of Laotians, hire some Flips or Thais or Mexicans. We run out of workers here, we move to Florida, no more winters, fill up a line with Haitians and Cubans."

"You forgot the Indians." Mack was one-eighth Cherokee himself, or so his grandmother on his mother's side, whose hair had remained jet black well into her seventies, had told him. Mack's own wavy hair was a mongrel mix of near black with hints of red and a few stray white hairs on the temples.

"Hell, Mack, you know Indians can't sew." Lars slapped Mack's back. "They're worse'n the goddamn Swedes." He laughed.

That was six months ago. They'd been sitting in Mack and Paula MacWray's kitchen drinking some peculiar raspberry-flavored beer that Lars had brought. Mack had just arrived home from his job at Linkway Sportswear. Lars had been sitting in his kitchen waiting for him, ruddy from eighteen holes at the Minikhada Club. He had pitched his big idea for nearly an hour, making it sound better and better, patiently overcoming each of Mack's objections and concerns, Paula with her back against the stove, listening, biting her lip, pushing her thumb in and out of the neck of her beer bottle.

"You know so much about it," Mack said, "What do you need me for?"

Lars looked at Mack. "You kidding me? You're the man. What do I know about manufacture?" He pronounced it *man-uh-fatcha*. "I'm just the people guy."

That had stuck in Mack's mind: *the people guy.* He had thought, What does that make me? The machine guy? No. Lars had called him something else.

"You're the rag man," Lars had said.

Mack MacWray and Lars Larson. Mac-Lar Manufacturing. The rag man and the people guy. What a team.

~

When Lars Larson had first been hired as national sales manager at Linkway Sportswear, he had made it a point to get to know the production staff. Mack, who ran the sewing operation, had been sitting in his glass-fronted cubicle looking out over the Linkway factory floor when a tall heavyset man holding an unlit cigar between his teeth walked in gripping an A-18430 men's golf shirt in his left fist. A large diamond set into a heavy gold ring adorned his middle finger. Red scalp showed beneath flaxen hair.

Mack, irritated that this big stranger had barged into his office, said, "Something I can do for you?"

The big man thrust out his right hand. "Lars Larson," he said, grinning. "The new sales guy." He held up the shirt. "This is one hell of a shirt. You really know how to make 'em."

Mack shook the man's big soft dry hand. "Mack MacWray," he said.

Lars laughed. "Lars Larson and Mack MacWray. Sounds like we're gonna make a hell of a team. You golf?"

Mack said, "Used to. No time, these days."

Lars laughed even harder. He had a good, hearty, appreciative laugh that made Mack feel clever. "Good! That's good! Very funny. What do they call that? Ironic! It's ironic!" He was referring to the fact that Linkway manufactured golf shirts, club protectors, golf towels, and other country club accessories. It really wasn't all that funny. Or ironic. But Lars Larson's laugh was infectious. And, Mack soon learned, the man knew how to listen. Once or twice a week he would drop by Mack's office to talk shop, letting Mack go on at length about the Linkway Sportswear product line, what was right with it and what was wrong, and how he would do things if he was in charge.

In time they had conceived starting their own company, and late last summer, over raspberry beers, Lars Larson had forced that dream to fruition.

～

Mack looked at the rows of sewing machines, exactly thirty-nine of them, many abandoned in midstitch, aprons hanging half sewn over the tables. He lit another Virginia Slim, silently thanking Gabriela Garcia for forgetting her smokes beside the pile of unsewn collars at machine number 19.

A few hours earlier, his workers had punched out for the last time. A lot of them hadn't even bothered. Mack had stood near the Simplex time clock and told his gathered employees, all forty-seven of them, not to return to work the following morning.

"We have to close up shop for a while," he said in his usual matter-of-fact, frozen-faced manner. God, he hated that, dying inside but

15

coming across as wooden faced as a goddamn cigar store Indian. No. Not a wooden Indian. A rag man, nothing inside. Forty-four women and three men staring back at him, waiting to hear the next thing. The date they were to return. Another place they could find work. The encouraging something. Anything. But he'd had nothing more to say, nothing to give them. Then came the questions, diminutive Asian women raising their hands like children in a classroom. How long was "a while"? He had no idea. Would they get their paychecks on Thursday? He didn't know. He hoped so. He would try to get them something. He could not promise anything, not anymore. Should they look for another job? After a long pause he had said, "Yes, probably."

One woman, Merlita Amurao, refused to believe it.

"Where Mr. Lar?" she demanded, stamping her foot. "Mr. Lar take care of!"

Mr. Lar, Mack wanted to say, is the reason this has happened. Mr. Lar is the one who is sitting on a beach somewhere spending your paychecks on seafood cocktails and rum punch. Mr. Lar—smiling, hand-shaking, back-slapping Mr. Lar—is the one who has ripped us all off, Mrs. Amurao. Every one of us, Mrs. Amurao.

But he did not say anything like that. It would do no good. Lars was gone, the money was gone, and unless a solid gold meteorite landed in his front yard, Mac-Lar Manufacturing was history.

And not one of them would ever believe that it was Lars Larson's fault. Everybody loved Mr. Lars. Mr. Lars could fix anything. Mr. Lars always had time to listen, always had a spare twenty if one of his "family," as he called them, came up short the day before payday. Of course, the twenty no sooner came out of Lars's pocket than it was replaced from petty cash.

"I'm sorry, Mrs. Amurao," he said. "I don't know where Mr. Larson has gone."

~

He remembered sitting in his kitchen with his belly full of raspberry beer after Lars had left; turning to look at Paula, finding an unfamiliar intensity in her umber eyes.

"Well?" she said, now sitting across from him where Lars had been.

"Well what?"

"Are you going to do it?"

Mack felt a raspberry belch climbing his esophagus. He let it emerge silently. "I don't know," he said.

"How much money can you make working for Linkway? Even if you get your raise you'll be getting what? Forty thousand?"

"I could make forty-five with the bonus."

"And I'm bringing in about thirty." Paula was a travel agent with Gold Coast Travel.

Mack drank the last of his third raspberry beer. It wasn't so bad once you got used to it. "That's seventy-five thousand dollars a year."

"Lars says you could make ten times that in your own business."

"Lars is a dreamer."

Paula leaned forward. Her nails dug into his wrist. "Maybe that's what we need."

~

The next week both Mack and Lars gave notice. Mac-Lar Manufacturing became a reality. Lars brought in close to half a million dollars in purchase orders before they had bought their first yard of poly-cotton twill. Mack remembered sitting in his kitchen with Lars just a few short weeks after their first meeting, paging through the purchase orders, adding up the numbers. Sixteen thousand tricolor smocks for the Pizza America chain. Seven thousand embroidered golf shirts for a Budweiser promotion. And the biggie: a contract to provide uniforms for Airlift International truck drivers—over $400,000 a year in shirts, vests, and jackets.

"How'd you know what to quote them?"

Lars had laughed. "I just know what people will pay. You can sew a jacket for eighteen bucks, can't you?"

Mack thought he could. The numbers looked good. Damn good. Too good to be true? Not according to Lars.

"This is a people business, Mack. People give me their business because they want to. They like me. They trust me. All we have to do is rent some space, buy a few machines, buy the fabric, sew it up, ship it, bill it."

"What am I supposed to buy fabric *with?*"

Lars grinned "We borrow against these." He pushed the purchase orders across the table. "You know a banker, don't you?'"

Mack's cousin Bob Seaman, a commercial loan officer at First Star Bank, fell in love with Lars and his purchase orders at first sight. One meeting resulted in a line of credit sufficient to lease space in a Maple Grove office park, buy machines and fixtures, and order enough fabric and thread to circle the globe. Mack hired a dozen Hmong sewers, a pattern man, a fabric cutter, three packing-and-shipping people. Lars paid an artist $2,000 to design a logo. He hired a statuesque blonde named Rita Monbeck as bookkeeper and office manager. He ordered thousands of embossed business cards, reams of stationery, two hundred Sheaffer pens, and six dozen coffee mugs imprinted with their new logo. They spent nearly $200,000 in three weeks.

It had been an exciting time—everyone fresh and eager, new orders and new challenges coming in daily, everybody feeling a part of it, feeling the company grow. Mack quickly gave in to Lars's heady, action-oriented business style. When their line of credit became strained, it seemed picayune to hold anything back. Mack put up his house, car, retirement account, and whole-life policy to coax another eighty thousand out of First Star Bank. Lars offered to sell his diamond ring, which he claimed was worth $10,000, but somehow— Mack wasn't sure how or why—that never became necessary. Lars insisted that Mack become the majority shareholder, since he was providing most of the collateral. Mack also got the title of president.

A mere six weeks after that first meeting over raspberry beer, Mack watched the first red-white-and-blue Budweiser shirts being pressed, folded, and shrink-wrapped in bundles of twelve.

"Think of them as money in your pocket, Macanudo," Lars had said. "Every shirt is another three dollars twelve cents, net-net." Lars Larson was not only a supersalesman, he was also a whiz with the numbers. He could calculate the profit margin on an order with astonishing accuracy. Mack, more comfortable with his hands on the product than fingering computer keys, let Lars and Rita Monbeck handle all the financial details of the business.

The twelve sewers soon became twenty-four. They added a second shift. Training was becoming a serious problem, and product quality, especially on the jacket line, was suffering. More than twenty percent of their light jackets were unshippable. He tried to get Lars to ease off on his delivery promises.

Lars said, "Macanudo, you either have to grab the gold ring or ride around in circles forever. I know you can do it, buddy." They were making money—a lot of money, according to the numbers—but cash flow was a serious problem. "It's all about how fast we can pump the stuff out the door," Lars explained. "Every hundred bucks you ship is forty in our pockets. Problem is, every hundred bucks we ship is costing us sixty now and we won't see the cashola for thirty to sixty. Hell, we're giving the Airlift people ninety days. Got to. By the way, Rita needs another body to help with customer service. She's handling a ton of calls."

"Maybe we're trying to grow too fast."

"Mack, buddy, pal, don't say that! All we need's another couple hundred thou, just for a few months. The Airlift money starts to come in, we're golden."

That was when Mack and Lars had approached Paula's parents, Hal and Joyce Byrnes. What was really pathetic, looking back on it, was how eager and excited the elderly couple had been to cash in their mutual funds and invest in a "real business." Mac-Lar gobbled up their $280,000 nest egg like a hungry possum.

Maybe he should have seen it coming. Of course he should have. But it wasn't until a few days ago that the alarm bells had started clanging.

Mack had been out on the sewing floor trying to solve a problem with Mrs. Lu's binding station. He liked working with the machines and fabrics. He'd always been a hands-on guy, more comfortable thinking with his fingers than juggling numbers. He liked solving production puzzles. In this case, the bias tape used to trim the edges of the Pizza America smocks was not feeding properly—either the metal folder on her machine was out of adjustment or there was a problem with the tape itself. Mack was kneeling before the machine, cranking it by hand, watching the way the tape inched through the sculpted steel folder, when his phone rang. He frowned, staring intently at the bias tape. It was the folder. It had to be.

He unclipped the phone from his belt and punched the talk button. "Mack here."

"Mack!" It was his cousin Bob Seaman, the banker. "I've been trying to get through to Lars all day. You know where he is?"

Mack did not know. Neither Lars nor Rita had shown up at work yet.

Bob said, "I really have to talk to him, Mack."

"Is there a problem? Something I can help you with?"

He heard Bob draw a shaky breath. "You've got a bit of an overdraw, Mack. I'm wondering if maybe Rita forgot to make a deposit?"

"I don't know, Bob. I'll check into it. But don't we have some sort of line of credit with you guys?"

"It's maxed out, Mack."

"Oh. How much are we short?"

"About a hundred sixty thousand dollars," Bob said.

Mack said nothing for a moment, his eyes fixed on Mrs. Lu's machine. "There must be some kind of mistake."

"I'll say. Have Lars or Rita call me, would you?"

"Sure, Bob." From this angle he could see the problem. The folder was not properly aligned. The two screws had probably loosened, then been retightened by Mrs. Lu herself. The sewers did not like to wait for Mack to fix their machines. They were paid bonuses for meeting production goals and so resented the downtime. Mrs. Lu had probably used a nail file or something to retighten her folder and had slightly altered its alignment—not that she would ever admit to it.

Mack hung up and went back to work on the folder. Five minutes later Mrs. Lu was back to binding smocks, and Mack was on his way to Lars's condo in Edina, expecting to interrupt Lars and Rita having themselves a little nooner.

Of course, they were gone.

~

He imagined them now, the two of them, lying out on a beach somewhere, bodies turning slowly brown against the white sand. Little umbrellas in their drinks. Lars sucking on a twenty-dollar Cuban cigar. Mack wished upon him melanoma, cirrhosis, and inoperable lip cancer.

He imagined himself driving home, opening the door, telling Paula what had happened. Telling her that Mac-Lar was bankrupt, gutted, destroyed. For the past two days, as everything had come crashing down, he'd said nothing to her, pretending that everything was okay at work, putting off the inevitable. What would she say when he told her they were broke, that they owed hundreds of thousands of dollars, that her parents' nest egg was gone? In his mind he saw her put on her brave face, trying not to blame him but failing. He felt her disappointment. His skin crawled with shame.

Mack pushed his finger into the wrinkled pack of Virginia Slims and tore through the top, looked inside. Empty. He crumpled it and dropped it on the littered floor. He slid down off the edge of the table and walked through the factory toward the front entrance. He needed more cigarettes. Real cigarettes. Winstons or Marlboros or something stronger. Make a solid commitment to his reawakened addiction. Having made the decision to start smoking again, he felt other inhibitions giving way. He would go to a bar where there would be a cigarette machine. He would have a drink. He would get drunk. He would get drunk and he would keep drinking until he figured out what he was going to say to Paula.

~

"You wanna know who I am? I'll tell you who I am. I'm the rag man."

The bartender, a slim, balding, middle-aged man with exceptionally long fingers, said, "Yes sir."

"You know who you are?"

"Sir?"

"You're Jeeves. I'm gonna call you Jeeves."

The bartender blinked. "Very good, sir."

An hour earlier Mack had walked into the Oasis, bought a pack of Winstons from the machine by the door, and planted himself on a stool. He had ordered a gin martini, and then another. Four plastic swords were now lined up on the bar. The pack of cigarettes was half empty. Mack tipped up his glass and emptied it into his mouth. "Gettin' dry," he said.

"Will you be driving tonight, sir?"

"No," he lied.

The bartender scooped a shakerful of ice, took a bottle of Gordon's gin in one hand and a bottle of Martini & Rossi in the other, and let the clear fluids slide over the cubes.

"You're good at your job," Mack said.

"Thank you, sir." The bartender swirled the shaker gently with one hand as he placed a clean glass on the bar.

"I was good at my job."

"Yes sir."

Mack watched the ice-cold mixture slither into the glass, marveling at the invisible transformation. The bartender stabbed an olive with a white plastic broadsword and balanced it across the rim of the glass. He set a napkin in front of Mack and carefully placed the fresh martini upon it.

"Thank you, Jeeves."

"You are most welcome, sir."

The corners of Mack's mouth drew back. He knew he was smiling but, thankfully, he could not feel a thing.

2

Mack usually called when he was going to be late. Was traffic bad? Had he received an important phone call just as he was walking out the door?

Paula MacWray busied herself in the kitchen. Friday was Mack's night to cook, but she was getting hungry. He could make it up to her. She put a pot of water on the stove for pasta, poured a jar of marinara sauce into a saucepan, and set it over a low burner. She made a green salad, then opened a bottle of Grain Belt and turned on the TV.

By seven-thirty she became concerned enough to call Mac-Lar.

The phone rang but was not answered, not even a recorded message. She began to think about car accidents. No, he probably had a meeting and had forgotten to tell her. Mack had seemed preoccupied the past few days. Something was bothering him but he didn't want to talk about it. Mack had never been much of a communicator. She tried calling Lars at his condo, but there was no answer there either. She moved from anger to dread and back again.

A little after eight she put a handful of fettuccine into the water, which had been simmering for an hour, and opened another beer. She ate her dinner while watching a *Seinfeld* rerun.

By nine o'clock she was bouncing between imagining Mack crushed beneath a runaway semi and seeing him in the sack with that bottled-blond secretary or bookkeeper or controller or whatever they were calling her this week, that Rita Manbait.

No. Rita had a thing going with Lars. Besides, Mack had never given her any reason to mistrust him. She considered drinking another beer but decided to have a cup of coffee instead. She might need it for whatever was to come.

~

Paula was half asleep in a living room chair when she heard a car coming up the street, raised her head, saw headlights flash across the ceiling. She heard tires crunching and a soft crackling noise followed by a dull *thud* that shook the house. She ran to the front door and flipped on the light. Someone had missed the driveway and driven across the front lawn into the spirea bushes, crushing them into the side of the house. The car door opened; a figure staggered out.

Mack.

~

How had he driven all the way across town without killing someone? The man could hardly walk. Even with her half holding him up, he fell twice on the way from the car to the front door. She finally got him inside and dumped him on the sofa.

23

"What's going on, Mack?" she asked.

His eyes roved, landed on her. "Gin martini please, hold the vermouth," he said, his voice remarkably clear. "Hold the fucking olive too." He laughed.

Paula was startled. Mack was no prude, but he never talked like that at home.

"Mack?"

"Christ, I don't know. Is that who I am?"

Paula wanted to smack him but she could not hold back a smile. It was so unusual to see him this way. "I'm going to get you a cup of coffee."

"Gin martini please, hold the fucking coffee," he called after her.

What had gotten into him? She had seen Mack drunk maybe twice in the ten years they'd been married, once after his father's funeral and once when an old college roommate had come to visit and they spent all night drinking rum and Cokes and reminiscing. She wasn't angry at him for being drunk. It was almost amusing. But she was plenty mad that he'd gone and done it without calling her—and then driven himself home. Paula poured a mug of coffee, not too full. He would probably spill it all over himself, so she added some cool water before bringing it to him.

"Your martini, sir."

Mack gave the mug a bleary examination. "Kinda dark," he said after a moment.

"So, what's the occasion, martini boy?" She was thinking that he and Lars might have been celebrating something. A big order, maybe. It didn't have to be something bad. She sat down across from him.

Mack let his head fall back. He closed his eyes and his jaw sagged. Paula thought for a moment that he had passed out, but his eyes popped open and he shook his head violently.

"I got the spins."

"Yeah, you're probably going to throw up. I feel real sorry for you."

"Not gonna get sick."

"Mack, are you going to tell me what's going on? You come home four hours late shit-face drunk, I think I deserve a story."

Mack swallowed, frowned at the taste. "I need a drink," he said.
"Drink your coffee."

"Get me a beer and I'll tell you."

Paula sighed and stood up. She might as well humor him—what difference could it make now? She went to the refrigerator, but she'd drunk the last Grain Belt. She moved a few things around—catsup, pickled herring, some jellies and jams, a big jar of pickles. There, way in the back, on its side, a bottle of that raspberry beer that had been there for half a year. She opened the bottle and carried it back into the living room, but by the time she got there Mack's head had fallen back, his mouth hung open, and he was snoring.

Paula sat down. Was she angry? Mostly she was glad he'd made it home. He would probably have a very funny story in the morning. He would be embarrassed. He would feel terrible, both from the booze and from making her worry. Mack was such a nice guy—considerate, thoughtful, honest, kind. And not bad looking in a squinty-eyed, Irish sort of way. All qualities that had made her fall in love with him. And now that he was partnered up with Lars Larson he was a business success, too, something she had feared might never happen. Mack could be *too* nice. He didn't have an ounce of ruthlessness in him. She loved him for his gentle nature, but she wished at times that he had a bit more of the rogue in him. Alone, he simply didn't have that passion, that drive to succeed. But he was a hard worker, and now he had Lars, and the business was thriving, and life was about to become very, very good.

Paula took a sip of the raspberry beer. It wasn't that bad.

3

Mack sat at his desk and watched the two auditors from the bank pawing through the file cabinets. Neither of the men spoke to him or made eye contact. They noticed him only as much as they had to, to avoid bumping into him or stepping on his toes. Bob Seaman, wearing a somber maroon-and-gray rep tie, stood in the doorway examining his fingernails. Bob was barely into his thirties but he had the confident air of a man who was going places. Tall, handsome, smart, personable, and ambitious, Bob had moved quickly up the First Star ladder. The Mac-Lar loan fiasco was his first major embarrassment.

Before, Bob had always made it a point to ask Mack how Paula was doing. He had always had a joke and a bright white even-toothed smile and a bit of family gossip to share—they were cousins, after all. On this day he was not smiling. He wouldn't meet Mack's eyes. It was part of the shaming.

Mack lit a cigarette. One of the auditors turned and sniffed the air with a puzzled, mildly shocked expression.

"Would you mind not smoking?" he asked, his eyes focused on a spot a few inches to the left of Mack's ear.

"It's my office," Mack said.

Bob Seaman cleared his throat and shuffled his polished black wing tips.

The auditor shrugged and, with a dry cough, went back to rifling the files. Mack took a couple more drags, then stood up and walked out. Bob Seaman leaned away, giving him just enough room to pass through the doorway. Mack carried his cigarette out into the factory. He walked past the dormant machines to shipping, opened the overhead door, and sat on the edge of the loading dock to finish his smoke. Over the past ten days the cigarettes had become a lifesaver. It was the one thing he could do that would always make him feel a tiny bit better, if only for a few minutes.

The back parking lot was empty. Beyond lay several hundred acres of wheat fields. The perimeter of the parking lot was this year's suburban threshold. Next year the threshold would move outward as the fields gave way to yet another office park. More businesses with an eighty percent chance of failure. That, according to Jack Price, his bankruptcy attorney, was the going rate for new businesses.

"You're in the majority, Mr. MacWray," Jack Price had said. "Successful businesses are the exception, not the rule." Jack Price was always glad to see him—as long as his retainer held out. Jack Price assured him that no matter what happened, they couldn't take away his self-respect.

"If they can find it they can have it," Mack said.

"Now, now," said Jack Price.

Mack imagined Lars rising up out of the wheat field. What would he do? He gave himself superhuman powers, lifted Lars high over his head, dashed him against the cinder-block walls of the building. No. He imagined striking at him, his fist sinking deep into Lars's thick abdomen. No. Mack contorted his face, obliterating the images. What would he really do? His imagination failed, revealing only a dark, pulsing void.

Mack lit another cigarette and redirected his thoughts. Would Linkway rehire him? Not likely. Not after he'd quit to start a competing business. He would have to move, go south and east, where there were still plenty of jobs in the rag trade. But Paula wouldn't want to leave her job, her family. He couldn't ask her to do that—he'd done enough to her. He would have to drive a cab, or bag groceries. Lots of things he could do.

Sensing a presence, Mack turned his head. A slight, bearded, forty-ish man wearing an ecru sport coat over khaki trousers stood on the dock, hands in pockets, peering down at him. The man's eyes were faded blue behind glasses with clear, round plastic frames. His hair was the exact color of his jacket. He nodded at Mack, his mouth forming a V-shaped smile that might be read as apologetic or complacent.

"How's it going?" His voice was soft and high.

"The rest of the vultures are out front," Mack said.

The man bobbed his head again and sidled closer. "You're John MacWray, aren't you?"

"Mack," said Mack.

"Mack." The man squatted down and offered his hand. "Jerry Pleasant. I'm an investigator with the Hennepin County Sheriff's Office."

Mack felt a stroke of fear. He looked at the man's proffered hand as if it were a steel-jawed trap.

"I just stopped by to talk to you about your partner." The V smile deepened. "Actually, I'm on your side, Mack."

Mack felt something in his chest crumble. He took Jerry Pleasant's hand and shook it. It was all he could do to keep himself from hugging the man. Jerry Pleasant's eyes crinkled and his upper lip lifted, showing white incisors and yellowed canines.

"So, how are you doing?" Pleasant asked.

Mack shrugged, took a drag off his cigarette. He saw the smoke drifting toward Pleasant's face, waved it away.

Pleasant said, "Don't worry about it. Actually, I like the smell."

"You smoke?" Mack asked.

"No. But I wish I did."

Their eyes touched. Both men laughed, suddenly uncomfortable. Jerry Pleasant stood up, his knees crackling. He touched the bridge of his glasses and put his hands back in his pockets. "What is that?" he asked, looking out over the field. "Alfalfa?"

"I think it's wheat," Mack said.

"Ah. What does alfalfa look like?"

"I don't know." Mack flicked his cigarette out onto the parking lot and stood up. "So, you're some sort of policeman?"

"That's right." Pleasant gave Mack a sharp look. "I suppose you're going to tell me I don't look like a cop."

"I wasn't thinking that."

"My wife says I look like an accountant." Pleasant returned his attention to the view. "How do you know that's wheat?"

"Somebody told me. I think it was Lars that told me."

Pleasant nodded. He removed a small notebook from his sport coat and consulted it. "Would that be Theodore William Larson?"

"Yeah. Lars."

"Your partner."

"That's right." They were standing shoulder to shoulder at the edge of the loading dock. "So . . . did the bank call you?"

Pleasant took a few seconds to reply. He said, "I was there, at the bank, on another matter. Nothing to do with you. Your situation came up in conversation and I thought I'd look into it. To be perfectly honest with you, no charges have been filed at this point. First Star's complaints are with Mac-Lar. To tell you the truth, they're more likely to go after you than they are to seek damages from your partner."

"Go after me? I'm the *victim* here."

"I know that, and so does First Star. But your name is on all the papers, you own sixty percent of the business, and, most importantly, they know where to find you."

Mack suppressed a surge of fury, locked it away. "Well, hell, *I'll* file charges against him."

Pleasant raised his eyebrows. "Oh?"

"Sure. Lars gutted the company. As close as I can figure, he took off with more than half a million dollars. My money, the bank's money, my wife's parents' money."

Jerry Pleasant nodded sympathetically.

"His girlfriend, Rita Monbeck, she was in on it, too." Mack lit another cigarette. "I've got nothing. I owe my suppliers close to a quarter million. I've got four hundred fifty thousand dollars in unfilled orders—some prepaid—and I can't even make payroll. Had to let everybody go. We borrowed two-eighty from my wife's parents. All gone. My father-in-law thinks I'm scum. And the bank, Christ! We borrowed three hundred grand against our purchase orders, then Lars went to their factoring division and borrowed another two twenty against receivables, which, incidentally, are about half that. Talk about your left hand not knowing what the right hand is doing! The same bank, and they're lending against purchase orders and turning around and lending all over again against the receivables— most of which turned out to be phony, just fantasy stuff that Rita typed up. He even maxed out his corporate credit card. Not that that makes much difference. Either way, the bank is taking over Mac-Lar and my wife and I are declaring bankruptcy. Hell yes, I'll file charges."

"Do you know where he is?"

"Lars? If I knew, I'd be all over him." Mack thought for a moment. "If I had to guess, I'd say he was in Mexico."

"Why is that?"

"He had a picture on his desk. He's standing next to this giant fish. A marlin, I think. He caught it in Cancún. He was proud of that fish. Also, he was hooked on these Cuban cigars he smuggled in from Mexico. You could charge him with that, too."

Pleasant scribbled in his notebook. "Mexico is probably a good guess," he said. "Larson speaks fluent Spanish."

Mack nodded, then looked at Pleasant. "You know him?"

Pleasant waggled his head vaguely, then nodded and grinned at his feet. "We've crossed paths. Actually, he's kind of a hobby of mine. You won't be the first person to file a complaint against the Larsons."

"Larsons? You mean there's more than one?"

"Teddy and his wife, Rita."

"Who's Teddy?"

"Teddy, Theo, Billy, Lars. All the same guy."

"Rita is his wife? Rita Monbeck?"

"Actually, her name is Larson."

"You're saying they've done this before?" Even after all that had happened, he still found himself thinking of Lars as a nice guy who had suddenly gone wrong, not as a career criminal.

Jerry Pleasant seemed to understand. Looking out across the field, he said, "Teddy Larson is a pro. Everybody that meets him likes him. I met him twice. He's a hell of a nice guy to talk to."

"He's the people guy," Mack said numbly.

"Excuse me?"

"He was the people guy. I was just the guy sewed it all together." Mack shook another cigarette from the pack, lit it. Thank god for cigarettes, he thought. Less painful than arsenic, and better tasting, too.

"You know, I believe that's actually alfalfa out there," Pleasant said.

"Wheat," Mack said, firing out a horizontal plume of blue smoke.

Pleasant said, "According to whom?"

~

Bob Seaman couldn't find Mack in the factory. He walked out to the loading dock—the overhead door was open—and saw Mack's car in the lot but no Mack. Strange. He was about to go back to the offices when he looked across the parking lot and saw two men standing hip deep in the field. One of them was Mack, holding up a stalk, pointing at it, talking. The other man, the cop, was shaking his head.

"Hey!" Seaman shouted, waving. The two men looked over, started walking toward him. Seaman did not like having the police involved. Even if they found Larson and charged him with some sort of fraud, it was unlikely that the bank would recover any money.

Also, it could be embarrassing. Very embarrassing. Best just to clean up the mess, take a few lumps, and get on with business.

Seaman waited, hands on hips, as they emerged from the field and crossed the tarmac.

Mack held up the stalk and asked him, "You know what this is?"

Seaman couldn't believe he was related to this guy. What a moron. Like a kid showing off a weed he'd found, not even knowing how much trouble he was in.

"That's rye," Seaman said.

"Rye?"

Seaman nodded. It was all he could do not to roll his eyes.

The cop, Jerry something, said to Mack, "I told you it wasn't wheat."

4

"We'll be okay. I've got my job at Gold Coast, and if Mack can find some kind of job we'll be able to keep the house. At least that's what the lawyer says." Paula MacWray stabbed a cherry tomato, examined it, scraped it off her fork, and went for a crouton instead. "What's really awful is the way people are treating us. I mean, we're the *victims* here. The only thing Mack did wrong was he trusted Lars."

"People want to think that it was your own fault. That way they can think that it won't happen. I mean to them." Julie Gorman laughed, jangling the bracelets on her thin wrist, pink nails flashing. "Like cancer."

"Cancer?"

"Yeah. You get cancer and the first thing people want to know is, did you smoke. Or live next to a nuclear reactor. Or you have a car accident, they want to know how fast you were driving. Or your husband has an affair and they want to know if he was getting any. At home." Julie laughed again, a little too loud. "Boy do I know that one! They want to know that you deserved what you got because god knows *they* don't. Deserve it, I mean. Like, I show a house that's on the market because of a divorce? Couples looking at it always want to know the reason. Was he running around? Did she get fat? It had to be *somebody's* fault."

"So, did you think that?"

"What?"

"That it was our fault that the business failed."

Julie produced her impish smile, an expression that had not changed since the second grade. "Just for a couple seconds." She dabbed the corners of her mouth with a napkin, a motion more symbolic than cleansing. The salmon fillet before her was hardly touched. She had scraped off the sauce and picked at the meat but if any of it had gotten inside her, Paula hadn't seen it go. Julie did not require nourishment. She would take the fish home in a white box and feed it to her cat. Even in the second grade she had been a frugal, picky eater. She would eat half an Oreo.

"Maybe it *is* our fault," Paula said.

"Oh stop it."

"I'm serious. Mack never checked into Lars's background or anything. He just let Lars tell him what to do. We put up our house, Mack's IRA, everything. My parents lost everything! They don't even know it yet. Mack is ashamed to tell them, and I'm sure not going to."

"I'm sure they'll understand."

"Maybe. But I don't think so. I just wish Mack was more, um, aggressive. Maybe if he had asked a few more questions none of this would've happened. He's such a trusting guy. Don't get me wrong—I love that about him—but sometimes I think he goes around wearing a *Kick Me* sign that a guy like Lars can read a mile off."

Julie caught their waiter's eye and made a complicated series of flashing pink-nailed hand gestures, asking him to box up her lunch. She said, "Lars was just impossible to resist. He had that grin." Julie had met Lars a couple of times. She had developed a minor crush on him but had gotten nowhere. "I think he read *Kick Me* on every back he ever saw."

"Maybe so." Paula pushed the salad aside, her appetite gone. "But this time it was my Mack that took the boot."

~

"You . . . *you* . . ." Hal Byrnes's voice rose in pitch. "You *lied* to us! *Cheated* us!"

Mack winced and held the phone away from his ear.

"You told us our money was *safe*."

"Lars said that," said Mack.

"Don't you tell me what I heard! I knew you were no good the first day my daughter dragged you home. I never should've let you talk me into giving you money. You, you better get this straightened out, mister." His voice was cracking. Mack imagined his father-in-law's face, red and popping with veins.

"Look, Hal, I'm sorry. I had no way of—"

"Don't you lie to me, *you*. I don't have to take this garbage. I'm getting that money back if I have to take it out of your hide."

"Take it easy, Hal."

"Don't *you* tell *me* to take it easy, you thieving little shit . . ."

Mack listened as the old man raved, taking it all in.

~

Mack was sitting under the locust tree with a pitcher of martinis when Paula got home. She watched him through the patio door for a few moments. He was sprawled on the chaise longue, his back to the house, his shoes and socks in the grass where he'd kicked them.

The small backyard, enclosed by a cheap pine fence, contained only patchy grass and a pair of spindly locust trees. They had never done anything with the yard or the rest of the place, because they had always thought of it as a starter house, a place to camp until they figured out what they wanted to do with their lives. Maybe they would get rich, buy a new house on Lake Minnetonka with a new kitchen, a four-car garage, and a boat. So much for that dream. They'd be stuck here for a while now. If they were lucky.

Maybe she would plant a rosebush or something.

Mack brought a hand to his face; a cloud of blue smoke formed a nimbus around his head. Paula despised the smell of cigarettes, but she wasn't going to say anything. He had been smoking ever since the day he'd let his employees go. Since Black Thursday. The habit was firmly in place by now. He'd go through hell again when he had to quit. He'd been drinking a lot the past couple weeks, too. Maybe he needed those crutches right now. She told herself that it was only temporary, that there were other, more important matters to worry about.

The Job Opportunities section of the *Star Tribune* lay open on the kitchen counter. She toed off her shoes and paged through the ads. A few were circled in blue ink. *Assistant Line Manager—Munsingwear.* That would be a big step down. *Salesman wanted—Lakeland Lincoln-Mercury.* Yeah, right. She could just see Mack trying to sell undercoating. *Retail Clerk—Quik Stop Market.* The poor man was having some serious image problems. She would have to try to be more supportive. Encourage him, make him feel manly.

Paula opened the glasses cupboard and fished through their mismatched assortment of drinking vessels until she located a martini glass. Actually it was a margarita glass, but it would have to do. She pulled open the patio door.

"Hey there," she said.

Mack craned his neck to look back. "Hey. You want a martini?"

Paula waggled her glass and sat down on the web chair next to him.

Mack poured her a drink. "It might be kind of diluted," he apologized.

"That's fine."

Mack topped off his own glass. "Bob Seaman came by with his goons today."

Paula nodded.

"He was a jerk about it."

"Doesn't surprise me." She tasted her martini. It was watery and not very cold. "He's never been through it himself."

"The cops were there, too. One cop, actually. Nice guy."

"Oh?"

"He knows Lars." He waited for Paula to look him in the eye. "Apparently I'm not the only half-wit on the planet."

Paula said nothing.

"I'm just the latest. He's been scamming guys like me for years."

"I guess we should have checked his references," Paula said.

"It wouldn't have made any difference. He was a pro. I bet his references would've checked out perfect."

"Maybe."

"I talked to your father."

Paula felt her heart thud. "How did he take it?"

"Not well."

Paula said nothing.

Mack said, "I keep hearing Lars telling me to grab the gold ring. That really got me, you know? The idea of this great opportunity flashing by, and all I had to do was grab hold and hang on. Well, shit. I grabbed it all right, and look where it got us." He displayed his empty hands.

They sat for a time, Paula trying to imagine a rosebush in front of the pine fence: a scraggly, thorny growth with a few tattered pink blooms.

"Maybe you didn't grab hold hard enough," she said.

Mack produced a faint grunt, absorbing the barb.

"You know what they want me to do?"

"Who?"

"The bank. They want to hire me. I'm supposed to go down to the bank tomorrow to meet with them. I think they want me to get the line up and running just long enough to fill the outstanding orders. Sell off the remaining inventory. They want to get as much of their money back as possible."

"I suppose you can't blame them. How much are they offering you?"

Mack shrugged. "Bob's acting like it's my fault, like I owe him personally. Like it's my responsibility to help him."

Paula recoiled from the whine in her husband's voice. "You don't owe him anything."

"Oh really?" Bitter and defeated.

"There's no one else who can get the factory going for them. Ask for lots of money."

"I'll take whatever." Shaking his head. "Besides, he's right. My name is on those loan agreements."

"Why should you care if First Star gets their money back? It's their problem. Maybe it's time to worry about Mack and Paula." She looked away. "I don't know why you can't be a little more mercenary."

"Mercenary?"

"Yes. As opposed to doormatty." Now she could hear bitterness in her own voice.

"Doormatty? When was I a doormat?"

"If you'd taken a look at the books anytime in the past six months you'd've seen what Lars was doing."

"Now wait a second. He was my partner. Partners are supposed to trust each other, in case you haven't heard. You trust me, don't you?"

Paula stared at her feet, toes blurred by nylon stockings. She *did* trust Mack. The man was safe and honest and kind and utterly predictable, but there were times—lots of times, lately—when she wished he would scare her a little. Stand up for himself.

"Well?" he asked.

"I trust you, Mack."

"Thank you! Christ!"

"But I still double-check your math in our bank account."

Glaring at her, Mack tossed his cigarette butt on the lawn and lit another. He smoked half of it, sucking hard, then sighed. "I guess I can't blame you," he said.

Which was exactly what she thought he'd say.

5

Waking up had been rough lately. Thinking it had been a dream, then a painful minute making a shaky transition to reality: Ripped off. Broke. Business collapsed. Owe everybody. Hungover. Head pounding.

Ten after ten on the clock radio. Was there something he had to do? A reason to rise?

The bank. He was supposed to be at the bank at eleven. Mack groaned and sat up. His stomach seemed to have broken loose, swimming in gut soup. He waited for it to settle, then climbed to his feet, oozed into his robe, and shuffled barefoot down the hallway to the bathroom, where he washed four aspirin down with a swig of Pepto-Bismol.

He continued his journey, feet dragging through carpet, to the kitchen. Paula had left a pot of coffee on the hot plate. Mack poured a dose of the overheated, stale brew into a Mac-Lar coffee mug. He sat in the window, lit a cigarette, smoked, sipped the sour coffee, watched the pictures in his head: fluorescent lights glancing off Bob Seaman's perfect teeth; Jerry Pleasant's closed, V-shaped smile; Paula's silhouette against the window last night after a prolonged and unsatisfactory bout of humping, both of them too drunk to make it work. Or maybe he was the only one who had been too drunk. He couldn't remember.

Mack closed his eyes, wishing something would happen. A tornado, an earthquake, a war. Something big enough and dangerous enough to make his problems seem insignificant. Winning a sweepstakes. A heart attack. The Rapture.

The telephone rang. It wasn't the Rapture, but it would do. Mack put his coffee down on the windowsill and answered.

"Mack? Jerry Pleasant here."

"Oh hi."

"Listen, I was wondering what time I could expect you today."

"Expect me?"

"You said you'd be willing to file charges?"

"Oh. Sure."

"It'd be easiest if you could come downtown. Say, this morning?"

"I, uh, I have to be at the bank at eleven. I could stop by after that. One o'clock?"

"One o'clock. Good. You know where I am?"

Mack said that he did. He hung up and lit another cigarette. Paula was right. He let people drag him around by the nose. First Lars, then Bob Seaman, now Jerry Pleasant. One of these days, he thought—but the thought went no further.

~

The secretary at the bank led him down a short hallway to a small conference room containing a round table, six chairs, and nothing else. Not even a bank brochure or a cheap lithograph on the wall. Mack sat down. The aspirin had reduced his headache to a faint, pulsing annoyance. He roamed the perimeter of the room, examining the wallpaper, a pattern of thin, uneven vertical lines in purple, orange, green, and three shades of brown. It did not look like anything. He supposed that was the point of it. The carpeting was designed to the same color specifications, but in a pulsing, pointillistic pattern that threatened to reignite his headache.

They left him to contemplate the wallpaper and the carpeting. Mack spent the time fending off thoughts. Lately, every mental pathway seemed to lead to shame, fear, and self-loathing. He lost himself in the grain of the veneer tabletop, looking for faces in the loops and swirls, finding only frowns and grimaces. After twenty minutes he heard the click of the doorknob and turned to it, grateful that they had not forgotten him.

It was his cousin Bob, dressed in a charcoal suit with overly subtle pinstripes and a solid-color tie of the most somber maroon. His black hair had been recently trimmed and carefully combed. His cheeks shone from a fresh shave. Mack caught a whiff of aggressive cologne.

Bob held the door open. A second suited man—shorter, and very straight in the spine—entered the conference room. He stopped as soon as he was clear of the door and gave Mack a quick visual assessment. His irises were extremely dark, giving him a rodentlike aspect that Mack found discomfiting. His hair was buzz cut, graying, and patchy on top, his wide mouth a four-inch slash of faded coral enclosed by double parentheses.

Bob Seaman closed the door and said, "Good morning, Mack. This is Jake Vink."

Jake Vink stepped in close and thrust out a hand. Mack automatically reached out, then nearly snatched his hand back when he felt the returning clasp. He looked down and saw that Vink was missing his three middle fingers. He brought his eyes back to Vink's black eyes. Vink's pincer grip was firm, just short of painful.

Vink smiled, his mouth changing shape without growing wider. "I've heard a lot about you, MacWray."

For some reason Mack had expected an accent, but Vink sounded local. Mack returned the smile, nodding and wishing that Vink would let go of his hand. Vink's thumb and little finger were compressing his knuckles. The squeezing and smiling went on for a few more uncomfortable seconds, then ended abruptly when Vink released him and seated himself at the table.

"Jake heads up our workout group," Seaman said.

For a moment Mack was puzzled, thinking in terms of workouts at the gym, still feeling the impression Vink had left on his right hand.

Seaman elaborated. "When one of our clients gets in trouble, Jake and his team go in and help them get back on their feet."

"They call me Jake the Pincher," Vink said.

"You're kidding."

Vink grinned. "I pinch costs."

"I already let everybody go," Mack said. "There's nothing left to pinch."

"Can you hire them back?"

Mack felt a splash of hope. "Really?"

Seaman and Vink exchanged glances.

"Oh." Mack's shoulders sagged. Nothing had changed. "You just want to fill the outstanding orders and then liquidate."

"That's right," said Seaman. "As cheaply as possible. We want you to head up production, and Jake here will step in as interim president to make sure we stay on track. You've got, ah, what do you have in-house? Purchase orders for . . . ?"

"About four hundred fifty thousand. But some of them, mostly the Airlift International account, are long-term contracts with delivery dates as far as two years out."

"They'll have to take delivery early," Vink said.

"And about a quarter of the P.O.'s were prepaid."

"Those we don't worry about," Vink said.

"How long to fill all the billable orders you have in-house?" Seaman asked.

Mack thought for a moment. "Six months?"

"We'll do it in two," Vink said.

"Like hell."

"We put your people on piecework," Vink said. "Pay 'em for what they turn out. Everybody on overtime."

"Not in my factory. Piecework means quality problems. Overtime makes it worse."

Seaman and Vink both stared at him, blinking.

"Quality is not an issue," said Vink.

Mack stood up abruptly and turned his back on Vink. The wallpaper pulsed purple and green. He wished for a window, evidence that there was still a world outside this room.

Seaman said, "It's not your company anymore, Mack."

"It's my name."

"Lars's name, too."

"Not really. According to the police his name was Theodore, not Lars." He turned back to the two men. "I'm going over to the courthouse when we're done here. I'm going to file charges, since you guys don't have the balls to do it. We're going to nail him."

Seaman nodded, being very serious. "I'm sure you will, Mack. But that won't help us here. Even if you find him, even if you are able to get some of your money back, that won't save Mac-Lar. We need to go forward. Salvage what we can. This is about survival. Nothing personal about it, Mack. Sit down."

Mack returned to his seat. He felt himself going numb, retreating to his core. The meeting went on for another twenty minutes, during which it was made clear to Mack that he had absolutely no say in how things would be. He signed some papers. When they finished, Seaman walked Mack down to the parking garage. As Mack was unlocking the car door, Seaman put a hand on his shoulder.

"Listen, Mack, about filing charges . . ."

Mack detected a note of uneasiness in his cousin's voice.

". . . that might not be such a good idea."

"Why?"

"Even if the police find him, bring him back, it might just make matters worse."

"Matters can get worse?"

"I'm only saying this for your benefit, Mack. Your name is on everything, you know. You're the majority shareholder. What do you think Lars would say if he was here? Where do you think he'd point the finger? Who do you think he'd blame? He'd say you engineered the whole thing. He'd say he left because he didn't want to be a part of your schemes. You and I both know that Lars is the bad guy. But you know how persuasive he can be. What I'm saying is, you might be cutting your own throat."

"But he's guilty."

"That doesn't matter. What *matters* is who pays. You could wind up in prison. Which would you rather have, justice or freedom?"

"I don't know."

"You have to realize that, technically, Lars never stole a dime from us, from First Star. The bank won't back you up on this. It was your corporation that committed the fraud, and you were both the president and majority shareholder. Lars may have stolen the money from Mac-Lar, but it was Mac-Lar that stole it from us."

"That's why I have to file charges."

"Don't do it, Mack. Let's just get this mess cleaned up and put it behind us. You pursue Lars, you're asking for more trouble."

Mack got into his car. He closed the door, started the engine.

Seaman hadn't moved. "Don't do it, Mack," he mouthed.

6

Ginny Bettendorf, the owner of Gold Coast Travel, knocked on Paula MacWray's divider and peered into her cubicle.

"Anybody home?" she asked in her low, chesty voice.

Paula looked up with a guilty start. She had been staring sightlessly at a Club Med brochure for several minutes, reimagining the rest of her life. An army of multicolored ants marched across her computer screen.

"Oh, hi Ginny," she said.

"Working late?" Ginny asked. "Or just moping?"

"Is it late?" Paula looked at her watch. Five-thirty. "Oh. I was just spacing out, I guess."

As always, Ginny was dressed in black. Today's ensemble was a silk pantsuit with an oversize jet-and-coral brooch pinned high on her right shoulder. Her hair, also black, was pulled back into a French braid. She stepped into the cubicle and wedged her ample hips into one of the two guest chairs.

"How are you doing?" she asked.

Paula shrugged. "I'm a little tired, I guess."

"How is Mack?"

"I don't know." Paula's eyes found a small dark spot on her wrist. A mole? She rubbed and it smeared. Ink.

Ginny said, "My dad lost a business once. He had a shoe store."

Paula smiled and nodded politely. Ginny liked to play mother to her employees, and she was good at it, but Paula resisted. She did not need another mother. One was more than enough—especially now.

Ginny said, "It wasn't really his fault. The state brought the four-lane highway to our town. All the merchants thought it was a great thing. The highway would bring new business. But all that happened was that the highway made it easier for folks to drive up to the Twin Cities to do their shopping. Dad hung on to the store for three years, but in the end he lost everything. It was rough on him, but I think Mother had the worst of it."

Paula looked up. "What happened?"

"We had to sell the house and move into an apartment. Dad took a job at the grain elevator. Came home smelling like wheat and corn every day. Mother went to work part-time at the Ben Franklin. We survived."

Paula thought, Is that what it's all about? Survival?

"There was about a year there when my folks didn't hardly talk. I used to hate to come home from school. It was like somebody'd turned off the sound. I think what it came down to was that no matter how much she understood what had happened, and why, Mother could not stand to look at the man she had married and see a failure. She just couldn't get over it."

"I can understand that," Paula said. "When I look at Mack—it's like he lied to me. But he never lied to me. It was all me, expecting him to be somebody he's not."

Ginny nodded. "Your house gets hit by a twister, everybody feels sorry for you. But your business goes belly-up and everybody thinks you're a loser."

"You know what I was thinking about when you walked in here? I was thinking about leaving Mack. Not seriously, but I was just trying to imagine how it would be if I was with another guy. I mean, sometimes in bed I pretend he's someone else." Paula blinked, her eyes filling with tears. "I can't believe I told you that."

"You're not alone, honey. Just because you fantasize a bit doesn't mean you don't love the guy."

"Yeah, I do love him. Sometimes I wish I didn't." She sniffed. "I look at him, this man I married, and I think maybe I made a mistake. Does that make me bad?"

Ginny smiled, shaking her head. "You aren't bad."

Paula looked at her watch. "I guess I ought to go home."

"You know what you really ought to do? You ought to take a vacation."

"I suppose. Maybe when we get back on our feet—"

"You're not listening to me, girl. You ought to take a vacation right now. You and Mack. Go away for a few days."

"I don't think we can. The bank has asked Mack to—"

"Forget the bank. Look, I've got some off-season freebies from Sun Country. Seven days in Orlando, Mazatlán, Cancún, or Oaxaca—take your pick."

"We can't afford to—"

"Air and hotel paid for. Take a trip with him, honey. You need it."

"But we owe all this money! I don't see how we can—"

"Don't worry. Your money problems will still be here when you get back."

Paula blinked, then laughed.

"You'll be drinking margaritas on the beach tomorrow. What do you say?"

~

Mack stared blearily up at his wife.

"What time is it?" He asked not because he cared, but to give himself time to wake up. He was on the sofa.

"Seven. Are you hungry?"

Mack licked his lips. Hungry? He had no idea. He'd drunk most of, or maybe all of, a pitcher of martinis. He grabbed the back of the sofa and pulled himself up. His head felt okay, which meant he was still drunk.

"I could use a bite," he said.

Paula faded away. Mack patted his pockets, found his cigarettes on the floor next to the coffee table, lit one. He sat smoking and blinking, listening to Paula moving things around in the kitchen. When his cigarette was nearly finished, he noticed several colorful rectangles on the coffee table before him. He forced his eyes to focus, identified the shapes as travel brochures from Gold Coast Travel. He picked up the one nearest to him, flipped through it. Mazatlán. He'd been to Mazatlán once, when he was in college. He had drunk a lot of tequila and gotten one hell of a sunburn. Those were the days. Mack tossed the brochure back on the table and stubbed out his cigarette. He made his way to the kitchen. Paula was frying bacon.

"We're having BLTs for dinner, is that okay?"

"Sure." He cleared his throat. "I talked to the bank. They want me to get the factory up and running."

"You knew that, didn't you?" She moved the bacon strips around with a fork.

"Now it's official. I'll be working with a guy named Vink. A real jerk."

"When do they want you to start?"

"Right away." Mack noticed that Paula had a beer going on the counter next to her. Good idea. He grabbed a cold one from the refrigerator, cracked it open. "They're paying me three hundred a week."

Paula compressed her lips.

"And they're agreeing not to prosecute me for fraud."

Paula washed a tomato and began slicing.

"Did you look at those brochures?" she asked.

"What brochures?"

"The travel brochures."

"Oh. Not really." He drank some beer. "Why?"

"We're taking a vacation."

"We are?"

"Wherever you want to go—as long as it's Orlando, Mazatlán, Cancún, or Oaxaca."

Mack frowned. "Why would I want to go to Orlando?"

"Disney World."

Mack laughed, shaking his head. "A vacation. Jesus Christ. We can't even make our house payment!"

"It's free," Paula said. "Air and hotel are free."

"I'm supposed to start rehiring my crew tomorrow."

"Let them wait a week. Nothing is going to change."

Mack sipped his beer.

"We'll still be broke when we get back, Mack. You won't miss a thing."

Mack rolled the mouth of the beer bottle across his bottom lip, his thoughts sluggish. "Where'd you say?"

"Orlando, Mazatlán, Cancún, or Oaxaca."

Mack felt a spark, a synapse closing, a passageway opening.

"Cancún," he said.

7

"Espérame, por favor." Teddy handed the *taxista* a hundred-peso note. *"Ahorita vengo."*

The driver took the note, held it up to the light. "No problem, amigo. I wait for you."

Teddy got out of the cab, ran his hands down the front of his guayabera to smooth it, brushed the brim of his panama with his fingertips, and entered Plaza Flamingo, an indoor conglomeration of shops and restaurants thick with U.S. franchises. Why anyone would travel thousands of miles to eat a Big Mac or a Domino's pizza was a mystery to Teddy, but they did. There was even a Planet Hollywood.

Plaza Flamingo did an enormous amount of business during the winter and spring, when hundreds of thousands of U.S. tourists descended upon Cancún, but this time of year the *tiendas* were quiet, free from the jittery crowds of pallid vacationers. Teddy passed a jewelry store, a gift shop, and a Subway sandwich shop—all with their gates open but few customers. He crossed the atrium with its chronically malfunctioning fountain. Today it was dry. Several people sat around its perimeter smoking cigarettes and speaking rapid Spanish. Strolling, window-shopping families from Mexico City or Mérida, spending a weekend in Cancún to escape the inland heat, dominated the sparsely populated corridors. At the moment, Teddy was the only non-Mexican in sight. He liked it that way.

The clerk at La Casa del Habano was cleaning the glass countertop with a blue rag, polishing with slow, circular strokes, a distant smile on his placid face.

"Buenos días," Teddy said.

The clerk looked up. *"¡Buenos días! Señor Larson!"* He folded the rag and put it away. "I have good news for you. We have just received a new shipment. You prefer the Espléndidos, no? One box?" He bobbed his round head, his slanted eyes disappearing as he smiled. Like many Mayans, he would not have looked out of place in Hong Kong. Or maybe he *was* Chinese. In Cancún, anything was possible.

"Sí, sí," Teddy said.

"No problem. I get them for you."

The clerk went into the humidor and climbed atop a short ladder. A few seconds later he came out with a cedar box of Cohiba Espléndidos, displaying it as if he had unearthed a great treasure.

"You see?"

"I see. *Bueno.*" Teddy pulled a money clip from his pants pocket and peeled off eight five-hundred-peso notes while the clerk undertook the laborious process of handwriting a receipt. Mexican merchants took their receipts very seriously.

"I meet a friend of yours," the clerk said as he wrote. "He come into the store yesterday. No. Day before."

"Oh?" Teddy felt his heart speed up.

"He ask if I know you."

"What did you tell him?" He strained to keep his voice calm.

"I just say I know you."

Teddy turned and looked out through the glass storefront into the atrium. A woman with her teenage daughter, walking quickly. An old man with a broom. A young Mexican couple carrying several shopping bags. Teddy ran down a list of names in his mind. People to avoid. "What did he look like?"

"Like a tourist. American. He ask me do you come here much."

"What did you tell him?"

The clerk shrugged, smiling uncertainly. "I tell him you come here sometime."

Teddy kept his eyes on the shoppers. He tapped the box of cigars with a forefinger. "How many more of these you got? *¿Cuántas cajas?*"

The clerk stopped writing. "Two, I think maybe."

"*Bien.* I'll take them." Teddy peeled more bills off his clip. He would have to avoid the area for a few weeks, stay on Isla. Whoever had been asking about him, he didn't want to run into them. "Anybody else comes in here looking for me, you tell them you don't know me. Like Pancho Villa. *¿Comprende?*"

The clerk's face lost all expression. "*Sí, señor.*"

Teddy watched the plaza traffic—still no gringos—as the clerk painstakingly amended the receipt, counted the money, gave him change, and loaded the cigars into a large plastic bag. Teddy pulled his panama low on his forehead and left the store on high alert. He walked directly to his waiting cab, took a quick look around, got in.

"*Puerto Juárez, por favor.*" He looked back as the cab pulled out into traffic, but saw nothing unusual.

~

At 10:30 A.M., side one of the Enya tape ended. Paula MacWray's hand followed the wire from her headset down to the Walkman. She pressed the eject button with an oily forefinger, reversed the tape, then rolled over onto her back. Sun crashed through the lenses of her dark glasses as the music—a slick New Age interpretation of Celtic rhythms—filled her ears. She squeezed her eyes closed, reached down, and groped for her bottle of Corona. Left side? No, right. She caught the bottle by its neck and lifted it out of the ice bucket. Frigid droplets of water tracked across her belly. She tipped the bottle to her mouth and swallowed. The beer went down like a rope of sleet, sending a chill up the backs of her arms and down her sides.

Paula pushed the bottle back into the ice and felt around for her tube of sunscreen but could not seem to locate it. Damn. Where was Mack when she needed him? She sat up and opened her eyes. There, right under her elbow. She squeezed a scribble of white goo, hot with stored sunlight, onto her thighs. She began to rub it in, taking her time. The tropical sun was unforgiving. Most of the other people around the pool were under the long *ramada* on the south side, in the shade. Another half hour and she would be sufficiently baked to join them. She coated the tops of her thighs, her knees, her shins and feet, enjoying the sensation of hands kneading flesh. Mack should be doing this for her. Where was he? Three days in Cancún and she'd hardly seen him. Every morning he took off, saying something about "seeing the sights." He would put on his new hat, a long-billed fishing cap with *Cancún* embroidered on the front, and walk up Paseo Kukulcán. She wouldn't see him again until sunset.

Paula made sure to get a heavy layer of sunscreen on her inner thighs, on her belly, and under her breasts—areas most susceptible to sunburn. The skimpy two-piece, purchased in the hotel swim shop that morning, revealed portions of her anatomy that had not seen sunlight in years. When her front side was completely coated, she let her arms fall to her sides and let the sun dig in.

Whatever Mack was doing with himself, he seemed to have regained his sense of purpose. Mexico had wiped off some of that hangdog look, and he was drinking less. On the downside, he hardly seemed to know she existed. They hadn't made love once since arriving in Cancún. Mack had entered a private world to which she was not invited—and she wasn't sure she *wanted* an invitation. She hadn't come to Mexico to share Mack's private hell. She'd come here to relax.

Maybe Mack needed the alone time. Maybe by the time they returned home he would be able to see things more clearly. Maybe they both would.

~

"Stay back! Not so close."

"No problem." The cabbie sped up.

Mack ducked down in his seat. "No! Don't get so close. I don't want him to see us."

"Okay, no problem." The cabbie laughed.

"Don't lose them."

"No problem."

"Don't let him see us."

The cabbie sped up.

"No!" Mack opened his phrase book. *"¡No santa sede!"*

The cabbie giggled, but he seemed to get the message. "No problem."

Mack raised his head. Lars's cab was two cars ahead of them. Lars! It was like a dream, as if he had stepped into another reality. A bad knockoff of a Hitchcock movie. He had flown thousands of miles to this garish speck on the map and actually found him. Unbelievable.

A bank of low gray clouds had settled upon the horizon to the north. Lars's cab followed the Paseo Kukulcán traffic through the *zona hotelera,* past the Hyatt Caribe, the Sierra, and the less expensive Miramar, where he and Paula were staying. Blips of ocean appeared between hotel towers. Mack's first look at Cancún had reminded him of Las Vegas. Today it looked to him like a twisted Disneyland, sprawling resorts made of Lego blocks and sand. Mack figured Lars would be staying in one of the biggest, most garish hotels—one of the places that looked like enormous Mayan pyramids—but the cab continued past the Caracol district, through the Club de Golf, and over the Playa Linda bridge onto the mainland. Mack hadn't seen this part of the city. They passed a series of small hotels. At one point a bus cut between the two cabs and they almost lost Lars's cab when it turned north at an interchange. The cabbie, responding to Mack's shouted command, circled the bewildering intersection; they caught up with Lars on Avenida Bonampak, the downtown bypass. The buildings became smaller and shabbier, and the signs advertising U.S. products—Burger King, Levi's, Coca-Cola—were replaced by unfamiliar Mexican brands.

Lars's cab turned onto a wide boulevard. They headed northeast, following the shoreline. A few miles later it pulled over to the curb at a busy intersection, people everywhere. Lars got out of his cab.

"Go past them, then pull over," Mack said. He counted to five, then sat up and looked back just in time to see Lars, plastic bag in hand, disappearing into a covered passageway between two long, low buildings.

"Where are we?" Mack demanded, fumbling with a fistful of U.S. currency.

"Puerto Juárez," said the cabbie. "Where you take a boat."

Mack handed the cabby thirty dollars, probably too much, hopped out, and jogged back to the entrance into which Lars had disappeared. He found himself in a wide alley shaded by a twenty-foot-high peaked roof. He could see the ocean at the far end, but Lars had disappeared. Mack walked quickly toward the water, emerged into sunlight at the base of a long concrete pier. Vendors on each side offered him seashells, baseball caps, pastries, cheap jewelry. Mack wove his way through the gauntlet, shaking his head, smiling, avoiding eye contact. A few dozen people were crowded near the end of the pier, boarding an ungainly-looking two-decker ferry.

Mack stopped. Was Lars on board? He searched the boarding passengers for Lars's straw hat. There? He thought he'd caught a glimpse of pale straw on the upper deck. Feeling exposed, Mack backed up to the base of the pier. Two teenage girls passed nearby; Mack caught their attention. "Where does that boat go?" he asked, pointing. Two young men were untying the boat and stowing the loading ramp.

The girls stared at him, uncomprehending.

Mack tried again. *"¿Dónde está . . . uh . . . boata?"* The ferry moved away from the pier.

The girls giggled and edged away. Mack looked around, ran over to the nearest vendor, a man selling sunglasses and plush toys.

"Excuse me," Mack pointed urgently at the ferry. *"¿Dónde? ¿Dónde?"*

"You want teddy bear?"

"No. I just want to know where the boat goes."

"Isla Mujeres. Next one, thirty minutes. You got plenty time. You sure you don't want to buy some junk?"

Mack walked out onto the wharf. The boat was moving out to sea. He squinted at the horizon. He could see land. Isla Mujeres?

"Hey, guy?"

Mack looked at the speaker, a teenage boy, rail thin, showing a set of large, crowded teeth beneath a neatly trimmed mustache.

"You want to go fast way, or slow way?" He pointed down the

beach to where several smaller craft—low-slung wooden boats painted in bright primary colors—were tied to a dock. "I get you there fast."

"To Isla Mujeres?"

"You wait for the big boat, it take an hour. Forty dollar I get you to Isla fast. Ten minute."

"Forty dollars?"

"Okay, guy. For you, thirty-five."

~

Teddy Larson used his time on the ferry to assess his fellow passengers. There were about fifty of them, but only a few who looked like Americans. Teddy wasn't too concerned about the Mexicans. The man asking about him at the cigar store had been American, according to the clerk. Lars moved around the upper deck, following the red wooden railing, looking at each passenger in turn, listening to their conversation. There were about a dozen non-Mexicans. Two German couples traveling together. Six of the passengers were Anglo women, paired off and standing close together. No surprise there. Isla de Mujeres, Island of Women, was a popular destination for lesbian couples. Teddy liked lesbians. He liked people that left him alone, that did not notice him. He'd spent a good chunk of his childhood fantasizing about being invisible. Maybe that was why he'd bought the condo on Isla.

The only passenger that concerned him was a heavyset middle-aged man wearing a Señor Frog T-shirt and a Toronto Blue Jays baseball cap. Could be American. Could be the guy looking for him. He was hanging on the railing, staring down at the passing water. Teddy sidled up to him.

"Looks like we got some weather coming in," he said.

The man raised his head. "Eh?"

Teddy pointed to the north, to a bank of gray clouds. "Weather," he said.

The man squinted. "Oh, yeah."

"You staying on Isla?"

"Me? Hell no. Wife's idea." He made a head gesture toward a perky-looking forty-something woman a few yards down the rail. "She wants to see the turtles. They got some kind of turtle farm. Me, I'd rather sit in the pool and drink beer and look at babes. That's my idea of fun, eh? But she says we come all the way from Winnipeg, we're gonna see the sights."

Teddy allowed himself to relax. He had nothing to fear from a Canadian. All of his business deals had occurred in the United States. "The turtles are all right," he said.

The man grunted. "Maybe she's right," he muttered, turning a red-eyed gaze on Teddy. "I think I had too goddamn much fun last night."

"That's what you're here for, right?"

The man laughed. His laugh became a cough. He spat into the ocean. "That, and look at the goddamn turtles."

Teddy echoed the man's laugh and moved on toward the stern. He felt slightly ill himself. He did not like to be around so many people, especially on a boat. They were animals, milling around the narrow deck, hanging on the rail like a bunch of monkeys. Making him nervous. He climbed down to the more sheltered lower deck. Two women wearing mud-flap hairdos and long-sleeved cotton shirts sat on a bench near the front; the other long benches were empty. Teddy sat down in the back row and opened one of the cigar boxes. He clipped and lit a fresh Espléndido. The two women rotated their heads, turning laser glares upon him. Teddy smiled at them and saluted with his cigar. The two women put on wide-brimmed straw hats, tightened the draw cords beneath their chins, and joined the other passengers on the upper deck. Perfect. Teddy lost himself in a Havana cloud, feeling, for the moment, safe.

8

The crossing to Isla Mujeres—no life preservers, the prow pointing skyward, slapping the waves with bone-jarring force, speed unknowable but certainly beyond what the tiny wooden craft had been designed for—terrified Mack sufficiently to keep him from thinking too hard about what he was going to do once he caught up with Lars. He sat in the prow, gripping the gunnels as if his life depended on it, which it probably did. The Mexican kid grinned at him from the stern, sinewy arms gripping the handle of the oversize outboard motor, black hair wet with spray whipping in the wind. They passed the slower ferry two minutes after leaving the dock. Mack kept his face averted.

They nosed up to the ferry dock at Isla Mujeres twelve minutes after departing Puerto Juárez. Mack unclenched his fingers and stepped shakily out of the boat. He fished out two twenty-dollar bills.

"Sorry, guy, no change." The youth grinned at him.

"No problem," said Mack, relinquishing the twenties. He could see the slow ferry, still a half mile out. The thought of being ahead of Lars for once sent a cold thrill through his body. When Lars got off the ferry Mack would . . . what would he do? He wasn't sure. He supposed he would tail Lars, gather information, find out all he could, and then, when the moment came, he would confront him. He stood on the dock watching the ferry grow in size. When he could pick out the individual people standing on deck he moved off the dock onto the street and stood off to the side, behind a fruit cart. He pulled his cap low on his forehead and hugged himself and waited, his body vibrating, trying to imagine how Lars would react to seeing him.

~

As the ferry glided up to the dock, Teddy emerged from his reverie and entered a state of alertness. He waited, smoking and watching through the windows, until the other passengers had disembarked. The waterfront was crowded with vendors, taxis, and tourists. He looked for anything or anyone out of place but saw nothing he had not seen before. He left the cabin and stepped onto the dock, scanning. There, across the street, behind a fruit cart, wearing sunglasses and a long-billed cap, standing perfectly still. Everyone else was moving, doing things, going places—but the one man stood still and watched. Teddy dropped his cigar into the water, walked quickly off the pier, and headed up Calle Morelos. The back of his neck crawled with the desire to look back, but he kept on moving. At Benito Juárez he turned left, passed the Tequila House and the Silver Factory, and ducked into a small shop. He backed into the shadows and waited, watching through the doorway. A few seconds later he saw Mack MacWray walk by, head swiveling rapidly.

Teddy let his breath hiss out through his nose. Mack! What the hell was Mack doing here?

"Can I help you?"

Teddy whirled, bringing his plastic bag full of cigar boxes around as if it were a shield. An Anglo woman wearing a long, heavily embroidered caftan stood with her hands clasped. He realized he was in a sort of hybrid art gallery/gift shop/jewelry store, one of several on the island. Brightly painted masks were displayed alongside porcelain necks loaded with necklaces. Soapstone and onyx carvings, mostly contemporary knockoffs of Mayan fertility dolls, perched on glass shelves. A long, glass-topped counter was loaded with coral and jet jewelry. The woman leaned toward him, smiling hard, lips compressed, head tilted, eyes bright.

"Just looking," Teddy said. He leaned out the doorway and looked to the left. Mack was out of sight, but it was likely that he would double back. Teddy jogged quickly back toward the piers. He followed the waterfront north for two blocks, turned up Calle Matamoros to the Hotel Caribe—now converted to condos—where Pepe, the wiry old Mayan who handled maintenance, landscaping, and building security, was filling a crack in the concrete steps leading into the lobby.

Pepe looked up as Teddy's shadow crossed his work. *"B'días, Señor Larson."*

"Morning, Pepe," Teddy said, looking up and down the avenue. "How's it going?" He stepped through and let the door close on Pepe's reply.

Safe. He let his shoulders drop, unclenched his hands. Mack! Of all the people he'd worried about running into, Mack was the least of them. What did the guy think he was going to do? Extradite him? Not likely. Teddy stood behind the door and watched the street through the tiny window. A handsome Mexican couple, laughing. Two women walking together. A taxi. A man pushing a cart full of mangoes and round watermelons. Teddy was about to head upstairs to his condo when Mack appeared, walking quickly toward the waterfront, the long bill of his cap swiveling from side to side, searching. Teddy backed away from the window.

Damn. Sooner or later Mack would catch up with him. The island was too small, and he was known to too many people. Mack would find him—or Rita. She was probably out there now, roasting her tits at the beach. The woman was the color of burnt toast; she just couldn't get enough sun. Probably get skin cancer before she turned thirty, but what the hell. She looked incredible.

What to do about Mack? Teddy started up the stone staircase to his third-floor condo. He and Rita could take a boat over to Cuba, make it a cigar-buying expedition, lay low for a few days. She'd like that. Go over and blow some Cuban minds with her tits and tan. Mack would eventually give up and go home. Or maybe he wouldn't. What to do, what to do? Teddy reached the door to his condo and went inside.

"Reet? You here, babe?"

No answer, as expected. Teddy opened a Negra Modelo and fired up another Espléndido. He took his smoke and his beer out to the bedroom balcony overlooking the courtyard. He sat in his favorite chair and looked down at the wading pool and the fountain, three stories below. The cigar burned slowly. He began to sort things out in his mind.

Teddy Larson had realized from a very young age that human beings could be easily manipulated. This knowledge had made life, in some ways, very easy for him. He had charmed, lied, and cheated his way through high school, and a few weeks after his graduation he had withdrawn $9,000 from his mother's savings account and fled to Mexico. He'd made the nine grand last for six months, bumming around the Yucatán, a couple months in Belize with some aging hippies, and finally a stint as a tour guide in Cancún. Eventually the money had run out and he had been faced with a choice: find a way to get more money in Mexico, or return to the States and acquire it there. A brief stint in a Cancún jail due to a misunderstanding over a wallet he had found convinced Teddy that it was best to be a tourist in Mexico and a thief in the United States. He had returned to the Midwest and took a job selling electronics at a Circuit City in St. Paul. He was good at it. Nothing easier to sell than a magic black box with lots of buttons. He sold a hundred grand in his first month, during which time he made the acquaintance of a pair of rudderless young men named Danny and Sport. Teddy made some suggestions. Shortly thereafter he brokered the sale of a truckload of high-end stereo systems to a discounter in Milwaukee, then hauled ass back to the Yucatán.

Over the next few years he worked with Danny and Sport on several other projects, and when they got caught and went to jail, he found other young thieves searching for guidance. Most thieves, he quickly learned, are looking for a setup man. They want someone to tell them what to do. They are willing to assume the risk and do the deed but are weak on strategy: what to steal, when to steal it, and what to do with the goods afterward.

He had discovered within himself a talent for motivating, organizing, and for spinning dreams. Over the years his methods became more sophisticated, the dollar amounts somewhat higher, and his time abroad more extended. By the time he met Rita, he had moved on from manipulating thieves, who were all unreliable at best, to working directly with the businesspeople who produced the wealth. People like Mack MacWray.

For the past six years, Teddy and Rita had called Isla Mujeres home. Teddy was not a greedy man. A few hundred thousand in the bank was all he required to feel safe. As long as he had sunshine, seafood, cigars, and enough cash to cover his greens fees at the Club de Golf, he could think of himself as reasonably happy. He did not need a big hacienda or a sixty-foot yacht, and he did not need friends. Why should he spend time with people he didn't respect? And why respect people who allowed themselves to be exploited? Human beings were ugly, greedy, frightened, stupid herd animals. That was how Teddy saw them. The only person he had ever loved—or whatever it was he felt for her—was Rita. Rita knew him for who he was, and she liked him that way. They shared a few simple desires—sex, sun, food, tobacco, and the desire to be left alone. Also, they each needed someone to occasionally confirm their existence. When Rita said good morning to him, Teddy took that as evidence that he was real.

They were a bit like drones, Teddy supposed, living out their years anonymously, asking only for comfort and safety. It was little enough to ask, but now his peace of mind was being threatened by one of the herd animals.

Mack MacWray? The guy had been nothing before they'd met. If not for Teddy, Mack would still be working for Linkway, slaving away at a dead-end job. Of course, things were probably a bit rough for him now, being stuck with all those loans, but that was part of life. He had given Mack months of drama and high living—at least by Mack's standards. So what if it hadn't worked out? What had Mack expected? If a guy didn't have what it took, he was bound to get screwed. One thing for sure, somebody had to be the screwer and somebody had to be the screwee. A guy like Mack MacWray was born to bend over.

Teddy smiled, thinking about Mack the worker bee running around that ridiculous factory trying to get those orders out. Like it made a difference. Like it was really about product when all that mattered in the end was cash flow and who it flowed to. The guy just never got it, which was why he would always be a pawn and never a mover and shaker.

So why worry? Teddy smiled. What was he hiding from?

~

Mack bought a bottle of Superior and sat on a bench near the ferry dock. An hour of walking the streets of downtown Isla Mujeres had gotten him nowhere. Lars would show his face sooner or later, and Mack planned to be there. According to the *Islander,* a freebie guidebook he'd been handed at the ferry dock, Isla Mujeres was only five miles long and less than a mile wide, not big enough to swallow up a guy like Lars. Mack sat and watched, sipping beer, reading the guidebook in snatches. This end of the island was mostly beaches, hotels, and shopping. The south end was less developed. There were a few larger resorts, a turtle preserve, some Mayan ruins, and a lighthouse overlooking rocky, treacherous cliffs.

A ferry arrived, gave up its passengers, took on another load, and left for the mainland.

He read about Fermin Mundaca de Marechaja, the fabulously wealthy slave trader who settled on the island one hundred fifty years ago and went slowly mad. One could visit the ruins of his *hacienda* and read the inscription, carved by Mundaca himself, on his tombstone: AS YOU ARE, I WAS. AS I AM, YOU WILL BE.

Mack bought a second beer. People came and went, and then, like an apparition, he saw a panama hat gliding through a cluster of pedestrians and, beneath it, Lars, driving a turquoise-and-pink golf cart.

Mack abandoned his bench and ran to a cab, fumbling with his phrase book.

"*¡Seguir! ¡Por favor!*"

The cabbie turned to him. "You talk English?"

"Yes!" Mack was too agitated to be embarrassed. "You see the golf cart? Follow it. Only don't get too close."

The driver shrugged his assent and put the cab in gear.

~

The land rose as they approached the south end of the island. Palm trees and hibiscus were replaced by low shrubs, tufts of grass, and rocky outcroppings. At a sharp bend in the road the golf cart turned right onto a narrow, single-lane road leading toward a lighthouse. The cabbie pulled over.

"You want me to follow?"

"Where does it go?" Mack asked.

"*El faro.* Lighthouse. Ruins. People go to look. You could walk."

Mack paid his fare and proceeded on foot. The road, paved with sand and crushed white rock, led to a small complex of buildings: a battered adobe residence, a low shed, a thatched *palapa,* and the lighthouse itself—an off-white, octagonal, forty-foot-high structure with several gaping skeletal sharks' jaws displayed at its base. Lars's golf cart stood parked a few yards away, but no Lars. Other than a small iguana sunning itself on a rock, he appeared to be alone. Where had Lars gone? To the lighthouse? He looked up but saw no one.

The low clouds that had been on the horizon now boiled over half the sky. Afternoon sun baked his back even as gusts of wind off the ocean chilled his front and threatened to dislodge his cap. Strange weather, he thought, but perhaps normal for this part of the world. Mack scanned his surroundings. He could see that he had almost run out of land. A couple hundred yards away, at the very tip of the island, he spotted a low structure of weathered stone blocks—the Mayan ruins? He followed a footpath through a landscape of low shrubs, grasses, prickly pear cactus, and small piles of rock, half expecting Lars to rise up out of the vegetation at any moment. As he neared the end of the path, he slowed.

The ruins were smaller than he had imagined. What remained of Ixchel's temple was only about ten feet high and twenty or thirty feet long. The upper portions of the structure were constructed of carefully cut and fitted stone blocks, while the base was a concretion of irregular chunks of rubble, as if the temple had grown naturally from the underlying rock and was now being drawn inexorably back into the earth.

The temple was situated a few yards from the end of the island, where, instead of pulverized coral beaches, the land ended in a jagged precipice. The air vibrated with the roar of waves hitting the base of the cliffs eighty feet below. As Mack reached the ruins he heard another noise, a faint *pok,* like the sound of stone striking stone.

Circling the ruins, he saw Lars standing near the edge of the cliff. Mack watched Lars pick a golf ball from a yellow plastic bucket and balance it on a golf tee set into a green one-foot-square patch of artificial grass. He lined up his golf club and with a short, chopping swing hit it out over the water. Mack moved closer. He sat down on the remains of a wall at the edge of the ruin, fifteen feet from Lars, who was balancing another ball on his portable tee. Lars looked out over the sea as if searching for the flag, shook his head, leaned the driver against his hip, removed a cigar from his pocket, and fitted it into his mouth. Standing very close to the edge, he hunched over the cigar and lit it. Mack imagined rushing at him, pushing, feeling the texture of Lars's shirt as his palms struck home.

Lars stood smoking and looking out over the ocean. Wind fluttered his loose white cotton guayabera and the legs of his chartreuse knee-length shorts. His thick calves bore a pelt of curly blond hair. He wore a pair of huaraches on his surprisingly small feet.

Seconds passed. Lars gave a faint shrug. He wrapped his hands around the golf club and addressed the ball. He raised the club slowly, paused for a count of two at the top of his backswing, then chopped at the ball. *Pok!* The ball shot straight out, then cut sharply down and to the right. Lars leaned out over the edge. Holding his hat down on his head, he watched the ball vanish into the spume.

Mack raised his voice over the sound of the surf and said, "You bring that right wrist over the top some, you'll lose that slice."

Lars, still looking over the edge, nodded. "I believe you have a point there, amigo." He turned his face toward Mack and grinned. "Macanudo! What a surprise!" He did not seem at all surprised. "Damn, but it's good to see a familiar face. *¿Qué pasa?* You doing okay?"

Lars had lost none of his power to charm. He really *is* glad to see me, Mack thought. He really *does* want to know how I'm doing. Lars could make anyone feel special.

Mack shook his head to clear it. "I'm doing lousy," he said. "Thanks to you."

Lars's grin became an embarrassed, self-effacing smile. "Oh. I guess I can understand you feeling that way." He produced another cigar from his pocket. "Cigar?"

"No thanks."

Lars tossed it to him. "Keep it for later. It's a Cohiba. Not what they used to be, but still one of the best."

Mack looked at the cigar in his hand, wishing he hadn't caught it. He set it on the crumbling stone wall.

"That's Ixchel's temple you're sitting on, Macanudo. Goddess of creativity. When Córdoba landed here five hundred years ago, this end of the island was guarded by statues of Mayan goddesses. That's why he named it Isla Mujeres, the Island of Women."

"I read the guidebook," Mack said.

Lars coughed out a nervous laugh. "Course you did. Hey, I'm just trying to break the ice here, Mackie."

"Is that what you're doing? I thought maybe you were trying to charm me out of having your ass extradited back home."

Lars blinked and reddened as if he had been slapped. "Jeez, Mack, why would you want to do that?"

"Why do you think? Maybe because you destroyed my life? Left me broke and looking like a complete fool?" He gripped the crumbling stone, leaning into his words, trying to drive them into Lars's blinking blue eyes.

"Is that how you see it, Mackie?"

"It's got nothing to do with how I see it."

Lars squatted down and moved his portable golf tee a few inches closer to the edge. "We had a good thing going. You took out, what, a hundred grand in salary?"

"Yeah, and now I owe six times that to the bank. Not to mention what I owe my wife's parents, our vendors, and the good people who worked for us."

"Mackie, Mackie . . ." Lars shook his head, walked over, and took a seat on the ruined wall. They were facing the sea, six feet between them. Lars pointed up at the clouds. "Looks like we got a little squall coming in."

"That's the least of your worries," Mack said.

Lars smiled. Mack held himself rigid.

Lars said, "You don't have to pay any of them, you know. Why don't you just walk away?"

Mack felt a surge of fury threaten to lift him from his perch. "I can't believe you're saying that to me."

"Why?" Lars lifted his eyebrows. "Because you're better than me? I'm such an evil son of a bitch that I'd screw my own mother while you're a paragon of morality and virtue? I didn't beg you to do business with me, my friend. You wanted it just as bad as I did. The only difference is, I got out first."

Mack did not trust himself to reply.

"It's your choice, Mackie. You want to let the bank and everybody else push you around? Christ, Mack, they're just as guilty as you and me. Everybody was sucking off the same tit and now, let me guess, everybody's calling me the bad guy. Am I right? Hell yes, I'm right." Lars sucked his cigar, red cheeks hollowing.

"You *are* the bad guy," Mack said.

"That's okay. I can handle the karma. I'm like Popeye. I yam who I yam. You can't change who you are, Mackie. That's the one thing you don't want to do." He took a few more agitated puffs, stood, and set up another golf ball.

"I talked to a fellow name of Pleasant," Mack said.

Lars shivered visibly. "Jesus Christ," he said. "What did that ass-hole want?"

"He wants you."

"Yeah? Well, everybody wants something." He looked out over the ocean as if searching for the flag on a par three, then turned back to Mack. "All Pleasant ever wanted was to lay a hurt on me, and do you know why? Because he feels sorry for himself, that's why. I feel sorry for him, too. Stuck in his sorry little life."

"Maybe he's just a cop doing his job."

Lars laughed. "That's another way to look at it. But hell, if I spent all my time worrying about guys like Jerry Pleasant I wouldn't get a thing done now, would I? Look, the problem is, nobody seems to see the big picture. They think of Mac-Lar as a failed business. They hold us responsible. Mack, we didn't fail. It's companies like Mac-Lar that drive the economy. We made some moves, took some risks, and got the money flowing. We created jobs, developed products, made a real positive impact on the community. Just because we went belly-up doesn't make us a failure. Look at Montgomery Ward. They went bankrupt, kaput, but for a hundred and some years they were this huge success story. Only difference is, we didn't last quite as long. Even now we're keeping people working: the bankers, the lawyers— even that carbuncle Jerry Pleasant. Wasn't for me he'd be directing traffic." He lined up the face of the driver with the ball. "Bring my top hand over more, you say?"

"That's right."

Lars shifted his grip, brought the club back, and swung. The ball sailed straight and true, rising above the horizon, seeming to disappear into the churning clouds.

"Damn!" He grinned. "For a guy doesn't golf anymore, you are one hell of an instructor."

Mack suppressed a spark of pleasure. "How much money do you have left?" he asked.

"Money?" Lars shrugged. "Maybe I spent it all."

"I figure you took about half a million."

"I wish!" Lars squatted down in front of Mack and balanced the golf club across his knees as if checking out the roll of a green. "Mack, I'm gonna be straight with you because I like you. Always did." He tipped his panama back, revealing a red stripe where the sweatband had gripped on his forehead. "Nobody's getting my money. Period. *Finiquito.* But that doesn't mean I'm not gonna help you out here. You don't have to let those guys push you around. Your cousin, Bob Seaman? Is he giving you a hard time now?"

Mack felt himself nod helplessly. Somehow Lars had taken control.

"Doesn't surprise me, that little weasel. You know how we got all those loans approved? No? I suppose you thought they were throwing all this money our way because we had a great business plan and a handful of purchase orders. Real world, Mack. We got the loans because your cousin Bobby had his eye on a new BMW. I kicked him back thirty. Called it a loan, actually. Of course, we both know he's never gonna pay it back, but I had him sign a note just in case. He was dumb enough to do it."

"What? You bribed Bob to give us the loan?"

"You got it, amigo. He loans us three hundred thou, I borrow him back thirty. Then I get their factoring division to come up with another two-twenty, based on the P.O.'s I brought in. Bob helped expedite that, too. By that time he was in too deep to say no. Of course, he figured we'd be good for it. You show a guy a little cash and he'll make himself believe anything. Lemme tell you a secret, Mack. You can buy just about anybody. Even people think they're not bribable, you show them enough money and they can't stop themselves. It's human nature." Lars used the golf club to help him stand up. "Whoo! Knees aren't what they used to be." He paced back and forth between Mack and the sky. Choppy gusts of wind tugged at their clothing. "It's a game, Mack. A guy like me gets the money moving, all that green swirling around, then *boom!* Everybody goes for it. You've still got Mac-Lar, right?"

"The bank's got it."

"But they need you. You're the man, Mack. You can start the tap flowing all over again. Just get your cousin to lend you the money and buy the company back from the bank. They'll not only have a shot at getting some of their original loan back, they'll also be booking a new loan. Of course, with that much debt you'll go bankrupt eventually, but the main thing is to get the cash flowing. Once it's coming in the door, you take care of yourself."

Mack blinked, stunned by the outrageousness of it.

Lars said, "You have to understand the way these guys think. They don't actually give a shit if you default. All they want is to look good. The money doesn't really matter."

"It matters to my in-laws. They're out more than a quarter million."

Lars shrugged. "Hey, I can't fix everybody's problems." He set up another golf ball.

"None of this gets to you, does it? You really don't feel bad about the people you've hurt?"

"I don't hurt people, Mack." Lars lined up his club. "I just create situations. I give people choices." He looked at Mack. "You've got a choice too, Mackie. Grab the gold ring or ride around in circles the rest of your life."

He brought the club back and swung at the ball, hitting it squarely just as a gust of wind came from behind and lifted his hat from his head. Off balance from the swing, Lars lunged toward the edge and shot out an arm, catching the hat by the brim. He laughed, balanced on one leg at the verge of a deadly drop, wind flapping his shorts, unafraid. Lars was teasing him, Mack realized, challenging him to act and knowing that he would not. Mack MacWray was not capable of revenge, or of saving his own business, or of any action requiring courage or commitment. He felt a deep sense of shame. He could no more grab the gold ring than he could throw himself off this precipice into the sea.

Lars shifted his weight, bringing his other foot back down—then he disappeared.

The golf club clattered to the rock.

For an instant Mack did not understand what had happened. Lars had been there, smiling, golf club in hand—and then he was gone, as if pulled over the edge by an invisible force. Only the sky and the sea, the sounds of wind and of surf remained. Mack replayed the last second, seeing it more clearly now. A rock had given way, the island eroding beneath him, and Lars had simply dropped.

Mack thought, Is this real? The golf club at the edge of the cliff was real. Did I push him? Did I do something without knowing it? No, he decided. He hadn't moved a muscle. He was glued to this ruin, devoid of volition. Was it possible that Lars had survived the fall? Not likely—it was nearly a hundred feet down to the jagged rock.

"Mack!"

Mack stood up, looked around. He was alone.

"Mack!" Lars's voice, coming over the edge. Mack approached the edge.

Lars was hanging on the face of the rock, his hands only inches below the edge, his eyes wide with terror.

"Gimme a hand, Mackie." White fingers gripped a narrow shelf. "C'mon, Mackie. I got a situation here."

He could reach over the edge and offer his hand. Lars could grab hold and climb up. It would be easy. Or he could offer him one end of the golf club. Either method would work.

Mack moved a few feet to the side to get a different view of Lars's predicament. One foot had caught a projection of stone, supporting most of his weight. The other hung free. Below, black rock chopped and slashed the waves.

"Macanudo?"

Mack stepped back and looked up at the low gray sky. The cloud cover was nearly complete.

"Mack, c'mon, buddy. Quit fooling with me."

Mack picked up the golf club and looked again at Lars. He felt bright and hard and jagged inside.

"Mack, look, you want money? Whatever you want. I'm telling you."

Mack liked how artificial this felt, and yet how realistic. The man hanging there talking, begging him to do something, but the words splintered and lost meaning in the wind.

"Mack?"

Mack looked Lars in the face: eyes round and blue as robins' eggs.

Mack had never seen that expression on Lars: fear and disbelief, as if confronted by a ghost.

"I can't hang on, Mack. For Christ's sake, have a heart."

Mack did not reply. He stood and watched—it only took another minute or two—until Lars's fingers began to slip. Mack thought, Is this how Lars felt, looking down at me?

"Anything you want, Mack! It's yours!"

Mack did not move. Lars made a desperate grab, trying for a new grip, but his fingers tore on the sharp rock and he fell.

~

Thick and thin, hot and cold, hard and soft: Paula MacWray jolted awake. For a moment, disoriented, struck with fear, she raised her hands to protect herself. The sky had gone gray; wind raised goose bumps on her thighs. She sat up. A plastic cup scudded across the poolside tiles. The other bathers had left the pool. Her beer bottle floated empty in the ice bucket. She pulled the headphones off and climbed to her feet. What was happening? Where had the sun gone, and where was the wind coming from? She picked up her Walkman. How long ago had the tape ended? She wrapped her towel around her shoulders, shivered. With the sun obscured, she had no idea of the time. She put her feet into her flip-flops and shuffled toward their room, wondering what had awakened her.

9

Mack could see nothing but a tumble of rocks and foam. He stood at the exact spot from which Lars had fallen and looked straight down but could not see where Lars had landed. Could he have survived? Lars's head had struck rock on the way down. He had seen a flash of bright red blood. Survival seemed unlikely. For a moment he imagined himself following Lars off the edge. Raising his head, he sought the reassuring flatness of the horizon, but the clouds now melded with the ocean in a broad band of shifting grays, offering no reference point. Disoriented, Mack backed away from the precipice.

What had happened? What had he done? Mack returned to his perch on the ruins. He lit a cigarette.

Lars had fallen. He had done nothing.

Mack hugged himself. His eyes fixed on the golf club, on the bucket of balls. He saw a scattering of pebbles, the ruin of Lars's makeshift tee, and beside him, on the crumbling wall, the cigar Lars had tossed to him. He had done nothing. He hadn't raised a finger. He was blameless. An innocent bystander. Witness to an accident. Yes, he could have saved Lars's life, but he had chosen not to do so. No, that wasn't quite right. He had *not* chosen to act—a minor but, it seemed to him, pivotal point.

Why did he feel so naked? The sound of wind in his ears rose and fell in pitch. Closing his eyes, he saw his knees pressing into cracked vinyl padding, saw his hands clasped before a perforated waxed screen. *Bless me, Father, for I have sinned . . .* He shook his head, casting the memory aside, searching for a thought that would make him feel better.

Lars's blue eyes, round with terror.

"You did this to me," Mack said.

Wind answered; he could hear Lars's laugh.

"It wasn't my fault, damn you." Waves of guilt pounded him, drawing him deeper. *It has been twenty-five years since my last confession . . .* He gritted his teeth and forced his thoughts to travel down new pathways. He needed to get outside of himself, see the big picture: Two animals, self-aware biological constructs with conflicting values, had come together. One had not survived the encounter. Only one might go on to produce offspring.

That was good. That way of thinking caused him no pain. He tried taking it in a slightly different direction: Two entities stand before God, awaiting judgment. The evil one is cast into the abyss while the good entity, who chose not to intervene, receives the gift of life.

That was better, except for the disturbing presence of a supreme being. He replaced God with fate, replaced judgment with the flip of a coin. He opened his eyes, saw the edge of the cliff in cartoonishly hard focus. He stood and surveyed the rocky point. The smooth walls of the lighthouse glowed yellowish white against the leaden sky, like a pillar of old bone. He cast his gaze out over the ocean.

This time, the indistinct horizon did not bother him. He felt himself on solid ground for once. He remembered something he had once read—that given a long enough lever, the will, and a place to stand, a man could move the world.

All he needed now was the lever.

~

The first few breaks in the cliff dead-ended a few yards from the top, and Mack had to climb back up. Then, after walking past it twice, he noticed a faint trail leading away from the main path toward a cut in the cliff. He knelt at the edge and looked down. A wide shelf, smooth with wear, lay a few feet below. He lowered himself, first holding on to a small shrub, then a rock, then feeling solidity beneath his feet.

From the shelf he could see a well-worn path leading along the face of the rock. Placing his feet carefully, Mack followed millennia of Mayan footsteps from the cliffs down to the sea. The descent took only a few minutes, and except for one spot where he couldn't see where to put his feet, it was easy. He reached the bottom about two hundred yards from the point of the island, the place where Lars had fallen. Between them lay a jumble of sharp rocks, slippery with seaweed, and breakers varying in size and fury.

I could die too, he thought. The clouds seemed lower and darker. Mack was not sure whether the spray soaking his shirt came from the waves or the sky. He pushed aside speculation and fear and scaled a mound of rock, staying as close to the base of the cliff as possible. He began to work his way toward the point with slothlike determination, using all four of his limbs. Halfway there, he came upon a foamy pool, about thirty feet across, filling a hollow in the cliff face. Every few seconds an enormous wave would crash into the hollow, foaming and roiling the pool. The rock face was smooth; he could see no handholds. In calmer weather he could have easily crossed, but these waves would pulverize him in seconds. What would the Mayans do? Undecided, Mack watched the waves pummel the base of the cliff. Was there a pattern? A brief period of calm seemed to follow each series of crashes. Enough time to cross the pool? He stood, undecided, then suddenly launched himself forward. Half wading, half swimming, he splashed his way toward the other side. He was nearly there when an enormous salty hand smashed down on him, driving him under the surface. His knee hit something hard. The pain galvanized him. Limbs churning, he clawed his way to the far side of the pool and dragged himself up onto the rocks just as another series of breakers crashed into the hollow. Mack hung on. When the waves subsided he climbed to his feet. His knee hurt but it wasn't bleeding. He continued around the base of the cliff, stepping from rock to rock, until he spotted Lars's straw hat bobbing in the foam.

Lars himself sat upright on a rock the size of a small car, his back resting against the cliff face. His legs stuck straight out and his chin rested on his chest. He might have been napping. Crashing waves sent a fine spray over the rock. In startling contrast to his chartreuse shorts, Lars's guayabera glowed pink with diluted blood.

As Mack moved closer he saw that the back of Lars's head had been crushed and torn open, exposing parts of his brain. No question about it: Lars Larson was stone-cold dead. Mack searched himself for feelings of horror or regret, but he found only a mild queasiness. The rain was definite now. Large, loose drops pocked the smooth backs of the waves and splashed his shoulders.

Averting his eyes from the ruin of Lars's skull, Mack took a few fortifying breaths and went to work emptying Lars's pockets. He found a wallet, a cigar lighter, a few pesos in loose change, and a set of keys. One of the keys was large, brass, and inscribed with the words *Hotel Caribe No. 4.* He pulled off Lars's belt and discovered a zipper pouch containing $700, all in fifties. He pocketed the money and tossed the belt into the sea. A flat bulge at Lars's hip caught his eye. He tugged out the waistband and found a small-caliber automatic pistol in a clip holster. Mack looked at the gun for a long time, considering its implications. He put the gun in his pocket and left the holster clipped to Lars's waistband.

Anything else? The diamond ring. Trying not to touch the cooling flesh, he worked the gold band over Lars's knuckle. It was astonishingly heavy. Mack read the inscription inside: *To My Teddy Bear with Love, R.*

Mack tried the ring on each of his fingers. Too big. Taking one last look at Lars, he pocketed the ring and said, *"Adiós, amigo."*

The rain was falling steadily now, but looking out to sea he could see sunlight sparkling the water. He returned the way he had come, this time crossing the pool without incident. By the time he reached the top, the rain had stopped and the clouds were moving off. Sun swept across the point. The temple of Ixchel, refreshed, glowed with golden light. The lighthouse had lost its yellowish tinge and now shone white as a new bolt of bleached poplin. Mack tipped his head back and let the sun bake his forehead. His T-shirt was drying, and the pain in his knee had subsided to a distant throb. He ran his fingers through his hair and realized for the first time that he had lost his cap, but he didn't care. He felt good. He felt better than he had in a long, long time.

10

From North Beach, Rita Larson could see the rain. The squall had come over from the mainland, carried by a raft of low clouds, and appeared to be soaking the south end of the island. Every few minutes she would look up from her Judith Krantz novel and peer over the tops of her sunglasses to observe the weather, each time noting with satisfaction that it would not interfere with her sunbathing.

At 3:45 the watch in the sand beside her beeped. She rolled onto her belly and, reaching back, adjusted the strings on her metallic gold bikini bottom. Her tan was nearing perfection. By employing an assortment of swimsuit bottoms—string bikinis, thongs, and one daring item that was less than a G-string—and by changing her position frequently, she had achieved a smooth, dark, even pigmentation over her entire body. Her skin had taken on the color of burnt caramel— darker than her lips or her nails, which were coated with ecru polish. Her hair was bleached nearly white, and the blue of her eyes had faded to the color of sky. She was without question the most striking female on Isla Mujeres—possibly on the entire Yucatán peninsula. It gave her great satisfaction to walk the streets of downtown Isla, turning heads. Or to take a seat at Daniel's and cross her long toned legs and sip margaritas for a few hours. With or without Teddy.

Rita propped herself up on her elbows and continued to read about powerful men and women, about betrayal, deceit, passion, and redemption. Two pairs of bare feet walked past, a few yards in front of her. The first pair stopped, the second ran into the first. She didn't have to look up to know that the two young men were angling for a better view. Her nipples, suddenly erect, brushed the nap of her beach towel. She lifted her shoulders an inch, giving the guys a better view. The feet did not move for several seconds, waiting for more. Rita continued to read. The feet moved away, slowly.

At four-fifteen her watch beeped again. Rita closed her book and sat up. She tied on her bikini top, stood up, shook the sand from her blanket, draped it over her shoulders like a cape. She tucked her book under her arm. She picked up her metallic gold high-heeled sandals, carried them across the sand to Calle Hidalgo, where she carefully brushed away the sand and put them on her feet.

She sensed eyes upon her. Every male within ogling distance would stop what they were doing to watch her pass by. She felt like a character in the novel she was reading. Even better, on this island of women she was royalty. More than that: a deity, perhaps the reincarnation of the goddess Ixchel.

Walking slowly, her beach towel flowing behind her, a pale smile fixed upon her divine features, she made her way to Calle Matamoros. Would Teddy be back from Cancún? She hoped so. She wanted to go out to dinner, maybe to the French Bistro Français for grilled lobster. She hadn't eaten lobster in a week. Too long. As she turned onto Matamoros, Rita noticed Teddy's golf cart parked in front of their building. Good, he was home. But why had he left the cart out front?

As soon as the lobby door closed behind her, Rita's shoulders sagged forward and her breasts dropped a good three inches. She removed her sandals. They looked great but set her calves ablaze. Tonight she would wear flats. She climbed the steps slowly, enjoying the feel of smooth, cool stone on her bare feet, looking down at the way her toes splayed, at the contrasting colors: gray stone, ecru nails, caramel flesh. She watched her feet ascend the three flights of stairs. Yes, lobster was exactly what she needed. She had once read that the pigments contained in lobster roe, when consumed with coconut meat, could deepen a tan. She would insist on a female lobster.

Rita unlocked the door to the condo and stepped inside. She dropped her towel, book, and sandals on the floor, untied and shrugged out of her bikini top, tossed it on the hall table. Much better.

"Teddy?"

No answer. She went to the refrigerator and opened a Diet Coke.

"Teddy Bear?"

Three boxes of cigars sat on the glass-topped rattan table. Good. Teddy liked his Havanas. When he couldn't find the kind he liked he was capable of sulking for days on end.

She heard a rustling sound coming from the bedroom and called out, "You in there, Teddy Bear?"

The goddess headed for the bedroom, dropping her bikini bottom as she walked, brushing a few stray grains of white sand from her bronzed hips.

~

The decorative iron scrollwork, thick with layers of cracking paint, cut into his fingers. He was hanging from the balcony railing, looking into the bedroom. Mack shifted his grip and looked down. The stone fountain was thirty feet below. From this angle it looked as deadly as the rocks that had claimed Lars.

Immediately below Mack was another balcony. When he had let himself over the railing, he'd thought that he would be able to reach the railing below with his feet, but no matter how he stretched he could find no purchase. Still, he knew the balcony was there, a foot or two below the tips of his toes. He could swing himself in, let go at the right moment, and land safely. Maybe.

"Teddy?"

He returned his attention to the bedroom and nearly lost his grip. The creature standing in the doorway looked like an Amazon queen out of a pornographic comic book: blond, buxom, bronzed, and stark naked. Her pubic hair, trimmed to a neat triangle, was lighter than the surrounding flesh. It took him several thudding heartbeats to recognize her as Rita Monbeck, former bookkeeper and, according to Jerry Pleasant, Lars's wife. Lars's *widow*. She looked around the bedroom wearing a confused expression. With her pale, close-set eyes and vapid smile it didn't take much. Her eyes swept across him without landing, seeing only the familiar ornate ironwork of the railing.

Mack's arms were burning. He didn't know how long he could hang on. Go back, he willed her. Please go back into the other rooms.

Still with the perplexed look, Rita's right hand drifted to her abdomen and strummed her belly button. She turned slowly around, giving him a look at her nicely proportioned buttocks. Under different circumstances he might have enjoyed the view.

Could he swing onto the balcony below while she was right there? Maybe, but he would have to start himself swinging, and that would make some noise. She would see him. That would be bad.

Please go away, he mouthed.

She started to leave, then stopped, catching sight of herself in the full-length mirror next to the doorway.

For god's sake, woman, move on! Mack's left hand was going numb.

Rita was turning, slowly, giving herself a seductive smile.

Now or never, Mack thought. He started his legs swinging.

The railing clanked; Rita turned. Her eyes found him. Pale lips fell open in astonishment. Mack's legs swung inward and he let go, arching his back, then curling forward.

He almost had it figured. His legs made it onto the second-floor balcony, but the railing struck his shoulder blades. Mack bounced off the railing and fell forward into a metal chair, knocking it through a set of glass doors into someone's bedroom. For a moment he lay there, the breath driven from his lungs, furious with himself for misjudging the drop. Sucking air, he scrambled to his feet and ran through the bedroom out into the hall and straight into a very frightened-looking Mexican woman. He pushed her aside, found the door, and seconds later was on the street, running. The papers he'd stuffed into his pants were working their way down into his left leg. Had Rita recognized him? He didn't think so. As he neared the ferry docks he looked back. No one was chasing him. Of course not! Did he think she would come after him buck naked? What was he worried about? He stopped and worked the papers out of his pants. Mack had grabbed everything that looked useful from Lars's desk drawers—bank statements, records, a calendar, and his passport. It would have to do. His shoulder blades throbbed where he had hit the railing. He reached back. His shirt was torn.

Enough. He had to get off this island. He crossed the street to the ferry docks, searched until he found a young man lounging near a small boat with an oversize outboard motor. He pulled a bill from his pocket, a fifty with three lengthwise creases from Lars's money belt.

"Cancún!" he said, trying to keep his voice urgent but not hysterical. "Take me to Cancún! *¡Cancún, por favor!*" He thrust the bill at the kid. "*¡Rápido! ¡Rápido!*"

~

Instead of being frightened by the window peeper—or balcony peeper—Rita was excited, amused, and flattered. It made complete sense that a voyeur would seek her out. As Isla's resident goddess, she would be the Holy Grail of window peepers. Think of all the effort he'd gone to just to get a look at her. He had risked his life! That one eyeful of her would keep the little creep's right hand pumping for weeks—once he recovered from his fall onto Señora Garcia's balcony. The poor woman wouldn't be sleeping peacefully for a long time.

Rita added a splash of rum to her Diet Coke and looked at her watch. She wished Teddy would get home. She couldn't wait to tell him.

11

The sun had set when Paula woke up again, this time on the bed in their room. The television set was tuned to a Mexican soap opera and the air felt like ice. Paula sat up, blinking, rubbing her arms. She looked at her watch. Seven o'clock. She frowned.

Two hours ago she had showered and changed into her sleeveless linen dress. She had turned up the air-conditioning and turned on the TV and thought about where she wanted to have dinner. Mack would want to find someplace quiet, while she craved noise and crowds. No doubt they would find a restaurant that suited neither of them. At some point she had fallen asleep. She'd been sleeping a lot, lately.

She heard a sound from the small sitting area outside the bedroom.

"Mack?" She felt her heart thud twice before he replied.

"Hi." The light in the sitting area went on. His silhouette filled the bedroom doorway.

"Where have you been?" She let her irritation show in her voice. "You scared me." She swung her legs over the edge of the bed.

"Sorry." He moved toward her.

"It's after seven. I'm hungry."

He grasped her shoulders, lifted her to her feet. He was not wearing a shirt.

"Mack?"

His hands moved up, cupped her head, pulled her mouth to his. She stiffened, then returned the kiss. His lips felt different, hungrier and harder than she remembered. His hands traveled down her back, over her buttocks, pulling her into him.

"Are you drunk?" she asked. Her voice was a squeak, her nipples stones.

His hands gathered linen; the dress came up and over her head. He tossed it over the television and pushed her down onto the bed, stripped off her panties. She opened her mouth to say something, but what came out was a gasp. He stepped out of his pants and was on her, tasting her, inhaling her, devouring her. Overcome by the intensity of his desire—of her own desire—she let her body respond freely, felt her vulva open, a rose uncoiling, demanding to be filled and, within seconds, the demand was answered. Her back arched and her legs clamped on and she gave herself to the primal rhythm, each thrust driving her deeper into the jungle. She saw Mayan pyramids, burning sun, tropical lightning, and then, in the prolonged moment at the brink of her orgasm, she realized that this time she did not have to imagine him as another man because in every way that mattered, for whatever unimaginable reason, he was.

~

"My god, what happened to your back?"

"I fell. It's okay."

"It's not okay. Let me look."

Mack sat on the edge of the bed, felt her fingers touch his back lightly.

"Does that hurt?"

"No."

"You've got a huge bruise!"

Mack shrugged. He picked a clean shirt from the closet. "I'll be fine. Don't worry about it. Where do you want to eat?"

Paula hesitated. She didn't want to ruin things by dragging him to someplace that would make him uncomfortable. "Did you have something in mind?"

Mack turned toward her, buttoning his shirt. "How about Señor Frog's?"

"Really?"

"Sure. I hear it's fun."

"It might be crowded."

Mack grinned. "The more the merrier."

~

Several times during the evening Paula wanted to say, "Who *are* you, mister?" But it seemed too corny. Also, she was afraid that by looking too hard she would change something. They were dancing! Mack hadn't danced with her in years. He'd been so clumsy and uncomfortable on the dance floor that she'd quit asking, much to his relief. But this time it had been his idea, and while he was as graceless as ever, he was having such a good time that it didn't matter. All she had to do was watch out for his feet. Had the hypnotic salsa rhythms seduced him? Or something else? Again, she didn't want to jinx the evening by inquiring.

In the end, she was the one who pooped out.

"No more, Mack. Look at me. I'm drenched!" But she felt great. The drinks they'd had, maybe half a dozen shots of tequila and a couple of beers each, had been burned up on the dance floor.

"One more," he said, signaling a waiter.

"Mack, it's after two in the morning!"

"What haven't we tried yet?"

"God, I can't remember what we *did* try."

Mack read from the tequila list propped on their table. "What about the Centenario Anejo?" He looked up at the approaching waiter, pointed at the menu. *"Dos Centenario, por favor."*

The waiter made an odd motion, almost a curtsy, and headed for the bar.

"Sir, are you trying to get me drunk?" Paula asked.

Mack—the *new* Mack—raised an eyebrow and grinned. *"Absolutamente."*

~

They made love more slowly this time, a swaying, liquid merging of bodies mellowed by tequila and fatigue. Paula was asleep moments after they separated. Mack lay on his back beside her, feeling the evaporating perspiration cool his belly, listening to her breathing. He waited until she began to emit a soft fluttering sound—Paula's version of snoring—before he rolled quietly out of bed, went out to the sitting room, and closed the bedroom door.

The papers he had grabbed at Lars's condominium were now in the drawer of the small writing desk, beneath the Cancún yellow pages and some coupon booklets. He sorted through them quickly. Deposit receipts from the Cancún Banamex, phone bills from Telmex, a calendar filled with cryptic notes, and Lars's current passport. Mack set aside the passport and the bank receipts and returned the rest of the materials to the drawer.

Lars's wallet, his keys, and his gun were stashed beneath the cushions of the small sofa. Mack removed Lars's Banamex identification card from the wallet. The photo showed Lars smiling, his eyes half closed. Mack stared at the photo, searching himself for signs of regret or guilt but sensing neither. Lars was dead. His death provided certain opportunities, which Mack was now able to perceive with chilly clarity.

He reached under the sofa and pulled out a paper bag. Inside were several items he had purchased that afternoon in downtown Cancún: a box of single-edge razor blades, a small tube of clear cement, and a dozen Polaroids—images of himself standing in front of a white wall smiling, frowning, gazing blankly into the camera, each one taken at a different distance by a friendly Cancún street photographer. He held the photos up against Lars's Banamex card until he found one with the same size head. The look of the photos did not match. The Polaroid had been taken outside in the sunlight instead of indoors with a flash. But they were close enough. Or so he hoped.

Mack unwrapped one of the razor blades and went to work on the Banamex card. Slowly, with excruciating care and patience, he began to peel back the laminate.

The most remarkable thing about the past twelve hours, he thought as he worked, was the great sex. His burden of self-consciousness seemed to have evaporated, freeing him to simply *take*. He'd simply gone after Paula, just taken what he wanted without thinking or caring what *she* wanted—and it turned out that *that* was *exactly* what she wanted. He smiled at the irony of it. Twelve years of trying to please her and it wasn't until he finally decided the hell with her and everybody else in this world that he was able to satisfy her. Life could be simpler and more rewarding than he had ever suspected.

Once he had the laminate peeled back, the photo of Lars came off easily. Mack used it as a template to cut out his own image.

The same with the dancing. Letting himself go, not caring what anybody thought, just bouncing to the beat. He hadn't had so much fun in years. Even more rewarding was that he hadn't really wanted to go dancing—his purpose had been to get Paula drunk and tired so that she would sleep while he performed the task at hand. Amazing how one good thing led to others.

A few drops of cement and the Banamex card was back together, now with his image in place of Lars's. It looked good. He put the card back into Lars's wallet and went to work on the passport.

Changing the passport photo presented a greater challenge. The lamination was solid—any effort to separate it would tear the underlying paper. Even worse, the underside of the laminate was printed with a complex seal, a portion of which overlapped the photo. After considering several strategies—most of which required equipment not at hand—he decided to simply glue his photo on top. It was crude, and would not pass even the most cursory examination by a customs official, but it might be good enough for Banamex. He hoped he wouldn't have to show it.

Yawning, Mack paged through Lars's bank statements once more to make sure he hadn't missed anything. The most recent statement showed 5,092 pesos—about $500—in an account held jointly by Lars and Rita Larson. The statement was in Spanish. He wasn't sure whether it was a checking or savings account. Not that it mattered. Rita could keep the five hundred bucks. What Mack was interested in was the one-hundred-peso fee on the previous month's statement. The item listed beside the fee was *"Caja de seguridad."*

One of the keys on Lars's key chain looked very much as though it would open a safe deposit box.

Using the signature on the passport as a guide, Mack began to practice Lars's loopy oversize signature: *T. W. Larson.* He filled the inside back cover of the phone book with signatures, each one looking a little better. When the page was full he went on to sign in the margins of the inside pages. *T. W. Larson, T. W. Larson, T. W. Larson.* When his fingers began to cramp, he shook out his hand, massaged it briefly, and continued signing, until *T. W. Larson* flowed effortlessly from his pen.

12

At precisely 10 A.M., Mack stood across the street from the Banamex, watching as the guard unlocked the door. He did not want to be the first customer of the day, so he waited until several others had entered the bank. He used the time to tell himself how easy it would be. All he had to do was pretend he was Lars. Move with confidence, speak without hesitation. The people working there would not really care. To them he would be just another transaction. He had to make it all seem routine.

He wished he knew the routine.

In a U.S. bank he would simply present his safe deposit box key, sign a ledger, and present some form of identification. In Mexico it might be different. It might be easier or it might be impossible. They might have a photo of Lars on file. That would be bad. Equally bad would be if they knew Lars by sight. That, he decided, was the greater risk. If Lars made frequent visits to his safe deposit box he might be well known to the staff.

Don't think about it, he told himself. Think too hard and you'll lose momentum. He remembered something Lars had once told him about golf: *Never let the ball know you're afraid.*

At twenty minutes after ten he crossed the street and entered the bank. He walked past the guard and into a lobby that looked more like an OTB parlor than a bank: a row of seven fortified teller cages, and steel doors at each end of the long room. Four customers stood in line at the only open teller cage. A long metal bench against the opposite wall supported several other customers. Even though the bank had just opened, they managed to look as though they had been waiting for hours. Mack returned to the guard.

"Excuse me?" He held up the key. *"¿Dónde está cajas de seguridad? ¿Por favor?"*

The guard stared at the key as if he had never seen such a thing.

Mack said, "Safe deposit box?" He inserted the key into an imaginary lock and turned it.

The guard licked his lips. *"Un momento, señor."* He lifted a walkie-talkie from his belt and spoke into it, listened to the brief reply, then motioned for Mack to take a seat on the long metal bench.

Ten minutes later one of the steel doors opened. A woman with jet black hair, a navy blue jacket, a tight matching skirt, and four-inch heels emerged. She said something to the guard, who pointed at Mack with the antenna of his radio. The woman clacked across the marble floor with short, rapid steps. She addressed him in English.

"You wish to access your security box?" She looked older than he had thought at first—maybe forty-five, but quite attractive in a heavily made-up, frozen-faced way. A pair of reading glasses hung from a chain around her neck.

"Yes." Mack smiled and stood.

The woman thrust out a hand. "May I have your key?" Her nails were long, red, and squared off at the tips.

He gave her Lars's key.

"And your card, please?"

Mack's heart began to pound as he gave her the altered Banamex card. She perched her reading glasses on her nose and examined the card without expression. She returned it to him. The corners of her mouth twitched, possibly in imitation of a smile. She lowered her glasses.

"Follow me, please, Señor Larson."

She led him through the steel door into a carpeted hallway, where a second guard was stationed. Mack followed her down a flight of stairs, past yet another guard, to a small room containing a desk, a computer, and a bank of files. The guard followed them into the room and stood quietly by the door. The opposite end of the room ended in metal bars, beyond which Mack could see another room, walled with safe deposit boxes of various sizes. Suppressing a shudder, Mack steered his mind away from visions of Mexican prison. The only decoration in the room was a framed bullfight poster on one wall. There were no chairs other than the one behind the desk. The woman sat down. She brought out a complex-looking, legal-size multiform and carefully filled in several of the blanks. This took about two minutes. She inspected her work, found it to be satisfactory, turned the form 180 degrees, and tapped a box at the bottom with the point of her pen.

"You will sign here, please."

Mack signed the form: *T. W. Larson.* His hand remained steady. The woman picked up the form and viewed it through her glasses.

Two faint horizontal lines appeared on her forehead. She once again placed the form on the desk before him.

"You must fill in your account number." She tapped a red nail before another blank box. He could see the tiny dent her nail made in the paper surface.

Account number? His heart rate doubled. He didn't know the account number. Could he invent one? Not likely. One half second passed.

"I'm sorry." He shrugged, smiling. "I don't remember it."

The woman's mouth tensed and he saw that she was irritated, but not alarmed or suspicious.

She turned to her computer and typed in his name—*Lars's* name—and stared into the screen, hitting the return key every few seconds.

"Four-three-nine-one-one-two-seven-six-five-five," she said, enunciating each word clearly. She tapped the form again with her nail and repeated, "Four-three-nine-one-one-two-seven-six-five-five."

Mack filled in the number. He watched, feigning boredom, as she pulled Lars's signature card from the files and compared the two scrawls. She took several seconds to make her examination. Had Lars signed his name the same for the bank as he had on his passport? Don't think about it. Mack turned away, smiled at the guard, then rested his eyes on the bullfight poster.

A jangle of keys brought him back around. The woman had come out from behind her desk and was at the barred gate, opening it. He followed her into the vault, his legs rubbery, moving through air gone thick and soft. She looked at the small key he had given to her, went to one of the larger boxes near the floor. She inserted the key, turned it, and drew the long, covered box out of its slot. It was about eight inches wide, four deep, and nearly three feet long.

"Will you require privacy, señor?"

"Yes, please."

She motioned to the guard, who had followed them into the vault. The guard pulled the box the rest of the way out of the slot and carried it to a tiny curtained alcove, where he placed it on a small table. Mack went inside and drew the curtain. As soon as he was out of their sight his knees went weak; he had to grab on to the table to keep himself upright. He held himself there, gripping the table edge, the hinged top of the box inches from his face. He could smell the cold metal, the odor of iron and blood. Counting his breaths: six, seven, eight. At the count of ten he pushed himself upright, took a final breath, held it, and opened the box.

~

A babble of Mexican voices reached up from the courtyard, floated over the balcony, through the French doors, and tickled Rita's ears. She covered her eyes with the sweaty crook of her elbow, as if sound were light. The voices continued, rising and falling like the surf, unintelligible but recognizable: Pepe's low, hoarse grumble punctuated by bursts of Señora Garcia's *español rápido*. She could almost understand what they were saying. Señora Garcia kept repeating something that sounded like *estuprador*. Stupid? No, that was *estúpido*. She would have to ask Teddy about *estuprador*.

Rita uncovered her eyes. She was alone, sprawled naked across of the bed, covers thrown back. It had been a long, hot night. Teddy had never come home. She imagined him with one of the local *putas,* or with a tourist—some grunting, thick-ankled fräulein. What if he . . . *no!* She sat up, her heart suddenly hammering. She crossed the room to the dresser, pulled out the bottom drawer, and flipped it over, strewing Teddy's underwear collection across the carpet. A manila envelope was taped to the drawer bottom. She opened the flap and pulled out a handful of thousand-peso notes and hundred-dollar bills—about $3,000. Tension drained; she became acutely aware of the sheen of perspiration covering her body, of the wool carpet pressing against her buttocks. She pushed the money back into the envelope and replaced the drawer.

Teddy would never leave her. And if he *did* leave her, he wouldn't go without taking their emergency stash.

She went out to the kitchenette, cool tiles drawing heat out through her feet, poured herself a glass of fresh orange juice, and sat on one of the rattan chairs. She sipped the juice, and tried to imagine where he might be. It was such a tiny island. Maybe he'd had to go back to Cancún for something. She thought about what she might do when he showed up with his abashed grin, saying how sorry he was and how it would never happen again. She stared off through the walls, imagining him on a boat, in a bed, on a beach.

She was sure he wouldn't leave her.

He would be back in a day or two with some reasonable explanation. It would all make sense when Teddy told it. It might be lies, but he would make it sound good. Her eyes drifted back into focus. The three boxes of Cohibas were sitting right there in front of her.

Rita smiled. He wouldn't be gone long. Not without his cigars.

~

Paula lay in bed fighting a faint headache, thinking. What had happened last night? Had the Mack she knew been possessed? She ran a hand from her breasts down over her belly, reawakening memories of their lovemaking. It had been wonderful—and strange and frightening. Something had happened to Mack. That huge bruise on his back that he wouldn't talk about—that had to be the key. He had hurt himself somehow, maybe scared himself so bad he'd decided to change . . . but what a change!

Paula shivered, feeling both aroused and afraid. Would it last? She wished there were a phone in the room. She wanted desperately to call Julie Gorman. She could talk to Julie. If she didn't talk to somebody she would explode. And where was Mack? She hoped he wouldn't be gone all day again. She didn't think she could stand it, waiting for him all day, not knowing which Mack to expect.

She'd make herself crazy lying there with her mind jerking all over the place. She rolled out of bed and took a shower. She put on shorts and a T-shirt and went downstairs to have a late breakfast by the pool. She lingered over coffee, yogurt, and a bowl of fruit, watching the couples, the mothers with their kids, the young women sunning themselves. She wanted to tell one of them about her hot night with her husband, but it wasn't a topic one could just launch into. Besides, they would have to know Mack to appreciate it.

It was after noon when she headed back upstairs, trying to figure out what to do with herself for the rest of the day. She opened the door to their suite and almost tripped over the suitcases standing in the doorway.

"Mack?"

"In here." He was zipping up her carry-on bag.

"What—what are you doing?"

"We're going home," he said. He looked at his watch. "Our flight leaves in forty minutes. We're all checked out."

"But—"

Mack stopped her by clamping his hands on her shoulders. "There are some things I need to do," he said, his eyes clear and narrow. "Everything's going to be okay now. Trust me."

Paula felt her will evaporate. They carried the suitcases downstairs and got into a cab. Paula did not say anything for several blocks, but as they passed the Plaza Kukulcán she turned to him and asked, "How many of you are there, anyway?"

Part Two

13

"You're joking." Bob Seaman dropped his pen onto his desk and leaned back in his leather chair. "Right?"

Mack shook his head slowly.

Seaman sniffed. "Well, it wouldn't be funny if you were."

Mack smiled. "So?"

Seaman lowered his chin. "So forget it." He sat forward and rested his forearms on the desk. "Frankly, I'm disappointed in you, Mack."

Mack's smile became quizzical. "Really? Why?"

"Why? You take off for a week, just when we're trying to get your business up and running, trying to get you off the hook. You just take off, leaving me and Jake hanging. You know how hard I worked to put this thing together? Anybody else, we'd just liquidate the business, take your house, take it all. Probably file charges, too." He picked up his pen and pointed it at Mack's nose. "The fact you're family is the only reason you're not in jail right now, cousin."

"That's a load of crap," Mack said in a quiet voice.

Seaman licked his lips, then continued, stabbing the air between them with his pen. "Then you have the chutzpah to come in here with your suntan and ask us to lend you the money to buy your own business back?"

"It wouldn't take much," Mack said. "Mac-Lar's not *worth* much."

"Forget about it. It's totally unrealistic. Look, Jake's over at the factory right now. Why don't you go out there and give him a hand?"

Mack said, "What would you take right now? The cash walks in the door this minute. What would you take?"

Seaman inhaled loudly through his nose, gathering patience. "You know what we're owed."

"Sure I do, but I also know you aren't gonna get it." Mack stared through him. "Best possible scenario, you'll net about a hundred ten on the receivables, then sell the equipment and the shell for, maybe, thirty. If you can find a buyer. And to do that you have to pay your man Vink. And me—except I won't do it. Plus your own time, plus you risk exposure to lawsuits and natural disasters and the possibility that any one of those customers waiting to take delivery might cancel. Or they might not pay. Maybe you'll ship them the wrong color aprons. Maybe they go out of business. The fact is, Bob, if a guy walked in here and offered you, say, fifty thousand cash to take the whole sorry mess off your hands, you'd be a fool not to take it."

"Jake says we can net two hundred."

"Jake is making work for himself."

Seaman shrugged. "I'm sure he's not that far off."

"He's assuming I'm on board, which I'm not, because it's not going to happen the way he thinks."

"Mack—"

"What do you say? Would you sell it for fifty?"

"Mack—"

"I'm serious, Bob."

"Look, I might take an offer like that to the board, but it doesn't matter. First Star is not going to loan you the money to buy Mac-Lar."

"Why not?"

"Let's just drop it, okay?"

"Tell you what. You write me a loan for twenty thousand and I'll come up with the other thirty."

Seaman gave Mack a sharp look. "How are you going to do that?"

"I'm holding a note."

"Then that note belongs to First Star. I didn't think you were concealing assets on us, Mack."

Mack pulled a folded sheet of paper from his breast pocket, flattened it, and slid it across the desk. Seaman stared down at it, his face slowly losing color.

"Where did you get that?"

"Where do you think?"

Seaman reached out a forefinger and poked at the paper as if testing it for signs of life.

"That's not a legal document."

"Oh?" Mack picked up the paper and examined it. "It says here that you borrowed thirty thousand bucks from our friend Lars. It says"—he pointed at the third paragraph—"payable on demand."

Seaman crossed his arms. "It's not legal. What you've got there, Mack, is a page of boilerplate from some office supply store. It's not witnessed, it's not legal, and that's not my signature."

"Sure it is, Bob. Only you would be dumb enough to sign something like this."

"Even if I did, the note is to Lars Larson. It's not a bearer note."

"Now, Bob, let's be realistic." Mack's voice flowed from his throat; his chest felt warm and powerful. "You and I both know that the thirty was a kickback. How do you like your new BMW?"

Seaman's face lost its last hint of color.

"And as far as its legality . . . what difference does that make? The important question is, will your employers believe it?"

~

Jake Vink sat at MacWray's desk working the phone, going through the Mac-Lar employee files. So far he had contacted a dozen of them, and all but two had agreed to return to work. That was pretty good. With a little luck he'd have the line up and running by Wednesday—even if that wuss MacWray never came back.

"Mrs. Nguyen?" He pronounced it *Nuh-GOO-yun.* Apparently that was close enough. Those gooks didn't give a damn how you said their names.

"This is Mr. Vink, down at Mac-Lar. We are calling all Mac-Lar employees back to work. Can you come in on Wednesday?"

He listened for a moment to some semi-intelligible gabble.

"Yes, this Mr. Vink. I the boss now." Like talking to an animal. "You to come back to work, okay? No, Mr. Larson not here, Mr. Vink here. Yes, that's right . . . Wednesday morning. Okay, see you then."

He hung up the phone and pinched the bridge of his nose with his half hand, thumb and little finger squeezing hard at the point where the bone became cartilage.

That fucking MacWray. He should be the one making these calls. He'd had a feeling about the guy from the moment he met him. A born loser, right down to his wimpy handshake. Jake Vink met a lot of failures in his line of work. Some were aggressive risk takers who had taken a few too many chances, but most of them were guys like MacWray—guys who didn't have the balls to make the tough decisions. Vink had no respect for guys like that. And MacWray, taking off like that, taking a vacation, for god's sake . . . what a schmuck. Back in Nam, a guy like that, they'd put him on point every time, use him as a human mine detector. Or if he was an officer, a guy couldn't make decisions, he'd get his ass fragged.

Vink was a buff; he read everything he could get his hands on about the Vietnam War. Sometimes he actually believed that he had been there.

He dialed the next number.

"Mrs. Amurao? This is Mr. Vink, down at Mac-Lar . . ."

He was on call number fourteen when MacWray appeared in the doorway. Vink looked up, held up his thumb and finger in a gesture that he hoped said, "Screw you."

"Yes, Mrs. Fong, Wednesday morning at seven. That's right. Good-bye." He replaced the handset in its cradle and gave MacWray a tight smile. "So, you're back." He raised one eyebrow and curled his upper lip. "Have a nice vacation?"

MacWray's eyes had a cold, blank look, like a guy who'd been in the jungle too long. A guy who didn't give a shit. Vink brought his good hand down into his lap, a protective gesture.

MacWray said in a flat voice, "Get out of my chair."

Vink had to process the words twice to extract any meaning from them. He said, "What's the problem?"

Mack shook his head. "There is no problem."

Vink considered the possible responses. MacWray did not seem to be upset. If anything, he was devoid of surface emotion. That made him dangerous. It wasn't the angry guys you had to look out for, it was the ones who felt nothing.

Vink stood up and came around the desk. He said, "What are we talking here?"

"I'm back. I'm in. You're out."

"You sure about that?"

MacWray smiled.

Vink shrugged. The guy was nuts, but it wasn't his job to tell him so. "Well, hell, I'm not gonna stand here and argue with you."

"Good."

Vink picked up his briefcase. He would call Seaman from his car, find out what was going on. He was out the door when MacWray said, "Hey, Vink."

"Yeah?"

"After you talk to Bobby, you give me a call."

~

Mack stood in the center of the factory floor, listening: the hum of the fluorescent lights, the exhale of air-conditioning, the faint ticks and pings caused by gravity tugging on chairs, tables, walls. He could hear his pulse, strong and regular. In a few days the hammering of sewing machines would bury these minuscule sounds. The hums, ticks, and hisses would become inaudible, as would his heartbeat, muffled by the sound of money being made.

Making money. Before, the process had been shrouded and mysterious. All he had known to do was work. Work, and the money will come. He had been naive. Dumb as a stump, his old man would've said. The truth was, money flowed in the direction of those who wanted it most, to those who were willing to do whatever it took. Money did not seek out the good, or the fair, or the deserving. It went to the ruthless. It went to the ones capable of pushing aside the shroud of ethics and making clearheaded, profit-motivated decisions. He was one of them now. The money would flow to him.

It had flowed already: $346,000, from Lars's safe deposit box into Mack's overnight bag, now safely stashed in the garage at home. It was flowing from First Star Bank, in the form of a new line of credit—all the money he needed to get the business back on its feet. And soon it would be flowing from his customers.

Sew it and ship it. He remembered cringing at the careless simplicity of Lars's vision. He had argued, insisted upon complications, laid out the intricacies of manufacturing: the buying, the design, the cutting, the maintenance, the effects of summer humidity on thread tension, the challenge of managing a multicultural workforce, the million things that could go wrong before a purchase order could be transformed into a tricolor smock.

Just sew it and ship it, Macanudo.

It would be so easy now.

14

On the third morning of Teddy's absence, Rita Larson sat down at his small desk and began to go through his papers, searching for some clue as to where he had gone. She was at it for no more than five minutes when she realized that certain items were missing.

She could not find his appointment calendar. She could not find his passport. The fear that he had left her returned full force.

But why would he take his passport and leave the money taped under the dresser drawer? Why would he leave his cigars?

Maybe he had gone to one of the other islands. Maybe he had gone to Jamaica—or Cuba, where there were plenty of cigars. Maybe he'd followed some bimbo onto a boat.

She thought about their safe deposit box in Cancún. Just to be sure, she should call the bank, ask them if Teddy had been there. She opened desk drawers, searching for their bank statements, looking for their Banamex account number. She was sure Teddy kept them right there in the desk. They had to be someplace. Was it possible that Teddy had taken them to Cancún to straighten out some problem with their account? No, it didn't make sense. Not for three days. Rita's mind ventured further afield. Was it possible that something had happened to him?

The idea struck her with physical force—until this moment she had not imagined it. Teddy was not a man that things happened to. Teddy happened to other people. But it was possible that he'd had an accident. Maybe he had been hit by a taxi, or robbed, or had a heart attack. And for three days she had been sitting around like a lump doing nothing, just thinking about herself, being mad at him when he might be unconscious in a hospital someplace. Rita stood up, suddenly frantic. What to do? What next?

~

"He was an animal, Jules. I haven't seen him like that since before we got married. Actually, I've never seen him like that before. Ever." Paula, on her back on the bottom bench, her upper body wrapped in a towel, stared up at the cedar ceiling of the sauna. "He just kept going." She turned her head slightly to look at Julie. "Like he couldn't get enough of me."

"Really?" Julie Gorman widened her eyes. She was perched on her folded towel on the top bench. Her entire body was slick with perspiration, but her makeup remained intact. "What got into him?"

"I don't know. But I liked it. I mean, I just went into this zone . . ." She laughed. "The love zone. He . . . Every time I thought it couldn't get any better, it got better." She shifted her legs. Beads of sweat broke, ran over her thighs, pooled on the bench. "I really liked it," she said again, a defensive note entering her voice.

"What's not to like?"

"Well, it was a little disconcerting. Almost like he wasn't really Mack."

"Even better. As good as cheating, only no consequences." Julie climbed down and scooped a ladle of water from the bucket by the door. She had a body like a mildly anorexic teenager: ribs showing, small breasts and buttocks, flat stomach. It was a body a lot of women would kill for, but Paula thought she could use another ten pounds. Still, she wished that she could pull off some of the outfits that looked so great on Julie's elfin frame.

"You ready?" Julie asked, then dumped the water onto the heated rocks and scrambled back up onto her perch as the water exploded into steam. Paula closed her eyes and braced herself as the scorching fog rolled across her. She felt it heating her toenails, her fingertips, her lips.

"Hot," she gasped, imagining blisters.

"Don't you love it?"

Paula wasn't sure whether Julie was talking about the steam, about Mack, or about sex in general. She said, "It's not just the sex, though. Whatever happened, he's turned into a completely different person. For instance, he quit smoking—just like that. We got back from Cancún and I noticed he hadn't had a cigarette lately. I asked him about it and he just shrugged, like it was nothing to him. You ever hear of anybody quitting like that? Now he says he's going to get Mac-Lar up and running again. I believe him."

"That's what you wanted, right? A more aggressive Mack?"

"I guess."

"What, he made you jolly, like, four times in one night and now you're having second thoughts? You don't want it, send some my way, girl."

Paula felt a familiar jolt of arrested indignation. Julie had been doing that to her since they were kids. Always pushing, being a little too crude, a little too daring. It was pure Julie.

"It was six times," she said, smiling, feeling just the right degree of naughty.

For a minute or two they said nothing, Paula wrapped in her towel, Julie perched naked and alert above her.

"I had a little thing with Comb-over Harold while you were gone," Julie said.

"Harold Nelson? Isn't he still married?"

"Yeah, but he doesn't care."

"My god, Jules, you have to quit doing that."

"It's not serious. Just a little thing. Harold is having his midlife crisis. You know."

Paula suddenly regretted boasting about Mack's sexual prowess. Since her divorce, poor Julie had been finding only two types of men: younger men who treated her like dirt and married older men searching for an echo of their youth. Harold Nelson, fifteen years her senior, fell into the latter category.

"He bought me dinner and after that he was all hands."

"What do you expect?" Paula grinned, trying to lighten things up. "You're hot."

"He's taking some kind of pill to make his hair grow back. You know—the one that has 'certain sexual side effects'? Funny thing is, it slows some men down, but others get really horny. Which was how it hit Harold."

"Oh."

"Only, Harold's also taking a blood pressure pill that makes it hard for him to get it up. He's horny but he can't get it up. So he has to take Viagra on top of everything else."

"Oh!" Now Paula was doubly embarrassed.

"I bet Mack has never had that problem."

Paula thought for a moment, wondering what she might say that would impress her friend, then she simply smiled.

~

"How can you be a cop here and not speak English?"

The young man—a boy, really—behind the desk laughed uncomfortably, his round, smiling face shiny with perspiration. The midday sun had heated the *estación de policía* to a sticky ninety-something degrees. Rita, wearing a short skirt, a sleeveless top, and a pair of braided flip-flops, could barely tolerate it. The boy in the polyester uniform had to be doubly miserable, but she had little sympathy for him.

"*¿Dónde está su . . . ah . . . superior?*"

The boy cocked his head, hearing sounds familiar but not meaningful. He probably thought she was ordering a beer, Rita thought. "*¿Capitán?*" she tried.

"*¡Ah!*" said the boy. He lifted the phone on his desk, punched a series of buttons, and filled the mouthpiece with rapid Spanish. He listened, hung up, then pointed to a row of wooden chairs at the end of the room.

"*Un momento, por favor,*" he said.

Rita clamped her jaw. *Un momento,* on Isla, could mean anything from five seconds to five hours. She would give it twenty minutes, she decided.

As so often happened in Mexico, her unspoken intentions were

95

understood. There had been times when she thought of it as a mystical phenomenon: the ferry arriving at the last possible moment, the waiter delivering dinner seconds before hypoglycemia set in, the price of a necklace suddenly lowered to precisely the amount she was willing to pay. In this case, the *capitán*—or whatever he was—strolled into the station just as she was getting up to leave. He looked at her through a pair of wraparound sunglasses, fired a burst of Spanish at the boy behind the desk, then turned back to Rita with a broad smile.

"I am Jorge Pulido." He lifted his sunglasses to reveal a set of protuberant bloodshot eyes. "I can help you?" Jorge Pulido was a well-fed man who carried his weight high in his abdomen, as if he were wearing a corset. He wore white trousers and a khaki shirt with epaulets and metal buttons, but no ribbons, badges, or other accoutrements. His thick black hair was combed straight back, held in place by some shiny, oily substance.

Rita introduced herself and explained that she was a local, not a tourist.

"I know you," he said, bulging eyes running up and down her body. "From the beach."

"Thank you," said Rita.

"How I can help you?"

"My husband has not been home for three days."

"Oh?" Jorge Pulido adopted a serious look. "This is a new thing?"

"Yes."

Pulido tugged at his earlobe with thick fingers and muttered something to the boy behind the desk. The boy answered in equally rapid and incomprehensible Spanish.

"What's that?" Rita asked.

Pulido shrugged and offered an apologetic smile. "Nothing. Your husband, can you tell me how he looks?"

"He's big." She measured the air with her hands. "About six foot two, two hundred twenty pounds, blond hair . . ." Seeing the puzzled look on Pulido's face, she translated: "Almost two meters tall, a hundred kilos. He usually wears a panama hat."

Pulido nodded, looking increasingly unhappy.

"I'm worried that something has happened to him," she said. "I mean, it's probably nothing. But I thought I should check. You know.

Just in case." She couldn't stop talking. "He's done this before, actually. Left for a few days without telling me. But I always kind of knew where he was . . . It's probably . . . nothing."

Pulido was not looking at her anymore. His eyes had found a place on the wall.

"The thing is," Rita said, "I just thought I'd check with you in case there was an accident or something, you know, if maybe he was in a hospital . . ." Pulido had grasped her arm, his touch gentle but firm, and was leading her past the front desk to his office. He was speaking, but she could not understand him. "Maybe I should just go home," she heard herself saying.

Pulido was talking, his voice quiet, his hands on her shoulders. He wanted her to sit down. Rita did not want to sit, but his hands were insistent and she felt the hard surface of a chair beneath her buttocks. Pulido's mouth was moving but instead of words she heard a roaring sound, the sound of a radio caught between stations, or of surf against rock.

15

"Harry, Harry, you're not listening to me. I need that bias tape."

"Hey, I believe you, Mack. But I've got a problem here. You're out a hundred days on that twill order. That's twelve thousand bucks. Nate won't let me ship so much as a spool of thread until you get current."

"I'll *get* current, Harry. The money will be here. Look, how long have you known me?"

"That's not the point, Mack."

"How much business did I give you when I was with Linkway?"

"It's out of my hands, Mack. Nate wants his money."

"You can handle Nate."

"No can do, Mack."

"Christ, Harry, we're only talking about a few hundred bucks' worth of tape here. You don't think I'm good for it?"

"It's the twelve thousand he's worried about, Mack, not eight hundred bucks' worth of bias."

"I'm telling you I'm good for it. You know what happened here. I need you to work with me, Harry. Lars is gone. The bank reupped our line of credit. Everything's coming together, but I've got to have that tape."

"Hey, Mack, I'm on your side. But you gotta look at it from our point of view. Two months ago you told me a check was in the mail—"

"I thought it *was*. Lars told me he'd paid it."

"—and nada. You know what they say, Mack: Screw me once, shame on you. Screw me twice and I'm a putz. I gotta see the money."

Of all his suppliers, Mack never thought Harry Goldblatt would be the one to hold him up. Harry was a friend. Not a guy he'd want to go fishing with, but a business friend. He'd thought they had developed some mutual trust, and here Harry was telling him to go screw himself. Mack suppressed the urge to slam down the phone. He needed that bias tape. He had thirty-seven sewers coming back to work the next day and without the tape he'd have half of his line idle.

Mack took a breath to calm himself. He had the money, actually. The line of credit he'd established with First Star would cover it, but that would leave him short of working capital. His payroll came first.

He leaned back in his chair. "Okay. Here's what I'll do. I'll cut you a check this afternoon and run it out to you tonight. But I need the tape, Harry. I need you to come through for me."

"You get me a check today and I'll have the tape for you by Friday."

"I'll bring you a check tonight and pick up the tape while I'm there."

"Mack! No can do! They're backed up three days in slitting."

"Slot it in, Harry. I'm writing you a check." Mack put his feet up on his desk and wound the phone cord around his index finger. "Can you hear it? That's me signing my name. You have that tape ready for me tonight and I'll have this check in your hands. You'll be a hero."

"I don't want to be a hero."

"Everybody wants to be a hero, Harry. You have that tape for me, you get the check. Otherwise I go to Zimmerman's and screw you for the twelve."

Harry did not reply.

"How much commission you make on me last year, Harry?"

"It's got nothing to do with commish. Listen, Zimmerman can't make your tape."

"Sure they can."

"Not in one day they can't."

"Maybe not, but it's sounding like you can't either. If this was an order for Linkway you'd be all over it."

He listened to Harry Goldblatt's asthmatic breathing.

"Linkway pays us in thirty," Harry said.

"So run the tape as an order for Linkway. I bring you the check and take delivery, and you're the man of the hour. You collect the twelve past due, plus you make a sale. Nate'll kiss your fat ass."

"Goddamn it, Mack!"

"You talk to all your customers that way?"

"Just you. Okay, look, tell you what. I'll run the order."

"You do that. I'll be over with the truck at seven, okay?"

"Seven? I dunno—"

"See you at seven, Harry." Mack hung up the phone. He dropped his feet to the floor. He closed his eyes and rubbed his temples. He rechanneled his thoughts, trying to ignore the faint thudding that threatened to become a raging headache. Problem was, he was wearing too many hats. He needed his own rag man. He had to keep his mind above the details, not get bogged down.

"You okay?"

Mack opened his eyes. Jake Vink stood in the doorway, his pincer hand gripping his left wrist.

"I'm fine," Mack said. He waited.

"I talked to Seaman," Vink said. He tipped his head and regarded Mack with curiosity. "He seems to have developed a new strategy vis-à-vis Mac-Lar."

"We came to an understanding."

"So I gather. Congratulations. Of course, this means I'm out of a job."

"It was only temporary anyway."

Vink nodded. "You really going to bring this turkey back to life?"

"That's the plan."

Vink pursed his lips and looked off through the walls. "You mind telling me how you think you're gonna do that?" He turned his black-eyed gaze on Mack.

Mack stared back at him. He said, "I'm going to bully my suppliers, cheat my customers, and exploit my workers."

Vink massaged his Adam's apple with his thumb and finger. "You need a hand?"

~

Harry Goldblatt's day went wrong starting with a bad breakfast burrito, and it never got better. Orders shipped wrong, an argument with Ellie over some billing, more high cholesterol test results from his doctor, and a nasty e-mail from his ex-wife. The call from Mack MacWray was the capper. Just what he needed: a super-rush order from a guy who owed him twelve grand. What was he supposed to do? He had good, solid, paying customers waiting for product. On the other hand, if he wanted to collect the twelve thousand from Mac-Lar he had to run the tape for the guy. Either way he came out looking like a jerk. He just hoped he could ram the order through the slitting department without it catching Nate's attention. Nate Coleman, Harry's uncle and the owner of Midwest Textile Services, was already livid over the twelve. He was holding Harry personally responsible now, even though he'd been happy enough to take the order six months ago and had told Harry that maybe he wasn't worthless after all.

Harry had to call in every favor he'd ever done for Al in the slitting department to get him to run the bias tape for Mac-Lar. Maybe once he collected the twelve Nate would lay off him, or maybe he'd just find something else to complain about, but whatever way it came down he damn sure wouldn't be a hero. The only thing he'd be for sure was sitting here waiting for Mack MacWray when he ought to be home eating Lean Cuisine.

The first good thing that happened all day was that Al came through for him. The bias was stacked up by the loading dock at six o'clock. Al and his crew punched out with only an hour of overtime.

Shortly after six-thirty Harry gave in to the rumbling in his belly and bought three Snickers bars and an orange soda from the vending machines. He was sitting alone in the break room chewing glumly on Snickers bar number three when the buzzer went off back by the loading dock. He walked back to the dock and rolled up the door. The Mac-Lar cube van was there, but the man—short, blocky, crew-cut, wearing an olive green suit—was not Mack MacWray.

"Jake Vink," said the man. "You Harry?"

Harry nodded. "Where's Mack?"

"He sent me." Vink jabbed a thumb over his shoulder, pointing northeast, the general direction of Mac-Lar, then gestured toward the open door of the cube van. Something was wrong with his hand. It was like a claw. "I'm here to pick up the bias."

Harry felt the first stirrings of a panic attack. "He was supposed to bring me a check."

"I got your check," said Vink. "And I'm in a hurry. You want to load me up?"

Harry hesitated. This didn't feel right. Vink's beady black eyes were on him, waiting.

"C'mon, let's get a move on!" Vink barked.

Reflexively, Harry started stacking the rolls of fabric tape on a dolly. Vink stood watching, not offering to help. Harry felt himself starting to sweat. He rolled the loaded dolly to the edge of the dock, then stopped, still not feeling right.

"Let's go," Vink said. "I got things to do."

Harry dragged a sleeve across his beaded forehead. "You said you have a check."

Vink reached into his breast pocket, pulled out a maize-colored check. "I got a check. Now load me up." He stuffed the check in Harry's shirt pocket and clapped him on the shoulder. "There ya go, sport. Happy?"

Harry wanted nothing more than to get this rat-eyed, claw-handed guy out of here so he could go home. He loaded the bias tape into the truck while Vink stood with his arms crossed, watching him. When Harry had finished loading, Vink closed the truck door.

"Thanks, sport, you're a hero."

"No problem," Harry muttered. He forced out a weak laugh. "Long as the check clears."

"Oh, it'll clear." Vink displayed a smile that produced a sick feeling in Harry's gut. He climbed into the cab, started the truck. Harry's panicky feeling returned full-force. He tore the check from his pocket and looked at it. For a second it looked right, then he counted the zeroes. There was one missing. "Wait a minute—"

But the truck was rolling.

~

"Mission accomplished, boss man."

"Good." Mack switched the cell phone from his left ear to his right. "Harry didn't squawk?"

"He's squawking now, but I've got the bias. Only thing is, we might need him down the road. My guess is he'll be kinda skittish."

"He'll be fine. Soon as we get our cash flowing we'll pay him off and it'll be like old times. Suppliers are like dogs. You kick 'em, then throw 'em a bone, and they love you all over again."

Vink laughed. "Damn, this is gonna be fun. Sayonara, boss man."

Mack disconnected and set the phone on the bar. He picked up his martini and swallowed half of it.

"You know, Jeeves, there are very few things in this world you can count on."

"Yes sir."

"Other than a martini."

"Yes sir."

"I don't know if I mentioned it, but I'm not the rag man anymore."

"I did not know that, sir." Jeeves, whose real name was Alan Whitman, had not seen this customer for several weeks, not since the night he had served the man five martinis in the space of an hour and sent him staggering off in a cloud of self-pity. He seemed happier tonight.

"Fact is, I'm something completely different now."

"And what would that be, sir?"

"Do you believe, Jeeves, that a single act can change who a man is?"

Jeeves took a moment before answering. It was rarely a good idea to express an opinion to a customer, even when solicited.

"I couldn't say, sir."

"Do you think that if you were to do something that you would *never* do, that it would change who you are? For instance, suppose that you would never kick a dog. You wouldn't kick a dog, would you?"

"No sir."

"Not even if it wanted to bite you? Suppose that one day, for whatever reason, you did. You kick a dog. One moment you're a man who would never kick a dog, then suddenly you're a man who kicks dogs. Are you a different person now?"

"An interesting technical point, sir."

"What I mean is, does the act change something inside? Or were you a dog kicker before you kicked the dog?"

"I've never thought about it, sir," said Jeeves, who had, in fact, very definite opinions on the subject. "Would you care for another martini?"

The customer pushed his empty glass forward. "Say a good man were to commit a crime. Would he still be a good man?"

Jeeves busied himself making the former rag man a second martini. There had been a time—back when he had thought of bartending as a temporary job, back when he had still aspired to a career in the arts—a time when he had believed that alcohol revealed a person's true character. This was no longer a viewpoint to which he adhered. Character, he now believed, was a fluid and ever-changing quality, and the concepts of good and evil were of purely situational utility.

Jeeves delivered the martini, saying nothing of Alan Whitman's thoughts.

The customer stirred his drink with an impaled olive.

"Do you believe in the soul?" he asked.

"I wouldn't know, sir," said Jeeves.

"You don't know what you believe?"

"At the moment, my beliefs elude me." Jeeves smiled. The customer smiled back. Their eyes made contact, then skittered apart, like eyes meeting accidentally in an elevator.

~

Paula could tell he'd had a drink or two, but he didn't seem drunk. More like preoccupied. She couldn't get a conversation started.

They were sitting at the kitchen table eating substandard Chinese takeout from the nearby strip mall. Paula had eaten her fill but Mack was digging another helping from a carton of something. She couldn't even remember what they'd ordered. It all tasted the same.

"Did you hire that man?"

Mack started. "Huh?"

"The man from the bank. You said you might hire him."

"Oh. Jake. Yeah." He gathered several small chunks of meat, probably chicken, on his fork and stared off into space as he chewed and swallowed.

"So . . . are you . . . you're really doing it, aren't you?"

"What's that?"

"Putting it all back together."

"You sound surprised."

"Two weeks ago we were bankrupt."

Mack shrugged. "We're still bankrupt. Puts us in a great negotiating position. Remember what Jack Price told us? He said, 'If a guy could figure out how to stay in bankruptcy all the time, he'd be rich.'"

"I don't like being bankrupt."

Mack did not reply. He attacked another carton, scooping out what looked like beef, peanuts, and celery in cornstarch jelly.

Taking another tack, Paula said, "I went to Julie's club with her."

"Oh?"

"You remember Harold Nelson? With the comb-over?"

Mack shook his head.

"Oh. Never mind, then." She watched him pick peanuts out of his pile of gunk and tried to imagine what he was thinking. Something had to be going on in there. Finally, she asked, "What's on your mind, Mack?"

Mack looked up. "Me?"

"No, the other Mack."

"Oh. I was thinking we should throw a party."

This was so unexpected that Paula laughed.

"Seriously," he said, suddenly interested. "A resurrection party. Spend some money we don't have. Hell, I'll get the bank to pay for it."

"What, here?"

"We'll have it at the factory. Make it a picnic. Invite everybody. Let 'em know we're back."

"Who's everybody?"

"Everybody. The whole address book. What do you say?"

~

The sex was not so good that night. Mack came at her the way he had in Cancún but his selfish intensity had lost its novelty and he finished before she got started.

Paula lay awake, watching her husband breathe. The rhythmic sounds she had once found soporific now seemed harsher and polluted with meaning, as if the air passing in and out of his lungs contained muffled warnings and gasps of pain. Of course, there was nothing to it. Mack's breathing had not changed, not really. Everything else about him was different, but the breathing was the same. She turned her head away and closed her eyes and imagined the old Mack sleeping beside her.

16

Jorge Pulido told her that Teddy had killed himself.

"Many people have jump," he said. "One last year, two the year before. It is a place where people do this thing."

Rita stared down at Teddy's body. His skin looked waxen, his lips gray and dry. Her own face felt numb. She had withdrawn deep inside, looking out through porthole eyes.

"Not Teddy," Rita said.

"Who knows what is in a man's secret heart?" said Pulido.

"I knew him." She turned away from the body. "I knew things about him even he didn't know. I know he wouldn't kill himself."

"Or maybe he slip. He stand on the edge, not sure, and then he slip."

Even in her stunned state, Rita saw that the policeman wanted very much for this to be a suicide. He could not be blamed for a suicide.

She said, "He just bought a thousand dollars' worth of Cuban cigars. There's no way he'd have jumped."

Pulido shrugged with Latin emphasis. "Then he just fall. I am very sorry." He led her out of the cold morgue and closed the door. "Is very tragic."

Rita nodded. A storm, dark and cold and wet, raged within her, but for the moment she had found a dry place to stand. She would fend off the tempest and get through this thing. The bone-colored hallway of the municipal building looked a mile long. Thoughts moved ponderously; she could see them coming before she knew what they were. None of this was really happening. She was playing a role: bereaved spouse. Soon she would be playing the role of beautiful young widow. She stopped and leaned against the wall, squeezed her eyes closed.

"Mrs. Larson?"

A hand grasped her arm. She shook it off. "No." She pressed her cheek to the smooth stucco wall and imagined herself at the beach, salt air caressing her breasts, sand between her toes. Where was Teddy? Back at the condo, smoking a cigar. The storm receded. Rita smiled.

"Mrs. Larson?"

She opened her eyes. Jorge Pulido's bulging eyes filled her field of vision. She saw he was afraid. You never know what a woman will do, he was probably thinking. Especially a woman so beautiful.

"I'm okay," she said. She allowed herself to be led down the hall to a small office. Pulido seated her in front of a small wooden desk. He wanted her to sign some papers. She forced herself to focus, to puzzle her way though the Spanish. One of the documents was an attestation as to the identity of the deceased. Another exacted her promise to make arrangements for burial of the body. The third document acknowledged receipt of Teddy's *accesorios personales*. She looked to Pulido for an explanation and received a manila envelope in response.

Rita poured the contents of the envelope onto the desk: several coins, a handful of plastic golf tees, and a plastic device that she did not at first recognize. She turned it this way and that.

"This was Teddy's?"

"We find it on his *pantalones*." Pulido pointed at his own waist-band, showing her where it had been clipped.

"Ah!" She recognized it now. The clip holster for Teddy's little pistol. Why would he have been wearing that? And where was the gun?

"I don't see his wallet in here," she said.

"This is all we find. It is a tall cliff. Things fall out."

"I bet they do." She stared at the small pile of *accesorios personales*. "No keys? You didn't find a set of keys?"

Pulido shook his head warily. "This is all we find."

"No belt either, I suppose?"

"No. No belt."

Rita was thinking more clearly now. Teddy's death was beyond comprehension, but she understood Mexican graft. At some point, either at the time his body had been discovered or shortly thereafter, Teddy had been relieved of his valuables. She suspected that the spoils had been divided up among the *policía*. Not much she could do about that.

Pulido said, "There were golf balls up above, in a . . . *cubo*. What you call it?" He made a shape with his hands.

"Bucket."

"*Sí*. Another thing." He got up and left the office, returned a moment later, and set a patch of artificial turf on the desk. "It is a golfing thing," he explained, pointing at the plastic tee set into the turf.

"I know what it is," she said, fending off a squall of sorrow and loss. It was only a piece of green plastic turf, nothing more. "He was hitting balls into the sea. He liked to do that." As she returned the golf tees and coins to the envelope, Rita realized that something else was missing. "Where's his ring?" she asked.

"Ring?" Pulido sat back.

"His diamond ring." She mimed sliding a ring on and off her finger.

Pulido was shaking his head vigorously. "No, no, this is everything."

Anguish turned to cold fury. "I don't care about the money," she said, "but I want the ring."

"There was no ring."

Staring into Pulido's red, bug-eyed face, Rita's anger suddenly broke as she saw an alternate reality: What if Pulido was telling the truth? What if Teddy had gone off that cliff without his wallet, his ring, his belt?

She said, "His golf cart. He would have driven his cart out to the point. But the golf cart is parked in front of our condo. How could he have jumped and then driven his cart back home?"

"This I do not know," said Pulido.

Rita turned away from the policeman as her mind began working on a new level. Teddy had been carrying his gun. Why? Tumblers rolled and clicked into place. He'd had the gun because he thought he might need it. Why would he need it? Because he had perceived a threat. But for some reason the gun had not protected him. Images whirled through her mind: Teddy, big and strong. Invulnerable Teddy. Her Teddy Bear. His wallet gone, his ring gone, everything but the empty holster and a few pesos. And the cigars. She saw the boxes in her mind's eye, stacked on the little glass-topped rattan table. A new connection snapped into place. When she had looked through his desk at home, his passport had been missing. And the bank statements.

The window peeper. Knowledge came like a series of blows to her abdomen, each one more solid and stunning than the last. Not just a window peeper. She saw him still, the unshaven face, the tousled hair, the open mouth. She had seen him for less than one second, but the image remained clear and hard-edged. She called it up again and again, a repeating slide, and each time the man's face became more familiar.

She knew that face. Again. Square jaw, wide nostrils. She almost had it.

Again.

17

A symphony of clicks, buzzes, pops, and hums. The whirr and chuckle of the sewing machines was constant, like wind in trees or the sound of waves. Mack stood at the front of the sewing floor smiling, his foot tapping to the regular popping sound of the riveter. Every *ptok* meant another 16.4 cents in added value. Every chatter, whirr, and clank coming off the floor was another coin in his pocket.

Before, when he had been nothing but Lars's tool, he had heard these same sounds through different filters, thinking in terms of looming deadlines, unfulfilled orders, malfunctioning equipment. He had been thinking not of money but of his own obligation to perform. He'd been worried about right and wrong, and whether or not the new die cutter would be able to keep up with the sewers, and whether the Pizza America smocks needed four, six, or eight bar tacks. He'd been a man without a vision, fixated on his own footsteps.

Not anymore.

The factory had been back up and running for two weeks now. The Pizza America orders were shipping daily. They'd be shipping and billing the Airlift International jacket order by the end of the month. Money would be flowing into Mac-Lar within thirty days. It was tight, but with the line of credit from the bank and the line of bull he'd been giving his suppliers, all his ducks were lined up in a neat— if precarious—row. He also had the $346,000 in cash, but he wasn't planning to use that unless it became absolutely necessary. From now on, he would risk only other people's money.

Mack smiled, thinking of Harry Goldblatt. There had been a time when he would have felt sorry for the guy. That was the kind of thinking that had got him in trouble.

Jake Vink appeared across the room and waved to get his attention, gesturing toward his glass-fronted office, adjacent to the sewing floor. Mack zigzagged his way through the sewing stations, followed Jake into his office, and closed the door. The sound of the factory went dull and distant.

Jake said, "We got a problem."

Mack sat down and waited for more information, feeling his heart pumping, bringing extra oxygen to his muscles and mind.

"I just got off the phone with Al Krupinski at Pizza America. They just received their first shipment of the smocks."

Mack relaxed. A production problem. Production problems were solvable. "Something wrong with them?"

"Yeah. According to Krupinski, they shouldn't even exist." Vink sat down behind his desk and stared at Mack, eyebrows raised.

Mack felt a flash of anger. "Don't play games with me."

Vink looked away. His tongue darted out from between his lips. He cleared his throat. "Krupinski said the order was supposed to be canceled."

"Canceled? A two-hundred-thousand-dollar order? That's bull-shit."

Vink's phone rang. He looked to Mack for permission, then answered, listened a moment, hit the mute button. "Sally says there's some guy out front asking for you."

"Tell her I'll be out in a minute."

Vink did so, then hung up.

Mack said, "What did Krupinski say, *exactly?*"

"He said, 'That order was never supposed to ship.'"

Mack thought for a moment. "Okay," he said. He stood up. "I'll take care of it."

"You want me to shut down the line?"

"Absolutely not."

~

The receptionist said she had just started working at Mac-Lar last week. Her name was Sally Grayson. The gold stud in her left nostril was a gift from her ex-boyfriend. The tiny scar on her chin was from a childhood bicycle accident, and her eyes were really that color. She called them caramel, which also happened to be the name of the lip-stick she wore and was very close to the color of her hair. Sally Grayson liked matching colors. She liked her job, too. Her boss was a really, really great guy.

Jerry Pleasant listened, smiling and nodding. He did not know why people told him things, but they did. It served him well in his chosen profession. His most successful interview technique was to simply sit across from the witness or suspect and ask them how they were doing. Once they got started, most of them couldn't shut up.

This receptionist, Sally, was no exception. Her words became a meaningless drone, and Pleasant's eyes traveled down her throat to her freckled bosom. The ribs of her scoop-neck cotton sweater expanded and contracted with every breath. She reminded him of his wife fifteen years ago, before her ass had dropped six inches and her tongue had grown sharp. He imagined his face pressed between Sally's speckled breasts. He smiled and nodded and rocked back and forth on the crepe soles of his Hush Puppies and waited contentedly for MacWray to appear.

~

Mack did not recognize the pink-cheeked man standing in front of Sally's desk, at first thinking the guy was probably selling something—except that his hands were in his pockets rather than clutching a sample case. Also, he was wearing a corduroy sport coat, blue jeans ironed to a sharp crease, and suede shoes: a look more Lutheran minister than sales professional. Mack thrust out a hand and smiled.

"I'm Mack MacWray. How can I help you?" He met the man's eyes: watery blue behind thick lenses.

"How's it going, Mack?" The man's mouth formed a V-shaped smile.

The smile triggered Mack's memory. The cop. He searched for a name. "Officer Pleasant!" He couldn't remember the first name. "How are you doing?" He looked carefully at Pleasant's face. "You lost the beard."

Pleasant grinned. "Life is change," he said. "Actually, I shaved it off just this morning." He took Mack's hand and gave it a gentle pump but did not release it.

Mack returned the man's inane smile. "So. What can I do for you?"

"I heard you landed on your feet here. Thought I'd stop by and see how you were getting on."

"Doing fine." He felt mildly alarmed that Pleasant had not let go of his hand. "It's a good, solid business. It just took a little talking to convince the bank of that." He pulled his hand free.

Pleasant buried his right hand back in his pocket and looked around, head bobbing, pale eyes blinking, smiling as if the walls of the reception area revealed all the workings of Mac-Lar Manufacturing. "You've sure done that. I'm impressed. Not too often a business facing bankruptcy can wrangle a loan."

"It was just a little cash flow problem."

"Your suppliers aren't giving you any trouble?"

"They want their money. Best way for them to get it is keep us in business, right?"

"I guess that's one way to look at it."

They were both smiling. Mack had a sudden powerful urge to tell Pleasant something that would shock him. Something that would blow that silly grin off his insipid face. *I killed Lars,* he wanted to say. *I let the son of a bitch die, and I took my money back. I blackmailed the banker. And that's not all . . .*

He suppressed the suicidal impulse and continued to match Pleasant's smile. After a few more seconds Pleasant shrugged. "You hear from your partner?" he asked.

"Lars?" Mack shook his head. "Not that I expect to."

"You never stopped by to file those charges."

"I got busy."

"Uh-huh."

"Even if you find him, the money will probably be long gone."

"You never know." Pleasant stroked his cheek with his fingers. "Of course, that's really not the point, is it?"

"It is, as far as I'm concerned."

"Actually, I thought you wanted to see him punished. You know. Justice."

"That's your job."

"Yes, it is. It certainly is. You know, Mack, there is evil in this world. There truly is."

"I don't doubt it."

"It's a disease." Pleasant cocked his head and smiled, his eyes locking onto Mack. "Like chicken pox."

Mack did not reply.

Pleasant studied him for a few more seconds, then straightened his head and shrugged. "Oh well, I'm sure he'll turn up sooner or later. They always do."

"To tell the truth, I hope I never see the son of a bitch again."

Pleasant laughed. "You're different than before," he said.

Mack smiled. "Life is change."

"I heard you took a trip."

"A few days in Mexico. Look, I don't mean to be rude, but I'm kind of in the middle of something . . ."

Pleasant stepped back and pulled his hands out of his pockets. "Say no more; I'm gone."

"Thanks for stopping by . . . Officer Pleasant."

"Jerry. Call me Jerry." He gave a wave and a grin and let himself out the glass front door.

Mack smiled until the cop was out of sight, then turned to Sally and said, "He ever shows up here again, I'm not in." Without waiting for her response he entered his office and shut the door.

~

Jerry Pleasant sat behind the wheel of his Ford and rubbed his right cheek, wishing he had not shaved off his beard. Wishing he had never grown it in the first place. Wondering how the hell MacWray had talked First Star into giving him a new line of credit. Maybe it was a family thing. Strange things happened when families and businesses intersected. One of the first things family businesses did when they got in trouble was to exclude outsiders, particularly the police. Bankers were the same way. The last thing any of them wanted was a bunch of government investigators pawing through their records. He couldn't blame them. But this one was odd . . . something about it he couldn't put his finger on.

Pleasant grimaced and started the car. It wasn't as if he had nothing else to work on. If something was rotting at Mac-Lar, sooner or later it would start to stink.

~

Decompress.

Mack breathed slowly and deeply through his nose. The cop was nothing, just a little man whose job was to make himself as irritating as possible.

He remembered something Lars had said: *If I spent all my time worrying about guys like Jerry Pleasant I wouldn't get a thing done now, would I?*

Lars was right. He had to focus.

His immediate problem was Al Krupinski and the Pizza America order. Mack reached for the phone but stopped before picking up the receiver. Maybe a phone call wouldn't be enough. Pizza America corporate headquarters were located in Shakopee, less than an hour away.

Some things were best done in person.

18

"Al Krupinski?" Mack offered his hand. "Mack MacWray. Mac-Lar Manufacturing. Sorry to bust in on you like this."

Al Krupinski, looking puzzled and slightly alarmed, stood up to shake hands across his desk. His eyes flicked over Mack's shoulder and his narrow lips tightened, giving his secretary a nasty glance through the office door.

"She told me you were busy." Mack laughed. "I just didn't listen."

"It's all right, Janice," Krupinski said, his expression making it clear that it wasn't.

Mack had a grip on Krupinski's hand, pumping it. "I thought we should meet."

Al Krupinski was a thin man, bald on top, gray haired on the temples, nattily dressed in a starched pink shirt and a parti-colored bow tie. Reading glasses rested near the tip of an attenuate nose; his lips turned down to form a short arc.

"Yes, well, I, ah, I spoke with a Mr. Vink this afternoon . . ."

"Jake said you'd called. Some misunderstanding about the smocks you ordered." Mack released Krupinski's hand and pointed at the chair in front of his desk. "May I?"

Krupinski pointedly looked at his watch. "Ah, certainly." He made a weak welcoming gesture, hitched up his gray trousers, and sat behind his desk.

Mack settled into the chair. "You were working with Lars Larson before. As you know, he's no longer with the company."

Krupinski cleared his throat. "Yes, ah, as I explained to Mr. Vink, we were surprised to receive that shipment this morning. I heard your company had closed its doors." His tone was that of a slightly impatient schoolmaster explaining school policy to a wayward student.

"Really! It's a good thing we're talking now. I don't know how these things get started."

"Yes, well, the fact is"—Krupinski's upper lip peeled back to reveal a crowded row of small, straw-colored teeth—"we have made other arrangements with another supplier."

"That's unfortunate."

"Of course, I had no idea you were going ahead with production."

"Let me be sure I understand. You heard a rumor that we were out of business so you went to another supplier? I wish you'd given us the courtesy of a phone call!"

Krupinski was shaking his head slowly, as if disappointed in his student's sluggish uptake. "The fact is, Mr. MacWray, that order was canceled some months ago. I explained as much to Mr. Vink."

Mack wrinkled his brow. "Are you sure? We have no record of any cancellation. I do, however, have a purchase order signed by you."

"I called Mr. Larson shortly after placing the order. I told him that we would have to cancel." He rolled his chair back and crossed his right leg over his left.

Mack looked carefully at the man in the bow tie. Was it possible that he was telling the truth? Had Lars left the canceled purchase order on the books simply so that they could borrow against it? Yes, Lars would have done that. The question now was whether the order had ever been genuine and, if not, how to make it so.

"That's all? You wrote out a purchase order for sixteen thousand smocks and canceled it with a phone call?"

Krupinski uncrossed his legs. "I have a letter from Mr. Larson." He smiled, a man about to display a winning poker hand. Opening his desk drawer, he took out a single sheet of paper and slid it across his desktop. Mack recognized the old Mac-Lar letterhead. He picked it up and read.

Dear Mr. Krupinski:

This letter is to acknowledge your cancellation of your purchase order number PA2-8903.

As Mac-Lar has incurred no costs to date, there is no outstanding balance.

Thank you for your interest in Mac-Lar.

The letter was signed by Lars. It was dated June 24, less than a week after Lars had supposedly landed the order. Mack read the letter again, a faint smile forming upon his lips. Even if the order had been canceled, why would Lars have written such a letter? Only one possibility suggested itself. Mack examined Krupinski, trying to imagine how Lars had worked him.

"I wonder how much he paid you," Mack said quietly.

"Excuse me?" Krupinski sat up straight, preparing to take umbrage.

"It was just for the loan, wasn't it?"

Krupinski's lips hardened, his face became concrete. "I don't know what you're talking about."

Mack considered his options. At this point, no amount of begging or cajoling would reactivate the order. Other techniques would have to be employed. What would Lars have done? Mack pushed the speculation aside. He was not Lars. The important question was, what could *Mack* do? How could he gain Krupinski's attention and cooperation? The best tools, as always, were fear and greed. It would take a lot of motivation for Krupinski to give the order back to Mac-Lar, especially since he apparently did not need or want the smocks. The man felt protected by his position, his experience, his bow tie. His equanimity would have to be shattered. It would take a lot of money, or a lot of fear.

Mack crumpled the letter.

"Hey!" Krupinski half dove across his desk and made a grab for the letter. Mack held it out of range.

"How much?"

Krupinski got hold of himself and sat back down. His mouth had become very small, his nostrils white and rigid.

Mack stood up, went to the office door, and closed it. Krupinski's brittle expression did not change. Mack went to stand directly in front of him, the front edge of the desk pressing against his thighs.

"Let me explain something," he said, displaying his fist. Bits of paper showed between his fingers. "Nothing Lars Larson did—nothing he said—matters anymore." He flicked the crumpled letter at Krupinski. It bounced off his arm, fell to the floor.

Krupinski said, "I'm going to have to ask you to leave."

"This is how I see it. You and Lars conspired to create a bogus purchase order so that the bank would loan Mac-Lar more money, and you asked Lars for this letter to cover your ass. He probably wrote it the same day you wrote the P.O. My question is, how much did he pay you?"

"That is both insulting and untrue. Now get out before I call security." Krupinski's watery eyes darted toward the phone.

Mack gave him a pitying look. "Oh stop it. Save the act for your wife or your boss or somebody else stupid enough to have you in their daily life. I'm not interested." He was seeing with astonishing clarity. Krupinski's neck had turned pink; the big vein on his forehead pulsed and his pupils contracted to the size of a pinhead. Krupinski was angry, but he was also afraid. Mack considered his options and was astonished by their number.

"I am asking you to leave." Krupinski pushed his jaw forward.

Mack shook his head. "You don't get it, do you? You really don't have any options here. The rules have changed."

Krupinski reached for his phone. Mack clapped his left hand on his wrist, cupped his other hand around the back of Krupinski's head, and slammed the man's face into his desk blotter. Krupinski yelped as his head rebounded. He clapped his hands to his nose and jumped to his feet. "You're crazy!" He made a dash for the door, but Mack caught him by the belt, walked him back to his chair, and sat him down. A trickle of blood appeared beneath Krupinski's hands, ran around his mouth, and hung from his chin. His eyes were wide, and his shoulders were shaking violently.

Mack waited for the shaking to subside, then said, "Let me explain something to you, Al. I've got nineteen thousand yards of custom-dyed fabric sitting in my factory. I am going to turn that fabric into red-green-and-white smocks, and you are going to pay me for them. That's the deal. That was always the deal. When you wrote that P.O. you entered into an agreement with me, Mack MacWray. Whatever special arrangements you made with Lars are history. Do you understand?"

Krupinski stared back at him.

Mack continued. "Now you're sitting there thinking that I'm insane, and that as soon as I'm out of here you're going to call the cops. And you're thinking you are about as likely to honor that P.O. as you are to regrow your hair. Am I right?"

Krupinski said nothing.

"But you are wrong. You see, when you fuck with me you enter a reality where I make the rules. There is nothing I won't do. Does that scare you? It should. It scares me." Mack stared down at the man with blood on his chin, feeling only mild repugnance. Was he getting through? It was hard to tell.

"I suppose you could make things inconvenient for me, for a while. Of course, the whole dirty little deal you did with Lars would come out. You know the police are investigating him, don't you? I'm sure your bosses would like to hear about how you conspired with a known criminal to defraud First Star Bank. And—keeping in mind I'm a raving lunatic—you'd have to worry about your family. You have no idea what I'm capable of. Do you have children? Grandchildren? No? Yes? I think you do."

Krupinski remained rigid.

"The point I'm making, Al, is that your best option is to do the right thing. Follow through on your original commitment and make sure I get paid for those smocks." Mack smiled. "There's an upside, too." He tossed an envelope onto the desk. "Go ahead, open it."

Krupinski opened the envelope with shaking hands and looked at the cash inside.

"That's five thousand dollars. Just so you don't think I'm such a bad guy. Now, don't you wish all of life's decisions were so clear-cut?"

Mack waited until Krupinski nodded. It wasn't a very enthusiastic nod, but Mack thought that he might have gotten through. He hoped that he had.

~

Mack and Lars had just finished lunch at Shelley's Woodroast, talking business, when Mack found a wallet in the parking lot. It was a nice wallet, almost new, plump with cash and credit cards. Mack had gone back into the restaurant and left it with the hostess. When he came out Lars had said, "Macanudo, you are a good man."

"Because I turned the wallet in? You'd have done the same."

"Sure, but only because you'd have been watching. But you, Mack, you did it because you thought it was the right thing to do." Lars had thrown his arm around Mack's shoulders. "That's why we love you, Macanudo. You're the last good man."

Mack remembered that as he drove back to the factory, thinking how Lars would have been laughing inside, not knowing how wrong he was.

19

The First Annual Mac-Lar Employee, Customer, and Supplier Appreciation Picnic was held behind the factory parking lot in what had, just a few days earlier, been a field of rye. Jake Vink had paid the farmer to cut down a half acre of his crop and replace it with fresh sod. The new field now held several rented picnic tables, three dozen folding chairs, a tented buffet and wet bar, a pair of volleyball nets, and about eighty people. Paula MacWray was attempting to organize a volleyball game, while Mack and Vink stood by the loading dock watching.

"Think everybody's having a good time?" Mack said.

"Sure they are. Look at the 'em. Free food, booze, nice day, what's not to like?"

"I notice Harry didn't show up. In fact, I don't see many of our suppliers."

Vink shrugged. "Most of them are from out of state."

"Don't see many customers either."

"They were invited, that's the important thing. Let 'em know they're appreciated."

"I thought Al Krupinski might come. We got a check from him Wednesday."

Vink shook his head. "I don't know how you do it, boss man."

"I threatened his grandchildren."

"Yeah, right." Vink laughed. "You know, sometimes I think that might actually be the way to go. I mean, why limit yourself to the usual sales techniques? Why not just put a gun to a guy's noggin and say, 'Gimme the fuckin' order'?" Vink sipped his beer. "*Godfather Part Four.* They should do that. They did all those *Rocky*s, they should do another *Godfather.*"

Mack, only half listening, watched the way people fell into their own groups. The Asian sewers sat with the other Asian sewers at three of the picnic tables. The Mexican sewers had their own table. Bobby and Theo from shipping were playing horseshoes with their wives, and the five women who worked in the embroidery department were lined up together at the buffet.

The only supplier to show up, Greg Strommer from Atlas Sewing Supply, had come with his four-year-old kid. They were out near the edge of the field, the kid spinning around, making himself dizzy, tumbling onto the fresh green grass. It looked like fun. Greg was one of the good guys—he had had no problem extending Mack more credit. Standing beside him was Porter Sell, who owned the Team One chain of sporting goods stores and had recently given Mack an order for five hundred warm-up jackets.

As far as customers and suppliers, that was it. Most of the people eating and drinking were employees, friends, and people from the neighborhood. The guy who sold him insurance was there, and so was Mack's barber. He had simply handed his Rolodex to Sally and told her to invite everybody on it. He had also told Paula to invite anybody she wanted, which apparently included all the neighbors.

Bob Seaman and his girlfriend, a robust blonde named Ceci, stood near the bar cart talking with Jack Price, Mack's attorney. That made

Mack a little edgy, but he figured Price knew what he was doing. He appeared to be telling a story—every few seconds his long arms would perform broad gestures. Price had been a semipro basketball player back in the seventies. He towered above Seaman, knees slightly bent to bring himself closer to his level, a can of Pepsi held loosely in his oversize left hand, sunlight glinting from his hairless dome.

Mack's in-laws, Hal and Joyce Byrnes, stood at the periphery of the conversation, smiling and listening to Jack Price's soothing line of bullshit. Mack wondered what Price could be saying to elicit such smiles.

Vink nudged Mack's arm. "Who's the big broad in the black?" he asked.

Mack followed Vink's glance. "That's Ginny Bettendorf. Paula works for her."

"She's got some style, don't she?"

Ginny was talking to Julie Gorman. The two women were both wearing expensive-looking, mostly black outfits. Neither of them had sat down since arriving, nor had they approached the buffet. Mack had noticed that very large women and very thin women avoided eating in public, and well-dressed women did not like to sit down. Julie held a plastic wineglass full of chardonnay; Ginny was drinking the zinfandel. The two women had been drawn to each other immediately—Julie because Ginny made her look thinner, and Ginny because Julie made her look voluptuous.

"I like a woman with handles," Vink said.

"Want me to introduce you?"

Vink made a face. "Nah, I'd just fuck it up."

Mack shrugged. Jake Vink's personal life was a blank to him. He preferred it that way. The more energy the guy had to focus on business, the better. Vink was proving himself to be an ideal first mate. He did exactly what Mack told him to do, he never complained, and he appeared to have no ambitions beyond doing his job. Mack marveled at the fact that he had once found the little man terrifying.

"I better go mix a bit," Mack said.

He headed toward the volleyball game. Off to the side he saw Hal Byrnes move to intercept him. The last time they'd talked, Hal had been screaming at him. Mack remembered some of the words Hal had hurled at him: *liar, thief, crook, worthless.* He slowed his pace to let Hal fall in beside him. Maybe he'd get an apology.

"Hey there, John." Hal Byrnes was one of the few people who refused to call him Mack. He said he just couldn't see his daughter married to a guy named Mack.

Mack said, "Hi, Halston," using Hal's full name, which he knew Hal hated.

"Great party," Hal said. "I've been over talking to that Jack Price fella. Hell of a guy."

"Jack's all right."

"I gotta admit, John, it looks like you've pulled your chestnuts outta the fire. I gotta admit, I'm impressed." Hal Byrnes stood an inch taller than Mack but looked smaller. He wore pale blue Sansabelt trousers, Nikes with Velcro closures, and a guayabera Paula had bought for him in Mexico. His hair was a stiff gray brush, unchanged since his service in Korea. Hal had been a supply sergeant and, in his civilian career, warehouse manager for a hardware store chain.

"We had a tough couple months," Mack admitted, still waiting for the apology.

"That son of a biscuit Lars. I tell ya."

"Yeah, well, he's gone now, and we're back on track."

"That Jack Price, he says this whole bankruptcy thing is just a legal thing. A definition, he says. But you got money now, right?"

"Well, we've got a line of credit. The real money is still down the road."

" 'Cause I was thinking, y'know, on account of we had a close call there, I was thinking Joyce and I might want to pull a few bucks out. I mean, since you got the bank behind you and all."

Mack stopped walking and looked intently at the older man. This was no apology, it was a dunning notice. "You'd pull out on me? Now?"

Hal licked his lips and shifted his eyes toward his wife, who was watching from several yards away. Mack saw in an instant that Joyce had been pounding on him. She had twice her husband's smarts, a real Lady Macbeth—only Hal was no Macbeth.

"Uh, I'm not asking you for all of it, John." He looked embarrassed.

"You want the benefits, but you don't want to take the risk—is that it?"

Hal squeezed his lips together and again darted his eyes in his wife's direction. "Look, John, it was up to me, I'd let it ride. Always willing to press my bets. But Joycie, she got pretty shook up when Lars took off like that. I mean, I was looking at bagging groceries. I'm sixty-eight years old, f'chrissake."

Mack regarded Hal dispassionately, thinking that at sixty-eight, veteran of two heart attacks, Hal wouldn't last long. How convenient it would be . . . Startled by his own thoughts, Mack looked away.

Hal said, "I mean, when we loaned you the money there wasn't any risk, at least that's what Lars said."

"There's no risk now," Mack said. He wasn't wishing his in-laws dead, not really. He was only imagining it.

"Maybe we could just start taking a little back—maybe a few thousand a month?"

"A few thousand?" Mack imagined himself standing before a coffin looking down at Hal's pasty face. "Look, Halston, lets talk about this later, okay? We're here to enjoy ourselves, right?"

Hal nodded eagerly. "Sure, sure, I just told Joycie I'd mention it. Ha ha." He moved off, head swiveling, looking for his better half.

Mack felt the tension ease. Where had he been going? His eyes were caught by the bar. He made his way over and asked the bored-looking bartender for a martini on the rocks. As he watched his drink being built, he noticed a slight man wearing a straw-colored sport coat standing at the buffet. Pleasant, the cop. What the hell was *he* doing here? Hadn't he told Sally not to invite him? Maybe not, but she should have known. He wouldn't let the cop ruin his day. Not this day.

Feeling another presence beside him, Mack turned his head.

"Hey, sailor." Julie Gorman gave him a friendly bump with her hip and set her empty wineglass on the bar. "Buy me a drink?"

"Hi, Julie." Mack shifted gears, leaving the cop behind. Mack thought Julie looked like Peter Pan's sister, or maybe a wicked elf.

Unlike Paula, she was delicate, irreverent, and impulsive. Paula had once remarked, "Julie's my alter ego."

Mack asked the bartender for a glass of chardonnay.

Julie said, "Nice party." Her lips were salmon, her eyes a mélange of brown and green. She had small, even teeth and a wide mouth, and when she talked he noticed her tongue.

"I figured it was the best way to see everybody."

"Best way for all of us to see you. Giving us a look at the new Mack."

Mack, startled, repeated, "New Mack?"

Julie cocked her head, puzzled. "Something the matter?"

"Paula has a big mouth. That was supposed to be a surprise."

Julie, still wearing her puzzled expression, reached out and touched Mack's chest, just below his throat, with a salmon-colored nail.

"You," she said, pressing her nail into his flesh, "are a nut."

～

"Jack Price! How you doing?" Jerry Pleasant offered his hand.

Price, not missing a beat, smiled and reached down and clasped Pleasant's hand. "Hey there, how's it going?"

"Super." Pleasant grinned, knowing that Price didn't have a clue who he was, even though they'd met on several previous occasions, all of them in court.

"Great party, huh? Nice bunch a people," Price said.

"Yep. Nice people."

"So . . ." Price pursed his lips. "I gotta confess, I can't remember where I know you from."

"Jerry Pleasant. Actually, I'm an investigator with Hennepin County."

"Of course you are! Of course you are! How's it going, Jer?"

"Can't complain. Plenty of bad guys to keep me busy."

"That's for damn sure."

They both laughed, eyes locked.

Price said, "So, Jer, you here on business, or pleasure?"

"Both, actually." Pleasant looked away. "I was wondering—you do divorce work, don't you?"

"A bit."

"I was wondering—this is for a buddy of mine—bottom line, what's the going rate these days?"

"Depends what you mean. He does it himself, all it costs is the filing fee. Of course, I wouldn't recommend that. His wife has a good lawyer, the alimony will kill him."

"Bottom line, say the guy's been married sixteen years and he wants out clean. What's it gonna cost him, bottom line?"

"Kids?"

"No kids."

"Wife employed?"

"Part-time."

"You got any idea of their net worth?"

"Less than a hundred grand, with the house."

"He got a pension?"

"Yeah."

Price nodded. "Call it three years."

"Three years?"

"Three years' salary. Spread out over ten years. Three years. Tell your buddy that's about what it will cost him to get single."

Pleasant whistled. "Jesus. Three years?"

"Give or take."

~

With the volleyball game under way, Paula looked about for her next task. Her eyes went from group to group, searching for signs of discontent. The Mac-Lar employees had settled at the tables with plates of food, the people from the neighborhood were centered around the volleyball game, and most of the rest were sitting or standing in scattered clusters, talking and drinking. Her parents? Sitting by themselves, looking a bit lost. Paula resisted the urge to go to them. If they hadn't learned to socialize by their age, there was nothing she could do.

Paula checked her watch. Two o'clock, almost time for Mack to make his announcement. She looked for a yellow golf shirt topped by a mop of curly dark hair and found him at the bar standing beside a svelte black wisp. Julie. Paula scraped her lower lip with her incisors, sucking in the last traces of lipstick, and looked away.

Where was Ginny? There, in the parking lot, talking to Jake Vink. Well, Ginny could hold a conversation with just about anyone, even the lobster man.

She turned her head and found herself looking at the buffet. Were there any of the shrimp kabobs left? She swallowed a sudden production of saliva and went to find out.

~

"What happened to your hand?"

Jake Vink looked down at his disfigured mitt, then raised it so that both he and Ginny could get a better look. Not many people had the chutzpah to come right out and ask him, but for those few who did, he had stories.

"Moray eel," he said, rotating his hand back and forth, cupping the image of her face between his thumb and little finger.

"No!" Ginny's mouth opened, ready to laugh.

Vink nodded, being very serious. "I was treasure hunting off of Ocho Rios. That's in Jamaica."

"I'm a travel agent," Ginny reminded him.

"Yeah, I knew that. Anyways, I was—"

"Before you go any further, I want to say a couple things."

"Yeah?"

"One, I think you're cute as a button, and two, there's no way an eel ate your fingers."

"You got a mouth on you," Vink said. This broad was a handful, but he liked her.

"So what really happened?"

"Antipersonnel mine. Vietnam."

"You're too young."

"I coulda enlisted in seventy-one."

"Yeah, but you didn't. You grew up on a farm, didn't you."

Vink compressed his lips and inflated his cheeks. "Okay, okay. John Deere tractor, alternator belt. You happy?"

Ginny touched a finger to the moon-shaped scar just below her left eye. "Holstein, left rear foot."

They both laughed. Vink looked at his hand, felt a twinge as he remembered the flash of the homemade cherry bomb. The smell of gunpowder and burnt flesh. The girl who had dared him to hold it, Rhoda Best, shrieking with hysterical laughter. The other kids laughing with her, then panicking as they got a look at his mangled fingers. He'd been, what? Nine years old and in love for the first time. And after that they called him Lobster Boy. Even Rhoda Best.

Ginny said, "I think your boss wants you."

Vink put his hand in his pocket. "It must be time for the unveiling," he said.

~

Keeping a smile on his face during his first conversation with Jack Price had given Bob Seaman an eyeball-searing headache. Now, Price had corralled him again. He was ecstatic over the rebirth of Mac-Lar. Here was a lawyer's wet dream that could go on for months, maybe years: a bankruptcy with positive cash flow. And he wouldn't shut up about it. Seaman tried to change the subject to sports, to the weather, to the stock market. All attempts failed. Price continued to describe his successes and his theories about the role of bankruptcy law in the new millennium. Anyone who failed to exercise their right to go bankrupt was missing out on the best things in life. He spoke of the varying forms of bankruptcy—Chapters 7, 11, and 13—the way a gourmet might describe the great cuisines of the world. One would be a fool not to partake of each of them, though perhaps not at the same meal.

Seaman looked at Ceci, who was nodding brightly, her glazed eyes politely locked on Price's long face. He could imagine what she was hearing: *Wurrawurrawurrawurra.* The sound of a car engine not starting. He would owe her big for this.

A stirring of bodies caught his attention. People were moving toward the parking lot.

Price sighed. "I could help them all—if only I had the time."

Seaman saw Mack standing on the loading dock, waiting for everyone to gather. He noticed a long white panel on the building above the dock. A sign? The surface rippled. A sign covered with cloth.

"We'd better go see what's happening." Taking Ceci by the arm, he followed the gathering crowd. Whatever this was about, he was going to use it to separate himself from Jack Price.

Mack had already started talking by the time they were close enough to hear.

"... and thank you all for coming today to help me celebrate. Now, I'm not big on public speaking, so let me just get right to the point. Six weeks ago this company was dead in the water. I had no money for payroll, the machines were dead silent, and the vultures were in here picking at the bones.

"Well, life is change. I convinced our good suppliers, our customers, and most importantly our friendly bankers"—he spotted Seaman and gave a nod—"that we had a good thing going here. And so we do. Our company is about growth and about opportunity. We are here to serve our customers, to provide income and security for our employees.

"Now there is one person, whose name I'm not going to mention, who was responsible for a lot of the problems we had in the past. Best thing for all of us will be to forget him, but that's tough to do when, every time we answer the phone or tell a friend where we work, we hear his name. So effective today, I am changing the name of this company."

Jake Vink, standing by the side of the loading dock, tugged on a cord. The fabric fell away to reveal a series of three-dimensional chrome-faced letters in a blocky, powerful font, spelling out NuMac against a navy blue background. Below, in small white lettering, was the word UNLIMITED.

～

Julie laughed and nudged Paula. "That's why he was so surprised!"
"Who?"

"I told Mack we'd all come to see the new Mack—I just meant the *new Mack,* you know? Not *NuMac.* He told me you had a big mouth."

"Oh. He wanted to be the one to show off the new name."

"But he *is* a new Mack. You're right. He *has* changed."

Paula nodded, watching the small crowd break up. Most of the Asians were moving toward their cars, another group was heading back for more food and drink. It had been a strange and uncomfortable party. Nobody having a good time, really, except for Mack. Nobody mixing outside their own group. She had the feeling that things would be breaking up soon. She hoped so. She had looked forward to seeing everybody and to meeting people she'd heard about. She'd wanted as much as Mack to show everyone that they were back on their feet. But the afternoon had become a confusing blur, and she'd had time to talk to no one.

"Excuse me, Mrs. MacWray?"

Paula replenished her party smile. She did not recognize the man standing before her.

"My name's Jerry Pleasant."

"Paula." She put out her hand, trying to place the name.

"I worked with your husband on the Lars Larson thing. Actually, I'm an investigator with the Hennepin County Sheriff's Office."

"Oh!"

Pleasant laughed. "Don't worry, I'm just here for the party. I gotta say, Mack has certainly turned things around. It's a pleasure to see a guy take a hit like that and come back fighting."

"Uh, Mack is pretty determined."

"What's really amazing to me is how he was able to get the bank to back him."

"He's a good businessman. I think they finally realized that."

"They sure are bending over backwards for Mack."

Paula shrugged and looked away from the policeman's smirking mouth. She felt guilty, but she had done nothing.

"We're still hoping to locate Larson." Pleasant looked up at the new sign. "But it looks like your husband has written him off."

"Mack doesn't like to dwell on the past."

"What about you?"

Paula felt a flutter of panic. She was hiding nothing, but she did not like being asked these questions.

Pleasant tilted his head. "Wouldn't you like to see Larson pay for what he's done?"

She called up an image of Lars and was surprised to find that she did not, at the moment, hate him. The other one, Rita, excited stronger feelings. "I guess both of them deserve something. Especially that Rita Manbait."

Pleasant frowned, then smiled. "Rita Manbait. That's good," he said. "Sounds like something Val would say."

"Who's Val?"

"My future ex-wife." He laughed.

"Oh." Paula looked away, embarrassed. "Anyway, Mack thinks we should put all that behind us. He has a business to run."

"Yes, he does. A remarkable recovery. I just can't figure out how he convinced the bank to back him."

Paula sensed that Pleasant was digging for something. Again, she was embraced by unfounded feelings of guilt. "Have you tried the buffet?" she blurted.

Pleasant blinked rapidly. "The chicken was delicious," he said.

Paula edged away. "I haven't had a bite to eat, myself . . ."

Pleasant waved her off. "Go! Go!" He pocketed his hands and stood smiling, turning his head back and forth, searching for another conversation. On her way to the buffet, Paula looked back and saw him talking to Bob Seaman. Bob did not look happy.

~

"We're taking over the next-door space next month," Mack said, pointing over the sea of idle sewing machines at the wall. "Going right through that wall. Putting in a screen-printing operation."

Julie Gorman was not sure what screen-printing was but she let her mouth fall open in an expression of amazed delight and watched Mack's chest inflate. "I really like your new name," she said. "It's so *right*."

Mack said, "Yeah, but Paula shouldn't have let it out."

"She—" Julie was about to explain, then thought better of it. It was Paula's problem. "It's so cool that you've done all this."

"Thanks," said Mack. "Have you ever seen an embroidery machine?"

"No!"

"This thing is amazing." Mack led her down the rows of sewing machines and down a short hall. "It's got eighteen heads. When it's running it can produce eleven hundred stitches a minute. These new threads they've got are incredible. Used to be, thread breakage was a real problem. Of course, you can only load and unload so fast, but Jake and the girls are working out a system. Pretty soon we'll—"

Julie stopped listening. After a few more seconds she put a hand on his biceps and said, "Mack, you're filling my head up."

"Oh. You said you wanted the tour."

"I do. Show me where *you* work."

~

She was standing very close to him, looking past his shoulder at the production schedule. "We track all of our jobs from this board." Something brushed the back of his left arm; he was sure it was her breast. Mack moved away.

"Over here is Lars's old office. I'm going to turn it into a conference room." He felt her follow, too close. Maybe she'd had too much to drink. He should get her back out to the picnic.

"Show me your office," she said into his shoulder blade.

He had always thought of Julie Gorman as an underfed clothes horse, but now, for some reason, she seemed distinctly . . . juicy.

"It's just a desk and chair."

"Is this it over here?" Julie opened the door to his office and looked inside. "Central command. This is where you run things from?"

"Yeah. Maybe we should get back outside."

Julie grew larger and was suddenly in front of him, as close as she could possibly be without touching. He could smell wine on her breath and something else, a subtle but powerful perfume.

131

"Mack, there's something I'd really like to show you."

"Oh?"

"A house. What are you doing Monday afternoon?"

"Uh, I've got a pretty busy day . . ."

"You eat lunch, don't you?"

Mack moistened his lips and nodded. Her eyes were only a few inches away from his mouth. She brought up a hand and hooked a nail under his top shirt button, pulled it out, let it snap back, smiled. Her teeth were shiny. Mack focused on a line of tiny saliva bubbles where her dark pink tongue met her teeth. His fingers hung thick and useless from his hands. He became acutely aware of his penis.

Julie's smile closed; she stepped back. "You're right. Let's go have another drink." She turned and walked away. Mack watched, imagining his hands cupping her small round buttocks. He followed her back through the factory to the loading dock and out to the picnic, thinking of all the reasons he should avoid Julie Gorman. Remarkably, not one of them seemed important.

20

"I talked to that policeman."

"Oh?" Mack poured himself a glass of orange juice, feigning disinterest. "We got any cookies?"

"Above the refrigerator. You didn't get enough to eat at the picnic?"

"I was pretty much talking the whole time. I'm hungry." He located a box of vanilla wafers and sat down with them at the kitchen table.

"He's kind of a creepy guy. He was asking a lot of questions."

"Such as?"

"He wanted to know why the bank is lending you more money."

"He must not have enough to do."

"And he seemed obsessed with Lars."

"Yeah, he's been chasing Lars for years." He ate a cookie. Paula stood resting her butt against the edge of the sink, arms crossed, trying to imagine what Mack might be thinking. Maybe he was just tired. It had been a long day.

"Ginny and Jake seemed to get along pretty good."

Mack nodded.

"Julie said you gave her a tour."

"I showed her around the factory." He dug another vanilla wafer from the box. "She thinks we should buy a new house."

"Julie thinks everybody should buy a new house. She's a realtor."

"She wants us to look at this place out in Eden Prairie." Mack watched his wife carefully. "She's threatening to drag me out there next week."

Paula smiled. "If Julie wants to show you a house, she'll just keep bugging you till you look at it."

"Maybe *you* should look at it."

Paula drew in the corners of her mouth. "You think we can afford to move?"

"We can afford to look."

"I'm not sure I want to look at something we can't afford."

"Well, maybe I'll drive out there, then. Get her off my back."

"Might as well." Paula yawned. "My folks had a good time. I think it helped for them to see how you're pulling everything together. They were pretty scared when, you know . . ."

Mack's eyes flattened. "Yeah. Hal asked me for money."

"He did?"

"We can't afford to be paying off our investors."

"Oh, well, I'm sure Daddy will understand." Paula did not like the way Mack was looking at her. Like it was her fault.

"It doesn't matter if he understands or not. NuMac is a long way from stable. I've got a lot of balls in the air. I can't afford to have your parents undermining my efforts."

"I'm sure Daddy didn't—"

"I don't need the distraction. Your father put his money into a high-risk investment and now he's asking for guarantees. It's not like he was there for us when things looked rocky. Two months ago he was calling me a worthless crook, and now he wants special treatment? He's got to get in line with the rest of them. You make sure he understands that. Okay?"

Paula wanted to scream, but her jaw was locked. She wanted to throw something at him, but her fingers were embedded deep in her biceps. She heard air whistling in and out through her nose.

Mack put another vanilla wafer on his tongue, drew it into his mouth, his eyes holding her pinned against the sink.

Paula said, her voice husky and tight, "I'm on your side, Mack."

Mack slowly chewed, staring at her the way he might look at an oddly dressed store mannequin.

Paula said, "If you don't believe that, then we've got problems bigger than Daddy. Bigger than money. We're partners. I want what's best for you. For us. I am not my father's agent. I'm not your enemy."

Mack swallowed and took another cookie from the box. "Good," he said.

~

His wife's features had become a bit coarse; her thighs strained against the fabric of her jeans. When had this happened? It seemed only weeks ago that he had found her mouth full and engaging, her body sweet and plump. Now he looked at her and saw a foreshadowing of ropy lips and sagging cheeks. What would she look like in another ten years?

Paula said, "It's late. I'm going to bed."

Mack nodded, trying to remember how she had looked at their wedding. No, before that. The first time he had met her. She'd had that apple-cheeked, bright-eyed look of a Gaelic peasant girl heading into the woods for her first tryst, but instead of a gingham dress and a bonnet she'd worn denim shorts and a skimpy little tank top that showed off her nipples. They'd been at a nightclub on Lake Minnetonka, lured there by mutual friends. After a few mai tais, Paula told Mack he looked like Charles Bronson, "only younger and with better skin. And your eyes aren't so squinty." Mack had liked that, so he told her she looked like Sally Field.

"Are you coming?" she asked.

"In a bit," he said.

She did not look like Sally Field anymore.

21

The house was hidden in a tangle of suburban streets a few miles south of the freeway. Mack became disoriented after the first few turns, but Julie's directions soon brought him to 10673 Cottonwood Lane. Turning into the driveway, he saw a black Lexus parked near the front door of a sprawling single-story house. Julie stood a few feet away in the shade of an oak tree, talking on her cell phone. She waved at Mack, folded the phone, put it in her purse.

"You found it!" she exclaimed, walking toward him. Her simple short-sleeved dress was made of a glossy chocolate-colored fabric. Silk? More likely one of the new synthetics, Mack thought. Whatever the fiber, it showed off her slim body in a way that on most women would have been indelicate, at best. On Julie it looked right.

"Good directions," said Mack.

Julie grabbed his hand. "You are going to *love* this," she said, pulling him up the flagstone steps to the front door. She lifted a hinged shingle to the left of the door and removed a key from the concealed niche. "It's one of a kind." The door opened into a tiled vestibule. "New tile. Italian marble. Installed just before the owners left for Europe. Last month. Living in France now." She turned to him, her eyes bright. "They're *desperate* to sell."

~

"Mac-La— I mean, NuMac Unlimited!" Sally Grayson listened, nodding. "I'm sorry, Mr. MacWray is not available. May I have him return your call?" She scribbled rapidly on the top sheet of her pink message pad.

"Thank you for calling NuMac!" Still writing, she hung up the phone. The front door opened. Sally looked up, hoping to see Mr. MacWray—he'd left for lunch two hours ago and she had a bunch of messages for him—but it was Jake Vink.

"Hi, cutie." Vink winked at her as he breezed past her desk and headed out into the factory. "Looking good!" he called over his shoulder.

Sally smiled. She liked Jake. He always had a friendly word, always acknowledged her. Except when Mr. MacWray was around. When the boss was there, Jake turned into a different guy. You didn't know if he was going to fire you or just rip your head off. Sally figured that Jake had to act that way because it was his job, like he was the vice principal of a high school. The regular principal, like Mr. MacWray, was way up there looking down. He would never get his hands dirty by dealing with the regular people.

The phone rang again.

"Ma— *NuMac* Unlimited!"

It was that Hal Byrnes again. Mr. MacWray had told her that when Hal or Joyce Byrnes called, she should be polite and take a message, but in no case was she to put the call through to him. Sally copied down the message and added it to the growing pile.

It was a fun place to work, always something going on. This morning, for instance, Mr. MacWray had taken an order for twenty-seven thousand tote bags. And all day the employees had been voting on new vending machines for the lunch area. Sally was hoping for Pepsi, but so far Coke was winning.

Jake reappeared.

"Sally? Have you heard from Mr. MacWray?"

"No. I got a lot of messages for him, though. He's been gone, like, two hours!"

"Okay, well don't worry about it. Just let me know when he gets back, okay?"

"I sure will."

"Thanks, doll." Vink disappeared back into the factory.

The phone rang.

"NuMac Unlimited."

"Sally? It's me."

"Mr. MacWray!" Good thing she'd answered the phone right. "I have some messages for you!"

~

Mack listened to Sally recite his messages, his eyes closed.

". . . and Hal Byrnes called again. Twice."

"You can toss those. My wife didn't call?"

"No. But Mr. Vink wants to talk to you."

"Tell him I'll be back in an hour or so."

He hung up the phone and opened his eyes to bare feet on Berber carpet. The muffled sound of running water came from the bathroom. Mack stood up and walked to the wall of windows overlooking the river valley. The view caused him to inhale, filling his lungs, making him bigger. What would it be like to wake up to such a panorama every morning? Would it lose its appeal?

The sound of the shower stopped. Mack heard the soft sounds of terry cloth on flesh, then Julie Gorman appeared, patting herself with an oversize white bath towel.

"Hey, stud." Grinning. "Nice view, isn't it?" Flat belly. Small, perfectly round aureoles. Neatly trimmed patch of pubic hair.

"In every direction."

Julie laughed. "Make a reasonable offer, it's all yours. The seller is highly motivated." She dropped the wet towel on the floor and picked up a scrap of filmy black material. "I guess we should get back to the real world." She pulled the black fabric over one foot, then the other. Panties. Fabric slid up her legs, wrapped her boyish hips. She ran her thumbs around the narrow waistband, adjusting it with a practiced movement.

Mack took a step toward her. "What's the hurry?"

Julie cocked her head. "You don't have to get back to work?"

"It can wait." The carpet felt harsh against the soles of his feet.

Julie took a step back and crossed her forearms over her breasts. "I've got things I have to do. I'm a working girl."

"C'mere a sec," Mack said.

Julie shook her head, but she was grinning impishly. "Paula was right—you *are* an animal."

"She said that?"

"She tells me everything."

"I hope the arrangement isn't mutual."

Mack launched himself. Julie made a feint to the left but let him catch her around the waist. He lifted her and threw her onto the bed. She landed on her back, suddenly still, legs and arms splayed wide, her eyes dilated solid black, her mouth open. Mack, blood rushing to his groin, took a moment to explore her with his eyes, then dove in.

~

The most surprising thing was that he felt okay about it. Mack had worried that it might make him feel guilty, but it had been a simple matter to shove his marriage into an out-of-sight closet and slam the door. He felt powerful and clean, as if he'd flushed his pipes with a new, more powerful cleanser. He wished he could tell someone about it. He was tempted to roll down his window and say to the driver next to him, "Hey, I just banged my wife's best friend!"

The light changed. Mack stomped on the gas and shot through the intersection. Two o'clock. There would be a stack of messages waiting at the office, and he had to meet with Vink to go over next week's shipping schedule. Putting Julie Gorman in her own mental closet, Mack focused on his driving, weaving from lane to lane, driving at twice the posted limit. At Lyndale Avenue he missed the light but accelerated through the intersection anyway, cutting off a maroon minivan. He caught a frozen glimpse of a woman's startled face as he narrowly missed taking off her front bumper.

Christ, he thought, that could have been damned inconvenient. A faint cry from the back of his mind said, *You could have killed her.* Mack turned on the radio. "I could have killed myself," he said aloud, punching buttons until he found some rock and roll, a gritty, pounding lament by the late Kurt Cobain. He turned the volume up until the speakers distorted, and blew through another intersection.

22

Sally looked up at the sound of the front door buzzer, again hoping to see Mr. MacWray returning, but instead found herself facing a tall black woman wearing a sleeveless saffron dress and wraparound sunglasses. Her hair swept low on her forehead and fell in platinum curves to dark shoulders. She approached to within a few feet of Sally's desk and looked around the room.

Sally ogled the woman with an envy approaching lust. Her body was a classic hourglass, and the yellow dress fit with such relentless precision that it could not have accommodated even the silkiest, most delicate undergarments. Few women would dare to wear such a dress, and even fewer could wear it well. How did she keep her boobs so high? It had to be wires. Or implants. Or magic.

The woman lifted her sunglasses and peered down at Sally, who was astonished to see bright blue irises. The woman wasn't black after all—she just had an incredibly dark suntan.

Sally said, "Can I help you?"

"Is Mack in?" Her full lips were painted a burnished gold, a shade lighter than her skin. Sally decided then and there to try that color herself, even though she knew it would be wrong for her no matter how many hours she spent in the tanning booth.

"I'm sorry, Mr. MacWray is not—"

The woman slashed the air with creamy gold nails, cutting Sally off, and walked quickly down the hall toward Mr. MacWray's office.

"Excuse me?" Sally was up out of her chair but then froze, not knowing what to do next. The woman opened the door, stood for a moment looking at the empty desk. "You can't just walk in here . . ." Sally said.

"Mack's an old friend," the woman said. "When will he be back?" She didn't look at Sally.

"I don't know. He might be back anytime now. If you'd like to leave a message?"

"No message." The woman stepped into the office and began looking through the papers scattered on the desk.

Sally said, "Hey!" She moved to grab the woman by the arm but couldn't bring herself to complete the act. If this was an old friend of Mr. MacWray's, she did not want to offend. Also, the woman frightened her.

"What's going on here?" Jake Vink appeared in the doorway.

Sally said, "I don't—"

The woman turned. For the first time, her mouth opened into a smile.

"Hello there," she said.

"She just barged in," Sally said.

Jake Vink took a moment, then said, "I'm Jake Vink. Is there something we can do for you, Miss . . . ?"

She laughed as if he had said something delightfully clever. "I'm sure you could do plenty, Jake Vink," she said.

~

Jake Vink believed that beautiful women were mostly evil and always dangerous. They were as likely to rip your heart out as they were to blow your fingers off. The best defensive strategy, he had found, was to be rude and unpleasant, otherwise they were likely to have you doing things for them before you knew what hit you. It helped to imagine them tied up and naked and begging.

He said, "You mind telling me who you are?"

"I don't mind." She moved closer, attacking with pheromones. Vink stood his ground, giving her his best reptilian stare. She stopped with her tits about eighteen inches from his chest, her eyes locked on his. Vink thought how she would look with a handkerchief stuffed in her mouth and her wrists lashed to a bedpost.

Her smile remained on her mouth, but her eyes went dead. She put her sunglasses back on. Vink knew that she had made him.

"You're one of *those,* aren't you?" she said.

"You haven't answered my question."

"Who I am? It's none of your business." She walked around the desk and sat down in Mack's chair. "I'll wait for Mack." She crossed her legs.

Vink said, "I don't think so, doll. You want to wait, you can wait out front."

He made a move toward her and almost had his hand on her arm when she said, "You touch me and things will get ugly, Jake Vink."

Vink hesitated. "Maybe they'll get uglier than you think."

She laughed. "You'll be in court for a year. Not to mention out of a job."

Vink set his jaw. It would almost be worth it. He thought how it would feel to bury a two-fingered fist in her left tit. To drag her out the front door screaming and kicking. He wished he knew who she was. One of Mack's ex-girlfriends? If so, he was impressed. One did not often see a woman like this outside the pages of *Penthouse*.

"Are you thinking," she asked, "or having an episode? I can't tell."

Vink turned to Sally, who was standing frozen in the doorway. "Call the cops," he said. Sally remained motionless for a full second, then broke and ran back to her desk. Vink settled into one of the visitor chairs. He scratched his chin with a ragged nail and said, "Now we wait."

"That's fine with me."

Vink sorted through his remembered conversations with Mack but came up with nothing in the way of statuesque blondes. He cast his mind back further, then remembered Bob Seaman talking about the Mac-Lar loans, and how they had come to be. He remembered Seaman describing Lars Larson, and Lars's girlfriend. The name eluded him, but he remembered Seaman using the phrase "tits out to here."

"I know who you are," Vink said.

"Good for you."

"You used to work here. You're in some serious trouble, doll."

She smiled. Five minutes passed with neither of them speaking, then they heard voices and a few seconds later Mack appeared in the doorway.

Vink stood up and said, "Mack, this—"

Mack cut him off. "It's okay." He stepped into the office.

"She said she was a friend of yours, but—"

"Take a walk, Jake."

Vink shrugged and walked out.

23

Mack closed the door, stood with his back to it.

"You look different," said Rita. "Are you wearing lifts?"

Mack lowered his chin, his eyebrows moving up slightly.

"Your secretary called the cops," Rita said. "Are you sure that's what you want?"

"Maybe. What do *you* want?"

"*Moi?*" Rita touched her nails to her sternum. "What makes you think I want something?"

"You're here, aren't you?"

Rita smiled, but her heart was pounding. This Mack was altogether too calm. What had happened to the fearful, uncertain Mack of old? She took her eyes off him and looked at the papers on his desk—production schedules, invoices, a handful of mail, and a Mercedes-Benz brochure.

"You must be doing well."

"No thanks to you and your husband."

"Late husband."

"Sorry to hear that."

Rita's throat tightened. It was intolerable that this cocky nobody had taken away her Teddy Bear. She said, "He was murdered. But you know that, of course."

"I do?"

"The Mexican police are looking for the killer."

"Is that a fact?"

"Yes. Apparently, there was a witness." Rita watched intently as Mack stared back at her, his face immobile. "The lighthouse keeper," she added.

Mack gave a faint shrug. "Lighthouse?"

"He saw what happened."

"And what was that?"

"I think you know."

"Hardly."

"We can discuss it with the police when they get here. Maybe we'll both end up in the can."

"The police aren't coming. I told Sally not to call them."

"That was smart. When did you get smart?"

"Just after you and Lars took off with my money."

"Your money?" Rita smiled, shaking her head.

Mack turned his gaze upon her. For a second or two she feared he might do something physical. She braced herself, ready for anything, but then his shoulders dropped and his eyes fogged and she saw that she was, for the moment, safe.

"What do you want?" Mack asked.

"What have you got?"

~

Thoughts came and went, a flickering, seething soup of memories and imaginings. Mack saw Rita sitting in his chair. His eyes and ears told him she was there, but for the moment he chose to regard her as a phantom. He could feel his heart beat, regular and slow. He would not panic. He remembered Lars falling, and the rain, and the lighthouse. He had seen no one in the lighthouse. And even if someone had witnessed Lars's death, they would know that Mack had done nothing. He put himself in Rita's place. What would *he* do? He would lie, he would bluff, he would threaten. This Rita phantom was blowing smoke.

Mack crossed his arms. "I'm going to do you a favor, Rita."

"Really."

"Really. You see, I have this friend, a fellow named Pleasant. And he is"—smile—"very pleasant. Do you know him?"

"No."

"Well, he knows you. I'm sure he'd be interested in talking to you. He's been a fan of yours and Lars's for a long time now. He's a cop."

Rita blinked rapidly, her smile frozen. Mack was reminded of a light on a processing computer.

"Oh." Her smile became pensive. "*That* Pleasant."

"That Pleasant." Mack watched, wondering what she would do next. For several seconds Rita stared back at him, blinking twice, then she laughed. The laugh had a visceral effect; Mack felt as if his intestines were unraveling. He tightened his abdomen, trying not to let her see that she had reached him.

"Mack—Macanudo—you do not want to play your Officer Pleasant card. Trust me. You get him involved and you'll come out of this a lot worse than I will." Rita stood up. Mack's eyes automatically scanned her body; somewhere in his hindbrain a few molecules of hormone were released. Rita gave him a moment, then said, "The law is not what you see on TV, Mack. It's got nothing to do with justice.

The law follows the money. Just like everybody else. You send the police in my direction and the next thing you know they'll be all over *you*. Think about it." She stepped out from behind the desk. Mack's eyes went to her legs. "And think about how you're going to pay me back the money you took. Cash would be nice." She moved to the door. "I'll call you tomorrow."

"Where are you staying?"

The left side of her mouth turned up in a smile. She walked out.

Mack stood still for twenty seconds, then followed her. He reached the lobby door in time to see Rita getting into a white Toyota. He considered tailing her, but what would be the point of that? If there was one sure thing, it was that he would be hearing from Rita Monbeck again.

~

Five thousand two hundred square feet. Four baths, and the bath off the master bedroom had a Jacuzzi, a commode, and a shower in the round with sixteen pulsating heads. The bed was enormous. Bigger than king-size. Where would she find sheets for a bed like that? Nine-foot-high French doors led out onto a deck overlooking the river valley. The deck was larger than her backyard. The distorted scale of it made her uncomfortable. Paula moved from the master bedroom into the six-foot-wide hallway, followed the hall out to the sunken living room. Twenty-foot ceiling, a fireplace big enough to burn a sofa, a wall of windows with remote-controlled blinds. Living rooms were supposed to be cozy. This one made her feel small. The house seemed to have been designed to make her feel insignificant and inadequate. What would they fill it with? The thought of buying that much furniture terrified her.

"It's really . . . big," she said. Her words were absorbed by the space.

Julie Gorman laughed. "Check this out." She guided Paula into the kitchen.

"My god . . ." Paula ran her hand across the countertop. "What is this? Pink marble?"

"Granite. Look at the stove."

Paula looked. Eight burners, two ovens, and a grill.

"My god, Julie, what would I do in here?"

"You'd cook, honey. You'd *really* cook."

"God, I don't know. You say Mack liked this place?"

"Honey, he was totally turned on."

Paula looked doubtfully at the spotless pink granite countertops. What, exactly, did Mack like about this place? Certainly not the kitchen. Mack could barely distinguish a microwave oven from a toaster.

"What did he like?" she asked.

"He liked it all," Julie said.

"I wish you'd shown it to us together."

"Divide and conquer, hon. Here's the thing: I show a house to a couple, all they do is worry about how the other one likes the place. I show it to you one at a time and you can each make up your own mind. It's better, hon. Trust me."

Paula looked out the kitchen window at the long sloping lawn. With Mack working twelve or fourteen hours a day, they would have to hire someone to take care of it. Had Mack considered that? Did it matter? How could he be considering buying a new house when they couldn't afford to pay her parents back? My god, what would *they* think of this? *Sorry, folks, we can't pay you right now, but how do you like our two-million-dollar house?* Her father would blow a vessel.

Julie was chattering on about the kitchen floor, some kind of imported tile. Paula imagined talking to Mack, trying to understand what he was thinking. Of course she wanted to move to a nicer house. She wanted a lot of things. She wanted a new fall coat, a week at a luxury spa, a vacation in Italy. Things they might be able to afford. She also wanted a red Miata and a baby girl. Could they afford those things, too? She pictured a toddler running clumsily across the imported tiles. Suddenly the kitchen seemed full of hard surfaces and sharp corners and she knew she could never live in such a place.

Julie said, "I have to tell you, hon, I can really see you guys coming into your own here. You deserve it. Mack said he could really *breathe* in here."

Paula half smiled and gave a shallow nod. That did not sound like

145

something Mack would say. It was possible—no, it was *probable*—that Julie was bullshitting her. It wouldn't be the first time, or even the hundredth time, that Julie had twisted the truth to try to talk Paula into an unwise course of action. Back in high school it had been an almost daily event. It was the foundation of their friendship—Julie spinning tales, Paula buying the fantasy. Sometimes she came to her senses, sometimes she simply let herself roll with it.

She said, "It's awfully nice, but . . ." She looked at Julie's eager face. "I'll talk to Mack," she said.

~

Mack sat slumped behind his desk. The thing with Julie Gorman and the visit from Rita Monbeck battled for ascendency in his thoughts. Rita was winning. He could smell her perfume. He could almost feel her hand in his pocket, groping for his wallet. He tried to find a rational line of thought, a strategy that would move her out of his life. He could stonewall her, assume that the Mexican cops would not care enough about Lars's death to launch an international investigation. What could she do? She could do a lot. She could ruin him this time as surely as she and Lars had destroyed him before. She might not get the money, but she could raise enough questions and suspicions to make things very, very difficult for him. With all the plates he had spinning it wouldn't take much to bring the whole show crashing down. Rita would know that. But what if he paid her off? What would it take? Here, the matter became even more convoluted. Was there a magic number? If he gave her, say, $10,000 or $20,000, would she go away? What if she wanted the entire $346,000? Or more?

Daunted by the complexity of the problem, his mind turned back to Julie. He felt the heat enter his groin, saw her arched spine, the fine down at the small of her back, her ragged gasps of pleasure—or had he been the one making those sounds? He let himself remember it fully, hearing the synchronated breathing and the sounds of flesh on flesh, and the creaking of the bed. Seeing her dark hair on the pillow, the sheen of sweat at the nape of her thin neck. Mack felt himself getting hard. He turned her hair to platinum, enlarged her slim frame, dug his fingers deep into her tanned buttocks. Fucking Rita. That fucking Rita. He should have . . . he should have . . . what? He sensed a void. His thoughts veered off, leaving him gripping the edge of his desk, his heart pounding.

For the first time since Cancún he felt afraid—not of Rita or the cops, but of himself. He thought back to his visit to Al Krupinski and remembered how it had felt to slam the man's face into his desk blotter. It was not an act the old Mack would have committed or even considered, but it had felt good. The old Mack might have fantasized such a thing, but only later, when he was safely alone with himself. The new Mack was not so tentative. He had no sooner thought it than he had done it. The same with Julie Gorman. If all his thoughts became reality, of what else might he be capable?

A sharp knock, repeated three times, brought him back to the moment. He cleared his throat.

"Come in."

Jake Vink entered, holding a thin sheaf of papers. "Got a minute?"

Mack nodded slowly.

Vink sat down across from him.

"I just wanted to run a couple things by you. We've got a bit of a bottleneck in sewing next week. I'm scheduled to ship a batch of smocks to the pizza folks, but I've also got a deadline on seven hundred aprons for that chili festival down in Dallas. You think it's okay if we hold up on the smocks for a week or three?"

"Sure," said Mack. He felt drained. "Whatever. It's your call, Jake."

Vink nodded, shuffled papers, cleared his throat. "That woman—was that who I think it was?" He had not come to discuss the production schedule.

Mack did not reply. He was not sure what, if anything, he wanted to share with Jake Vink. He needed time to think this thing through.

Vink said, "None of my beeswax, eh?"

"Not really."

Vink shrugged and stood up. "You're the boss, boss."

Mack watched him leave, feeling very alone. The instant Vink was out of sight, Mack raised his voice and said, "That was Rita Monbeck. She used to work here."

He wasn't sure Vink had heard, but a few seconds later he reappeared in the doorway.

"You say something?"

"That was Rita Monbeck."

"I thought that's what you said."

"Her real name is Larson. She's Lars's wife."

Vink returned to his chair. "We got a problem?"

"I'm not sure," said Mack.

"She's a real stone-cold bitch, that one," Vink said.

Mack nodded, surprised by Vink's intensity.

"What does she want?" Vink asked.

"What everybody wants."

"She got some reason to think you're gonna give it to her?"

Mack considered carefully before answering. "She thinks she does."

The two men sat in silence. Mack had no intention of elaborating. He wanted to see what Vink would do with what he had.

After nearly a full minute, Vink contracted his wide mouth into a wavy slash. "I guess maybe it's personal, eh?"

Mack gave the ghost of a shrug.

Vink nodded. "Okay then, I'm cool with that. I just want to say, if there's anything I can do—and I mean anything—you let me know."

"I appreciate that, Jake."

24

A few years back, succumbing to a local fad, Paula MacWray had painted the front door of their home turquoise. At the time it had given her great satisfaction. Now it looked cheap and contrived. Paula turned the doorknob with its chipped brass plating and let herself into the house. She breathed in the familiar smell, welcoming herself home. She set her purse on the small table beside the coat closet.

Everything seemed small.

Cozy, she corrected herself. Not small. Cozy. The house had served them well for almost eight years. It wasn't a mansion, it was a perfectly normal three-bedroom ranch with a two-car garage and a full basement and more than enough room for a childless couple in their mid-thirties. It was a good, solid house with a reasonable-size yard in a nice, neat, blue-collar neighborhood. She and Mack had built their marriage there. They'd had good times and bad. She kicked off her shoes and went into the kitchen. The refrigerator, a ten-year-old Amana, rumbled to life. She could feel the vibrations through the floor. The shallow stainless-steel sink was piled high with dishes, some from that morning, some left over from last night. The stove was a Kenmore electric with grease permanently baked onto the burner pans and a clock that ticked loudly but always read 7:32. She thought about the enormous, perfect, perfectly clean stove she had looked at that afternoon. She turned away from her kitchen, her eyes stinging with envy and shame. Everything was so . . . *shabby.*

She felt a flash of anger at Julie Gorman, both for showing her the house and for having borne witness to her shabby lifestyle for all these years. Paula admired Julie's taste when she did not find it absurd, and the thought of Julie looking at that turquoise door so many times without comment produced a skin-prickling rush of embarrassment. Paula opened the refrigerator and took out a beer. She twisted the cap off and was about to take a sip when she saw herself, a thirty-six-year-old woman, twenty pounds overweight, standing in her stocking feet, sink full of dishes, drinking beer from a bottle. She looked at her fingernails—short, uneven, unpolished. She touched her face. When had her flesh become so slack and doughy? How could she expect Mack to want her, now that things were going so well for him?

She poured the beer down the sink. She would not let it happen.

~

Mack left NuMac as soon as the second shift arrived. On the way home he spent a half hour tooling around the Minneapolis lakes, watching the joggers and skaters and dog walkers. He thought about parking the car and doing some walking himself, but could not quite see himself as one of them. They were going around in circles, staying on the six-foot-wide paved paths. He had rejected all such restraints. He understood now why business tycoons and film stars and top ath-

149

letes go to such lengths to insulate themselves from ordinary people. It was not a matter of protecting their privacy or providing security for themselves. The simple fact was that they lived in another reality, one in which the ordinary boundaries and rules no longer applied. They had stepped outside the lines. They made their own rules, just like him.

He thought about Julie Gorman stretched small and naked on that enormous bed. Did Julie make her own rules? He was not sure. He thought about Paula, seeing her in sweatpants and a T-shirt trimming the hydrangea by the back door. His mouth turned down. Paula was not a rule breaker. He searched for a feeling about her. Did he love her? Probably, but at the moment he felt nothing other than a faint discomfort, possibly the shadow of guilt, or perhaps pity. He turned off the parkway and headed east, toward home. He was tired of driving and he had nowhere else to go.

The sun was setting as Mack pulled into his garage. Seven o'clock. Paula would be angry at him for not calling. Although he had not been home for dinner in weeks, she still expected him to call. He used the remote to close the garage door, steeled himself for whatever lay in wait on the other side of the door, then entered his castle.

The house was dark, and it did not smell like cooking. Soft jazz was playing on the stereo. He heard the clink of glass against glass.

"Paula?"

He walked through the kitchen into the small living room. Several candles burned on the faux mantelpiece. It took him a moment to find Paula in the flickering half-light. She was reclined on the sofa holding a champagne flute.

"Hey, Mack," she said in a low voice. Her lips were dark.

"What's going on?" Mack asked, suspicious and bewildered.

"Pour yourself a drink." An open champagne bottle and a second flute sat on the coffee table next to a red votive candle.

As Mack's eyes adjusted to the light he saw that she was wearing a cocktail dress, a black number that he hadn't seen in years. Her hair was pulled back. Her nails had become long and dark red to match her lips. A pair of dangling garnet earrings glittered with candlelight. She sipped her champagne.

"Did we have plans for tonight?"

Paula shook her head. Mack sat down on the easy chair facing the sofa and poured himself some champagne. The bottle was more than half empty.

"What's the occasion?" he asked.

"Oh, I don't know. Maybe a new home?"

Mack sipped his champagne, waiting for more information.

"Julie showed me the house," Paula said.

"She did? When?"

"This afternoon."

Mack gulped more champagne. It could have been Dom Pérignon or 7UP—he would not have noticed the difference.

"So?" he asked.

"She said you really liked the place."

Mack nodded.

"She says it's a good buy."

"The market's pretty soft right now."

"I guess what I'm saying is, if you really like it, maybe we should buy it."

Paula pushed herself to a sitting position. Her breasts and thighs strained against the thin fabric of the dress. She held out her glass. Mack filled it, then topped off his own, emptying the bottle.

"There's another one in the fridge," Paula said.

"What exactly did Julie say?"

Paula laughed. "She never stopped talking the whole time we were there. She was trying to talk me into loving the house."

"Did it work?"

Paula stared at the votive candle through her champagne. "It half worked. She convinced me that we should be living better." She saluted him with her glass. "I mean, now that you're a big success." She laughed and tipped her head back and drank.

Mack sat back in his chair and watched her throat pulse as she swallowed. A fine gold chain encircled her neck. He asked, "How come you're all dressed up?"

"I got dressed up 'cause I'm sick of looking like a schlub."

Mack nodded. "You look good." And she did. Even though the

dress was a size too small and her lipstick was smeared from repeated applications of the champagne flute. So different from the small, cool, impish Julie Gorman. Paula was meaty and juicy by comparison. Just last night he had been thinking her coarse and unappealing, but now that coarseness went straight to his groin. A few hours earlier he had thought that he would never want to touch his wife again, but now, the more he thought about Julie Gorman, the more enticing Paula became.

"Thank you," Paula said, touching her face.

"For what?"

"For looking at me like that."

"Oh. So, did you like that house?"

Paula nodded, smiling hard. A part of him saw that she was lying, but the rest of him didn't care. He stood up.

"Let's go."

"Go?" Paula held her smile, but her brow wrinkled.

"Come on," Mack said, holding out his hand. Paula reached out uncertainly; their hands clasped. Her palm was warm and moist. She was nervous. Mack felt his heart speed up. He pulled her toward the kitchen, grabbed his car keys and the other bottle of champagne, opened the garage door.

"Where are we going?"

"Going to look at a house."

~

It wasn't as good as that time in Cancún, but it was damn good, Paula thought. She sat with her back propped against the headboard, sheets pulled up over her breasts. Moonlight flooded in through the bank of windows. She could see lights from the other side of the river valley, twenty miles away. How would she feel, waking up in this room every morning? It was so big, and there were so many windows, and the view was so spectacular it made her feel naked and small. Mack, sprawled sideways across the mattress, seemed oblivious to the scale of their surroundings. They were sharing the same bed but were separated by more than four feet. He lay on top of the spread on his back, eyes closed, his limp penis flopped against his thigh, completely relaxed and unself-conscious.

Maybe she was agoraphobic. Of course, they could have a smaller bed. She could close the blinds. There were things she could do to make it cozier.

Her stomach growled, reminding her that all she'd had for dinner was a bottle of champagne. She slid her foot forward under the covers and nudged Mack's hip.

"Hey," she said.

Mack's eyes opened. He turned his head and looked at her.

"I'm hungry," she said.

Mack sat up. "Let's go, then." He stood up and began to dress, starting with his briefs, following the uneven trail of discarded clothing from the bedroom and down the hallway toward the front entrance. Paula followed suit. She found her dress hanging over the stairway railing, one shoe in the front hall, the other on the steps outside the front door.

She said, "I should at least make the bed."

"Why?" He seemed genuinely puzzled.

"Because we messed it. What if Julie has to show the house to another client?"

Mack shrugged. Paula went back to the bedroom and straightened the sheets and fluffed the pillows. She tried again to imagine herself living there. She would have to change. Maybe that would be a good thing. Life is change—she had heard that once, someplace. To live is to grow, to grow is to change. She would become a different person. Like Mack. She smoothed the bedspread, wondering what sort of person she might become.

25

Sally handed Mack four messages when he arrived at work the next morning. Rita had called at nine-fifteen and said she would call back, Jerry Pleasant had called at nine-twenty and left a number, and Bob Seaman had called twice, at nine and at nine-thirty. His call slips were both marked *urgent*.

"What exactly did Bob Seaman say?" Mack asked.

"He said to write *urgent* on the message slip," Sally said.

Mack nodded, dropped the messages in a wastebasket, and shut himself in his office. Five minutes later Sally sent a call through on line two. Mack took a deep breath and picked up.

"MacWray," he snapped, hoping to intimidate whoever was on the line.

"Mack! Jesus Christ, it's Bob. How come you didn't call me back?"

"I just got in, *Bob*. What can I do for you?"

"Do? You're three days late on your loan maintenance!"

"So?"

"Jesus Christ, Mack! There's only so much I can do!"

Mack laughed. "Okay, take it easy. Give me another couple days. I've got plenty of cash coming in the next few weeks. Hey, I was going to call you about something anyway. Paula and I are thinking about buying a new house."

"Really?" Seaman's voice became cautious. "With what?"

"Well, we figured we'd borrow some money from you."

"I don't do home loans. You have to go through HomeStar, our mortgage company."

"Yeah, but you can talk to them, can't you?"

Seaman gave forth an audible sigh. "Jesus Christ, Mack . . ."

"Just put in a good word for me, Bob. Listen, I gotta go."

He hung up. It really *was* easy if you didn't give a shit. He put his feet on his desk and leaned back, smiling. The call from Seaman had put things back in perspective. A bit of bluster and bullshit would take care of Rita Larson and Jerry Pleasant. And as far as Julie Gorman was concerned, his dalliance had actually seemed to *improve* his marriage. He was reliving yesterday's sexual conquests when Sally sent through another call.

Mack punched the speaker button. "Mack here."

"Good morning, Macanudo."

Mack lurched forward and picked up the handset. "Mrs. Larson. What can I do for you?"

"I just wanted to let you know I'm planning to drop by the courthouse this afternoon."

"Oh?"

"I have some materials to drop off for your friend, Officer Pleasant."

"I see."

"I thought I might stop for a bite on the way. Do you have lunch plans?"

"No, I don't."

"Do you know where the Lotus is?"

"Yes."

"If lunch goes well, I might not have time to stop at the courthouse. I might go straight to the airport."

Mack nodded and cleared his throat. "What time?"

"Noon."

"Okay."

"Have something for me, Macanudo." She broke the connection.

Mack replaced the handset in its cradle and took several deep breaths to calm himself. He leaned forward over his desk and pressed an index finger to each temple. He had to think quickly and clearly, setting aside his anger and his ego. He had a problem and he needed to solve it by the most efficient and cost-effective means available. It was no different from a marketing or production problem, and like most business problems, the most direct and obvious solution was to add money. The specific question he had to answer was, how much?

There were two ways to look at it. The first was to figure out how much money it would take to make Rita go away. She wanted everything, but she might be satisfied with some lesser amount. She wouldn't want any trouble if she could avoid it. Going to the police would be a kamikaze move on her part. She might do it, though. He did not think she was bluffing. Not entirely.

He put himself in Rita's place. What would she take? A hundred seventy-five thousand would represent half of the money he had taken from the safe deposit box. Would that be enough to get rid of her? Perhaps. Which brought him to the second way to approach the problem: how much was he willing to part with? Of the three forty-six he'd brought back from Cancún, he had about three hundred thousand left. The rest had gone for bribes, kickbacks, and miscellaneous expenses. If he paid Rita, say, ten thousand, it would be a bargain. But he didn't think she would go for that. Fifty thousand? It would depend on how desperate she was. Massaging his temples, Mack continued his analysis of the situation. After a time, he got up and left his office, telling Sally that he would be back in a few hours.

~

It was almost ten o'clock when Paula woke up. Mack had left for work hours ago. She picked up the bedside phone and called Gold Coast. She told Ginny that her car had broken down, that she would be in by noon. The lie came to her easily and rather to her surprise, as Ginny would have accepted a simple apology and confession of having overslept. Paula shook her head, putting the pointless lie behind her. She shuffled into the bathroom and looked at herself in the mirror. Her left cheek was deeply creased, her eyes blurry with makeup, her hair twisted and off center. Good thing Mack isn't home to see this, she thought. She turned on the shower and washed her body, watching the water spatter and clump and run over her breasts, her belly, her legs. It's not a bad body, she decided. She still had it. She could still get his attention.

She dressed in a tight wool skirt and a white silk blouse and took some extra time with her makeup. Since she had overslept, it seemed important to look good. She worked her hair with a brush until it stood out, framing her face, giving her cheeks a concave look. She put on a faux pearl necklace and real pearl earrings and took a few extra minutes to touch up her nails. By ten-forty she was ready to go. That was when she heard the garage door go up.

~

Mack was surprised to find Paula's car still in the garage. He had expected her to be at work. He stood in the garage, listening. When, after a minute, the door leading into the house remained closed, he decided that she must have caught a ride in with someone else. Or maybe she was still asleep in bed. He removed the wooden stepladder from its hook and carried it to the back of the garage beneath the loft, where they stored their luggage and other rarely used items. He climbed the ladder. His black nylon overnight bag was crammed in back, behind a folding table and beneath some empty cardboard boxes. He pulled out the bag, balanced it on top of some other pieces of luggage, and opened it. Bundles of cash greeted his eyes. He let out his breath, realizing as the tension drained away that he had been afraid the money would be gone. He had to come up with a better place to keep it.

He picked out several bundles, stuffing them in the pockets of his sport coat. As he did so he considered the other items in the bag—Lars's diamond ring, his passport, his pistol—three of the most incriminating items he could possibly possess. He'd been foolish and reckless to keep them. One suspicious customs agent and he'd be in jail right now, not only for transporting the cash but for bank fraud as well. Maybe even murder. Only the most extreme self-confidence had driven him to retain such souvenirs.

I should take these things to the nearest river and toss them in, he thought. Especially with Rita threatening to blow everything wide open. He opened Lars's passport and looked at the photo, the Polaroid of himself he had glued over Lars's photo.

Paula's voice startled him. "Mack? What are you doing up there?"

"Nothing!" Mack dropped the passport back into the bag. He grabbed Lars's diamond ring, put it in his pocket, zipped the bag shut, and pushed it back into its niche.

"Well, you're doing *something*."

"I was just looking for something."

"What?"

"I lost something, my, ah, you know that little manicure set?" He climbed down the ladder. "I hadn't seen it in a while and it just occurred to me I might have left it in my suitcase."

Paula laughed. "You goof. You drove home to look for your manicure set? It's in the bathroom cabinet."

"Oh. I, uh, didn't come home just for that. I left some papers in the house." He folded the ladder and returned it to its hook. "What are you doing here?" he asked as he walked past her into the house.

"I overslept," said Paula, following him inside, down the short hall to the spare bedroom, where he had a desk set up. Mack shuffled through the bills and unopened junk mail, picked out an envelope at random, stuffed it in his pocket.

"I've got to get back to the factory," he muttered, brushing by her as if she was a stranger in a crowd.

Paula watched him walk quickly out through the garage door to his car. He took off, spinning a tire on the loose gravel at the end of their driveway. She stood in the doorway, a bit stunned, wondering what had just happened. After a time she went into the garage, lifted the stepladder from its hook, and carried it back to the loft.

26

"I'm sorry, Mrs. MacWray, but he's in conference right now."

"With who?"

"He's meeting with Mr. Vink. He told me not to interrupt him."

"Tell him it's me."

"I don't think he—"

"Do it!"

Sally stabbed the hold button. She closed her eyes and bit her lower lip and waited for the wave of discomfort to pass. This was way too much like her last job, where her boss had been having an affair with his sales manager and his wife kept calling to check up on him and Sally had to lie to her almost every day or get fired, and finally she'd had to quit. At least Mr. MacWray wasn't asking her to lie. But it gave her the same icky feelings being between the boss and his wife, and she didn't like it any better. Maybe she could just tell Mrs. MacWray that her husband had left the building. But she'd already said he was in a meeting, which was true. It was also true that Mr. MacWray had told her he did not want to be interrupted. Sally took a breath and punched the illuminated button on the phone.

"Mrs. MacWray? I'm sorry, could I have him call you back in just a few minutes?"

She heard a hiss, a sudden intake of breath. The line went silent. Sally winced and gently replaced the handset on its cradle.

It was almost noon when Mr. MacWray and Mr. Vink emerged from their meeting. Sally told Mr. MacWray that he had to call his wife right away. He thanked her, said he would be back later that afternoon, and left the building.

~

Rita had chosen the most conspicuous window table at the front of the restaurant. Sunlight slanted in through the plate glass and lit up her hair like the mantle of a kerosene lamp. She wore wraparound sunglasses and a black zipper jacket–some shiny, synthetic fabric— not quite large enough to close over her breasts. Mack stood in the entryway and watched her drinking iced tea and eating a spring roll. He had $40,000 in the pockets of his sport coat, and he was still trying to decide how much to offer her. He had been watching her for nearly a minute when she turned and looked at him and smiled as though she had been aware of him all along. Mack crossed the room to her table.

"You're late," she said.

Mack could see himself in her sunglasses. "I have a business to run."

Rita sipped her tea. A waiter appeared. Mack ordered a cup of coffee.

"You're not eating?" Rita asked.

Mack shook his head, watching his reflection, wondering what he would do next. What would Lars have done?

Rita said, "You're still trying to decide what to do, aren't you?"

Mack thought for a moment. "I'm thinking that you've got a lot to lose, too."

Rita laughed. "Me? I don't have a thing."

"You have your freedom."

"I'll always have that."

"Not if Jerry Pleasant gets his hands on you."

"He should be so lucky."

"At the very least, it would be inconvenient."

"For both of us."

Mack felt himself make a decision. "I'm going to make you an offer." He took his wallet from the inside pocket of his sport coat and counted out five hundred-dollar bills.

Rita frowned. "What's that?"

"Airfare back to Cancún." He set the money on the table next to her spring roll.

"That's a joke."

"Not at all. Wait, there's more." He dug into his pants pocket, brought his hand out, and placed Lars's heavy gold and diamond ring on top of the $500.

Rita's mouth opened and her hands came together. Was she looking at him, or at the ring? Her hands unclasped and she picked up the ring. She squeezed it in her fist. Her knuckles whitened.

"I thought you might want it." Mack bared his teeth in a humorless smile. "You know—to remember him by. So you don't forget what happened to him."

Rita stood up. She walked out of the restaurant. Mack watched until she was out of sight, then turned back to the table. A cup of coffee had appeared on his place mat. He took a sip. Good coffee. Somewhere deep inside a debate raged, but the voices were distant and dilute, affecting him no more than a political argument in a bowling alley affects a head of state. He picked up Rita's unfinished spring roll. As long as he was getting stuck with the bill, he might as well get something out of it.

～

It could be a business meeting. The woman in sunglasses might be a customer or a supplier, but she looked like neither. Not dressed like that. It was hard to see with sunlight glancing off the glass, but the woman did not look like a customer. Paula MacWray considered walking into the restaurant, going right up to their table, and saying, "Mack! Hi! What on earth are you doing here? Who's your friend?"

What would he say? Would he know that she had followed him there?

Mack was giving the woman something. Money. He was paying

her. Was it some of the money from the loft? Paula felt something cold squirming in her gut. All that money in the garage—what had he done to get it?

Mack placed a small object on the table. The woman took it. Mack said something. He was smiling.

The money in the bag had to be connected with Lars. Lars's passport had been in there, but with Mack's picture in it, as if Mack was really Lars—but that was impossible. And the gun. What was Mack doing with a gun? Paula was scared, but she wanted fiercely to know the truth. Her first impulse had been to confront Mack. She had called him, and when that little bitch Sally had refused to put her through, she had driven to the factory. Face-to-face, she would demand an explanation. Where had the money come from? And why, with all that money in the garage, was he refusing to pay her parents some of the money they had loaned to Mac-Lar? And most of all, why hadn't he told her about it?

Paula had arrived at the factory just as Mack was pulling out of the parking lot. He had not seen her. She had followed him here, to this restaurant.

The woman was on her feet now, walking toward the door. Paula waited on the sidewalk. The woman stepped out of the restaurant. They were only a few feet apart. Recognition hit hard. Rita Manbait! Paula heard herself make a sound, something between a gasp and a squeak. Rita's head snapped around and she looked Paula full in the face. Her wide mouth opened, her lips pulled tight against her teeth. She laughed, a harsh metallic cough, then moved quickly off down the sidewalk. Paula wrapped her arms around herself as if she had been struck in the belly. She held herself like that for a few seconds, letting her insides settle. *Rita Manbait!* Thoughts clattered and flashed in a crazy, high-speed slide show. She reached up and pinched her earlobe, hard, until the pain forced a halt to the reeling images. She took a deep breath, squaring her shoulders. She looked at the restaurant entrance, turned away, walked slowly back toward her car.

~

The white Toyota moved erratically through the midday traffic, sometimes going with the flow, sometimes lagging, drifting from lane to lane without signaling, occasionally speeding up and passing other cars. At one intersection she stopped on a green light. At another she stopped, then drove through the red light as if it had been a stop sign. At first, Jake Vink thought that she was trying to lose him. Then he wondered whether she might be drunk. Then he decided that she was simply a lousy driver.

He followed her down Lake Street. Now and again her hands flew into the air and her head jerked from side to side. She was talking to herself. She was furious. Vink grinned, wondering what Mack had said to her.

At 35W she turned onto the freeway and immediately brought the Toyota up to eighty miles per hour. Vink let her get a quarter of a mile ahead of him, far enough so that she wouldn't notice him but close enough so that he would see her exit, which she did at 494 westbound. He caught up with her as she exited 494 at Highway 100. She turned into the Radisson Hotel, pulled up to the entrance, and gave her keys to the valet. Vink drove into the side lot and parked his car. He gave her a few minutes to get to her room, then called the hotel on his cell phone.

"Radisson South."

"I'm calling for one of your guests—a Rita Monbeck."

"One moment . . . I'm sorry, sir, we have no one by that name registered."

"She's probably registered under her married name. Try Larson."

"One moment . . . I have a Mrs. Theodore Larson."

"That's her."

"Thank you."

The phone rang. On the third ring a woman's voice answered. "Yes?"

"Mrs. Whitman, this is room service. You ordered a—"

"You have the wrong room."

"This isn't Mrs. Whitman?"

"No, it isn't."

"Is this room four thirteen?"

"You have the wrong room."

"Are you sure? What room am I calling?"

"Two-oh-seven. Please do not bother me again." She hung up.

~

The knock on the door came just as she was getting into the shower. Probably that idiot who had called, still trying to deliver Mrs. Whatserface's order to the wrong room. Rita considered ignoring it, but she was still steaming from her meeting with Mack MacWray. She needed to yell at someone, and it might as well be some poor sap from room service. She put on her thin travel robe, belted it, and opened the door.

Jake Vink.

She tried to slam the door in his face but he blocked it with his foot. His sharp, two-fingered fist shot forward, hitting her hard in the left breast, knocking her back onto the bed. He closed the door. She sat up on the edge of the mattress, nails digging into the bedspread, her breast a knot of agony. She imagined silicone gel leaking into her chest cavity.

"How's it going, Rita?" he asked. His mutilated hand curled into a distorted fist.

Rita felt herself shift into robot mode. That was what Lars had called it when you were running a game and could not afford to look at your emotions. Like walking through customs with a half million in U.S. currency. Like being interviewed by the cops. Like laying out a story for a mark. Just do the act. The pain in her breast grew distant and unimportant. She glared at Vink.

"Nothing to say? I'm surprised. Did you have a nice meeting with Mr. MacWray?"

Rita nodded.

"That's good." Vink massaged his half hand. He stepped closer, his eyes dilated and shiny, his lips parted. Rita flicked her eyes to his crotch. The guy had a hard-on. "I just dropped by to make sure that you understand your position. You do, don't you?"

"Better than you know," she said, amazed by the confidence in her voice.

"Oh? What am I missing?"

"You like money?"

The corners of his mouth tightened, and his shoulders dropped slightly. He liked money, but did he like it enough? She sat forward, bringing her face within range of his hands. "There's plenty to go around, you know."

~

Never in his forty-four years had Jake Vink beat up a woman—but he had always wanted to. It wasn't until now that he'd had a good excuse. Sure, he'd slapped a few of his girlfriends around, but he'd never before used his fist. Punching this one in the tit had felt just about as good as anything he had ever done.

MacWray had told him to put the fear into her. He hadn't actually said to *hit* her, but in Vink's judgment nothing less would make an impression on this stone-cold mantrap. Nothing short of pain and fear of disfigurement would do. He was ready to go again, but she had stopped him, for the moment, with her talk of money.

"What are we talking here?" he asked.

"Why don't you sit down?" She pointed toward the chair at the writing desk.

Vink did not want to sit down. He wanted to hit her again.

As if reading his mind, she said, "You want to beat the shit out of me, go ahead. But if you want to make yourself a nice chunk of cash first, sit down. You can always beat me up later."

She has a point, Vink thought. He walked four steps to the writing desk, leaned a hip on it. If she made a break for the door he wanted to be ready. He crossed his arms so that he would look confident and relaxed.

Rita said, "You might not know this, but Mack MacWray is sitting on a pile of cash right now, and I'm not talking about the business."

"Really?" Vink did not believe her, not even a little.

"Let me show you something." She stood up, moving slowly, and reached for her purse, which was hanging on the bathroom door.

164

"Hold on there, sweet stuff," Vink said. "Sit your pretty ass back down."

Rita sat down obediently. Vink walked around the bed and picked up the purse. He unzipped it and pawed through the contents, checking for pepper spray, stun guns, or other weapons, but finding nothing. He looked at her quizzically.

"Well? What did you want to show me?"

Rita held her hand out for the purse. Vink gave it to her and stood above her watching as she took out a Banamex passbook and a spray bottle of perfume.

She said, "During the time Mack and Lars were in business together, Mack embezzled more than half a million dollars from the company."

"I thought it was Larson who did the embezzling."

"I won't lie to you. We did take a little, but only after we realized what Mack was up to. Once Mac-Lar started to go critical, Lars and I decided to leave town for a while. We figured there was nothing else we could do. But then Lars was killed, and I discovered that Mack has a safe deposit box at a Banamex in Cancún, Mexico." She looked him full in the face. "I won't bullshit you, Jake Vink. I want a piece of it, and I intend to get it, but I'm willing to share."

Vink was not sure he believed her. But it was possible.

"What did you want to show me?" he asked.

"This is Mack's passbook." Rita opened the passbook to the last page. She folded it back and showed it to Vink. The page was blank.

"What am I looking at?" Vink asked.

"The access code, written in invisible ink." She pointed the perfume bottle at the page and depressed the plunger. A rich, musky aroma enveloped them. "The alcohol in the perfume will bring up the numbers. There. See?"

Vink couldn't see any numbers. He moved his face closer to the book.

"I'll give it another squirt," said Rita. She pumped the atomizer again, but this time the jet of perfume went straight into Vink's eyes. He let out a roar and clapped his hands over his eyes. Something hit him hard between the legs and he knew, even before the pain wave reached his brain, that it was going to be bad. Very bad.

~

Rita kicked him twice more before picking up the chair and swinging it against the side of his head. Vink went down. Rita lifted the chair and brought it down again, snapping off two of the legs. Vink curled into a whimpering ball. She hit him with the chair three more times before his mouth went slack and his eyes fell open, showing only the whites. Was he unconscious, or faking it? She found the perfume bottle where she'd dropped it and gave him another squirt in the eyes. No reaction. She took three minutes to get dressed and pack her two suitcases. She hauled her bags down the hall and summoned the elevator. When the doors opened she blocked them with her suitcases and ran back to the room. She called the front desk and told them that a man had broken into her room. She screamed into the phone, dropped it, ran to the elevator, and descended to the parking garage. She didn't stop shaking until she was back on the freeway, heading east, with no destination in mind.

27

"Sorry, sorry, sorry." Paula walked quickly past Ginny to her desk. A stack of phone messages and god knew how many e-mails. She hung her purse on the back of her swivel chair, sat, flipped her computer on, and as it warmed up, scanned the stack of pink message slips. Three repeat calls from a Marriott sales rep. She tossed those. One was from Mack. She tossed that, too. She had just started to check her e-mail when a large black-clad presence eased into her cubicle.

Paula looked up. "I'm really sorry I'm late, Ginny."

"Hey, everybody has a bad morning now and then. Are you all right?"

"I'm fine. Just a little frazzled. That damn car."

"It's not a problem, honey. Say, I enjoyed that party. Pretty impressive, what Mack has done."

Paula nodded, forcing herself to smile.

"I even landed myself a little date while I was there."

"Really? Who?"

"Jake Vink."

"Oh! I saw you talking to him."

"I think he's cute."

Paula was not about to argue, although in fact she found Jake Vink to be about as cute as a mange-ridden bulldog.

"And he's a tough guy. I like tough guys." Ginny grinned. "I know how to handle 'em."

Paula laughed. It was a real laugh. Ginny *did* know how to handle a certain breed of tough guy—Paula had seen her do it. She treated them like little brothers, kidding them along, and they loved it. Vink might be perfect for her.

"Maybe I should get some lessons from you. Learn how to handle Mack."

"You don't handle a man like Mack, honey. You just hang on. That man is going places."

"Yeah, well . . ." Damn! It was coming up. She had been holding it down so well, and now it was coming up. She turned abruptly back to the computer.

"You sure you're okay?" Ginny asked.

Paula shook her head, her fist pressed to her mouth.

"You want to talk about it?"

She shook her head again. What could she say? She couldn't tell Ginny that she had found hundreds of thousands of dollars in the garage. She couldn't tell anyone.

"Well, you let me know if you do, okay?"

Paula nodded.

"Promise?"

She nodded again.

Ginny stayed where she was for a few seconds, then was gone. Paula sat very still, feeling as if she had narrowly escaped disaster. She wanted desperately to talk to someone, but she couldn't. She did not know what Mack was up to. How had he gotten all that money? It had to be illegal, or he wouldn't have concealed it. And what was he doing with Rita Manbait? Some sort of secret deal with her and Lars? She couldn't imagine what it might be. The image of Mack's face in Lars's passport kept flashing before her. That and the gun. It was too much, too impossible, too utterly weird for her to make sense of.

She would have to confront him. That was all there was to it. She should leave work now, drive back to the factory, and have it out. What could he say? He would have to tell her the truth—or else.

Or else what? Could she leave him? The thought left her head spinning. Even in their darkest moments she had never seriously considered leaving him. Where would she go?

Her phone began to ring. Paula grabbed it, saved from her thoughts.

"Gold Coast Travel, this is Paula."

"Paula MacWray?"

"Yes."

"This is Jerry Pleasant. We met Saturday?"

"Oh?" She wasn't connecting.

"I was the cop."

"Oh!"

"How are you?"

"Fine! What can I do for you?"

"I was wondering if you could give me some advice."

"Oh?"

"I've got some vacation time coming up, and I was thinking about spending a week or two in Mexico."

"Mexico is nice."

"I was thinking about Cancún. You and Mack were just there, right?"

"Yes. We stayed at the Miramar. It was nice. Not too fancy."

"So you think Cancún would be a good choice?"

"It depends on what you want. You'll find plenty of shopping, nightlife, golf, and other things to do in Cancún. A lot of people go inland from there to visit the Mayan ruins."

"I just want to get away for a while, you know? Lie in the sun and read."

"Cancún would be perfect."

"Somebody suggested I check out Isla Mujeres."

"Isla? I haven't been there myself, but it's supposed to be very quiet. Not a lot going on."

"You and Mack never went there?"

"We stayed in Cancún the whole time."

"Really!"

"You sound surprised."

"Do I? Hmm. Well, Cancún sounds very nice."

"Would you like me to send you some information?"

"I don't think that will be necessary. How about you just book me a flight?"

"Oh, sure . . . Do you have a date in mind?"

"The sooner the better."

"Will this be for you and your wife, then?"

Pleasant was silent for a moment, then he said, "Actually, it'll just be me."

~

Mack's car was in the driveway when Julie showed up at the Cottonwood Lane house. She rang the doorbell, and when he opened the door, she pushed her sunglasses down her nose and peered over them. "Ding-dong, Avon lady." She winked. "You called?"

Mack grinned and stepped aside to let her in. As soon as she cleared the threshold he yanked her skirt up over her hips and slid his hands into her panties, grasping her buttocks, lifting her. Julie gasped with surprise and pleasure. Her legs locked around his hips and their teeth clacked together as their tongues entwined. Mack backed into the door, slamming it shut.

"Right here," he said, his voice husky. "Right now." He lowered her to the tile floor of the entryway.

Julie was ready, but the floor was cold. She made a move toward the carpeted living room, but Mack was tearing off her panties with one hand and undoing his belt buckle with the other.

"Wait a second, Mack!" She tried to take off her sunglasses, at least, but he knocked her hand away.

"Leave them on."

And with that he was in her, skidding her butt across the tiles with each thrust. The last coherent thought Julie had was that the fresh grout would scratch the hell out of her ass—and then she came.

28

Mack drove back to the factory seeing the cars, the buildings, and the trees as if they were props on a board game. He followed the roads and obeyed the laws because it amused him to do so, even though a large part of him believed that he could simply point his car in whatever direction he desired and go there. The buildings would prove to be nothing more than cardboard facades, the trees would be soft as cooked broccoli. Even the people were insubstantial. He smiled, feeling powerful and cool and safe, enjoying his waking dream.

He had been very tense after seeing Rita. Now he felt better. He had left Julie standing in the entryway looking at the scratches on her ass in the mirror and complaining about his technique. Instead of feeling remorseful for hurting her, he felt satisfied, and he felt good about how he had handled Rita. He hoped Jake Vink had made an impression on her, too. Scared the shit out of her. Jake would be good at that sort of thing.

He pulled into his parking place. The NuMac building looked more solid than anything he had seen on the drive back. He sat in his car for a minute, sorting out the rest of his day in his mind. He had to phone a couple of clients, do a walk-through of the factory to make sure his employees knew who was signing their paychecks, and make an appointment to test-drive the new Mercedes.

Sally was on the phone. She saw him enter and her eyes darted toward the waiting area, four side chairs and a coffee table where salespeople and job applicants were sent to wait. She made a helpless, shrugging gesture. Mack followed her glance. The man slumped in the nearest chair wore sunglasses, a wide-brimmed straw hat, and a short-sleeved shirt covered by giant red hibiscuses. Baggy khaki shorts were connected by pale legs to a pair of white stockings in leather sandals—obviously neither salesman nor job seeker.

As soon as he saw Mack, the man lifted a hand from his lap, gave a little wrist wave, and smiled.

Mack recognized him by the smile. "Officer Pleasant," he said. "New dress code?"

"I'm undercover," said Pleasant. "I'm practicing to be a tourist."

"That's very good. You blend right in."

"Ha ha," said Pleasant. He stood up. A camera hung by a thin strap from his shoulder. "Got a minute?"

Mack shrugged his assent and motioned Pleasant toward his office. He told Sally to hold his calls, then followed. Pleasant sat down and propped one sandaled foot on his knee. Mack stood behind his desk, his fingers resting lightly on the blotter.

"What can I do for you?" Mack asked, smiling. Why should he worry about a man who wore socks with his sandals?

"First, I'd like to say that your receptionist did everything she could to get rid of me."

"She's a good girl."

"I wouldn't want to get her in any trouble."

"Don't worry about it."

Pleasant nodded, satisfied. "I have some sad news, actually," he said.

"Oh? Should I sit down?"

"It's about your partner."

Mack stared at the sunglasses, trying to remember the color of Pleasant's eyes.

Pleasant's mouth twisted into something resembling a smile, but it was not a smile. "He's, ah, dead."

"Lars is dead?" Mack froze his face, not trusting himself to react.

"You don't seem surprised."

Mac shrugged. "I feel a bit numb where Lars is concerned."

"He was found dead in Mexico, on an island called Isla Mujeres."

Mack nodded and sat down.

"You've been there?"

Mack shook his head.

"It's near Cancún."

"I know where it is."

"You haven't asked me how he died."

"Okay. How did he die?"

"He fell off a cliff. The police think it may have been an accident." He showed his teeth in a momentary smile.

Mack decided that, behind the shades, Pleasant had blue irises to go with his sandy hair. It helped to imagine the eyes.

171

Pleasant said, "Or maybe not."

"That sounds pretty conclusive."

"He may have killed himself."

"I'm sorry I wasn't there to help him." The words came out loud and wrong.

Pleasant cocked his head. "Really?"

"Let's just say I'm not grieving for him," Mack said in a quieter voice.

Pleasant nodded. "I understand."

Like hell you do, Mack thought.

"I talked to your wife a couple of hours ago."

Mack felt his heartbeat jump up. "Why did you do that?"

"She's a travel agent. She found me a ninety-nine-dollar flight to Cancún—one of those insider deals."

"I see."

"Your wife recommended the Miramar."

"It's nice enough. When do you leave?"

"A week from Friday."

Mack's head nodded and his face smiled. His eyes had found his hands resting on the desk blotter. The pale, pinkish edges of his fingers shimmered against the pale green. He sensed Pleasant doing something with his hands, doing something with his camera.

"Smile!"

Mack looked up and was blinded by a flash.

~

Julie Gorman was on her way to meet a client when Paula called.

"Jules. I've got to talk to you."

Julie felt her heart jump; her foot came off the gas pedal as she forced a cheerful response. "Sure! What's up?" She became acutely aware of her sore buttocks.

"I mean, we have to *talk*. What are you doing right now?"

"I'm on my way out to Delano."

"Where's that?"

"About halfway to South Dakota. Or it might as well be. I might not get back in town until six or so."

She could hear Paula breathing.

"Paula?"

"Yeah, I'm here. How about breakfast tomorrow?"

Julie had nothing scheduled, but she said, "Can't do it, hon. I'm in a sales seminar all day."

"I thought you didn't do seminars."

"Have to do this one."

"How about— Oh, never mind. I'll call you."

Paula hung up. Julie let a lungful of stale air hiss out. A red Jeep honked and blew past her. She looked at the speedometer—thirty miles an hour—and stepped on the gas, bringing the Lexus back up to highway speed, thinking, *It's not worth it. I just don't have that many real friends.* She drove for a few minutes, thoughts flitting about in her head but not settling long enough to make an impression, aware mostly of certain points on and in her body: hands sticking to the leather steering wheel cover, dampened road vibration traveling through the accelerator to her right foot, a faint throb from her bruised ass. Momentarily, she saw Paula's face. The corners of her mouth turned down, but the spasm of guilt was relieved by a flush of triumph. The phone began to ring again. This time she ignored it.

~

Mack told Sally he did not want to see or speak with anyone for the rest of the day. Unless Jake Vink called. He would talk to Jake Vink. He closed his office door and sat behind his desk with his elbows on the blotter and his chin cupped in his hands and his feet flat on the floor. He closed his eyes and concentrated on blocking out all the feelings and emotions that had been stirred up by Jerry Pleasant. He needed to relocate himself, to find that place where the world became his board game.

He was still working on it twenty minutes later when his phone rang. His hand shot out and picked up the handset.

"MacWray."

"Mack. This is Jake."

Mack opened his eyes. "Jake. How did it go?" He could hear men talking in the background.

"Well, she knows we're serious."

"Good. What's wrong with your voice?"

"I, ah, I had a little tussle. Cut my lip. You know."

"You didn't hurt her, did you?" He was not sure what answer he wanted.

"She's okay. I think she might have left town, but I'm not sure." Someone in the background was shouting. Mack distinctly heard the word *motherfucker*.

"Where are you, Jake? In a bar?"

"Not exactly. I'm in jail."

Mack's throat tightened. He forced himself to swallow and said, "You didn't . . . What did you do?"

"Well, not much, I'm afraid."

"Why are you in jail?"

"As near as I can tell, they're still trying to come up with something."

～

"You know what would be the ultimate superpower?"

"No sir."

"Go ahead, guess. Just take a stab at it, Jeeves."

Jeeves's shoulders rose and fell in a shallow shrug. "Would it be omniscience, sir?"

"No. Omniscience would be terrible. It would be boring as hell."

"I imagine you are correct."

"It wouldn't be anything like that." Mack took a sip of his martini. He was getting tired of martinis. "I'll tell you what would be the ulti-mate superpower, Jeeves."

"Yes sir, I'm sure you will."

Mack frowned. Was that a shot? Had Jeeves just taken a shot at him?

The bartender stood attentively before him, his face free of all expression.

Mack decided not to let it bother him. Jeeves was hired help, just like Vink and the others. Mack was paying the man to pour drinks and listen. Nothing more.

"It would be the ability to control your memories." He waited a moment to give Jeeves a chance to respond, but Jeeves simply stared back at him, politely attentive. Mack continued. "If you could remember only what you wanted to remember, and forget precisely what you wanted to forget, there would be nothing you could not do." Mack drained the last of his martini. "Imagine it, Jeeves. Think what you could do if you did not have to live with yourself."

Part Three

29

After his third *Superior*, Jorge Pulido began to relax. His innards moved from his rib cage down toward his pelvis, his face took on a ruddy glow, and his command of English improved markedly. Pleasant told him a funny story about the bank robber who fired his gun into the air and set off the sprinkler system. He had some trouble getting across the sprinkler system concept, but once he did, Pulido roared with laughter.

Pleasant waved, catching the waiter's attention. *"Uno más,"* he said, pointing at Pulido.

"¡Dos más!" Pulido corrected, pointing his cigar at Pleasant's nearly full beer bottle.

Pulido launched into an anecdote about a sunburned German—or maybe it was about a German with red hair—and an amorous sea turtle . . . or tourist . . . or turkey. Pleasant listened, understanding almost none of it, laughing at Pulido's gesticulations and facial contortions. The man had a wonderfully toothy and pop-eyed storytelling face. He could blow out his cheeks to astonishing dimensions and flare his nostrils like an enraged bull. Another beer, Pleasant decided, and he would ease the conversation back to the late Teddy Larson.

At first, things had not gone well. Small-town cops were the same all over the world—overly protective of their jurisdiction and resentful of intrusion by external organizations, suffering both from feelings of inadequacy and from a stubborn tendency to defend their capabilities beyond all reason. Pulido was no exception, and his first reaction when Pleasant had shown up at the *estación de policía* had been to simply glare at him and affect not to understand a word of English. Fortunately, Pleasant had had the foresight to pack several trade items in his bag, and he was able to offer the obstinate Pulido some gifts for his grandchildren—he did have grandchildren, did he not?

It turned out that he had two of them, and yes, he thought that they would very much like the Minnesota Twins baseball cap and T-shirt. Pulido had adjusted the band on the cap, put it on his head, and smiled for the first time.

The dead man, Larson, had been living on Isla for several years, Pulido told him. He had a very beautiful wife with *pechos grandes*. Why would a man with such a wife throw himself into the sea? Who knew what secrets a man holds in his heart? Very tragic but—Pulido produced an elaborate shrug—*que será será*.

It seemed that the cap and T-shirt would buy him no more, so Pleasant had asked Pulido if he smoked. Pulido had nodded disinterestedly, but brightened when Pleasant offered him a *Romeo y Julieta* corona he had bought from the tobacconist in Cancún.

"¡Ah, puro cubano!" Pulido said. He slipped the cigar into his shirt pocket and gave it a delicate pat. *"Muchas gracias."*

Rather than follow up the cigar gift with more questions about Teddy Larson, Pleasant had immediately suggested that he buy lunch for the *capitán,* an offer to which Pulido had no objections, and so they had ended up at Daniel's sitting at a rickety table drinking *Superiors* and trading war stories. The *capitán* fired up the *puro* after his second beer. So far he showed little interest in ordering food.

When Pulido finished his sunburnt tourist story, Pleasant took a photograph out of his pocket and showed it to him. Pulido blinked and focused.

"Who is this?" he asked.

"Have you ever seen him?"

Pulido took a closer look. "I don't think so. He is a bad guy?"

"Could be. I showed this to the man who sold me that cigar—"

"Very good cigar."

"Yes. He thought this might be a friend of Teddy Larson's."

Pulido said, "This Larson, he did not have many friends. I ask around, but nobody know much about him. Him and his wife, they keep to themself."

Pleasant nodded and returned the photo to his pocket. "How did she take it?"

"*¿Perdón?*"

"The wife. Was she upset?"

"Oh, *sí,* very upset. She do not believe he do this to himself."

"Really? Why?"

Pulido shrugged and swallowed several ounces of beer. "She crazy *loca.*" He belched. "She think we rob him."

"Who? The police?"

"He was missing his wallet and some other thing. I don't know." He took a few puffs on the cigar, getting a good cloud going. "I think somebody maybe see him jump, maybe climb down and take things. Not the *policía.* He was there all one night and most of a day before we find him."

"How did you know *when* he jumped?"

"We know from the wife what day he leave. The last time she see him is twenty-two *Junio.*"

"Is she still here? On Isla?"

Pulido shook his head. "I have not seen her. Someone say she leave a week or two ago."

"But they actually have a place here, right?"

"*Sí.* A condo. She will be back, I think."

Pleasant caught the waiter's eye, held up one finger, and pointed at Pulido. He thought the *capitán* would need to be a bit drunker before he made his next suggestion.

~

Rather to Pleasant's surprise, Pulido cheerfully agreed to take him to Teddy and Rita Larson's condo. Pulido finished his sixth *Superior* and coaxed a few final puffs from his *Romeo y Julieta.* Pleasant paid the check and they left the restaurant. Pulido made an effort to suck his extra poundage back up into his rib cage but gave it up after the first fifty feet. They walked around the corner to the Hotel Caribe, a well-maintained three-story building.

"He lived in a hotel?" Pleasant asked.

"Is condominiums now," Pulido said, pushing through the double doors.

Pleasant followed him up the winding marble staircase to the third floor, where Pulido again sucked in his gut and pounded on a door. He shouted something in Spanish. He listened for a response, got nothing.

"It is like I tell you," he said. "She is not on Isla."

Pleasant pulled out his key chain, which held several lock picks. "How about we go inside and take a look around?" he asked.

Pulido regarded the picks with interest. He shrugged and watched Pleasant attack the lock. The three beers Pleasant had consumed did not help, but eventually the lock gave way. He pushed the door open and entered the apartment. Pulido followed.

Over the years, Jerry Pleasant had been in many homes, the vast majority of them belonging to suspected criminals. There were certain things that most criminal abodes had in common: they were dirty, they had expensive sound systems and large-screen TVs, and there were rarely any living houseplants. The Larsons' condo did not fit this profile. It was extremely tidy, it had no television, the stereo was a small bookshelf system, and there were dozens of houseplants—all of which looked as if they needed water.

Pleasant walked from room to room, touching nothing at first, feeling a sense of wonder at being inside the late Teddy Larson's home. He paused before the small desk in the bedroom and looked at the papers scattered across its top, a Telmex bill and a Visa bill in Rita Larson's name. He read the summary of charges but saw nothing of interest. The phone bill showed only a few calls to Cancún. He checked the desk drawers and came across a four-month-old statement from a Banamex in Cancún showing, insofar as he could decipher the Spanish, a modest balance. He folded it and put it in his pocket.

Pulido was sitting in the tiny kitchen drinking a Dos Equis. He was holding three boxes of cigars on his lap. The name on the boxes was *Cohiba,* a brand Pleasant remembered seeing in the tobacconist's humidor at about twenty bucks a stick. Pleasant found a pitcher and filled it from the tap.

"You find what you want?" Pulido asked.

Pleasant shrugged. "You?"

"No, I don't find nothing." Pulido winked.

Pleasant took one last tour, watering plants as he moved through the condo. He hated to see a houseplant die.

When Pleasant returned to the kitchen, Pulido was on his feet, hugging the cigar boxes to his gut. "We go now, okay?"

They left the condo and made their way down the staircase, Pulido moving with the excessive caution of a man who knows precisely how drunk he is. "We go back to *restaurante,* no? You like lobster, no?"

Pleasant did not see that he was going to get much more from Pulido that day, but he had promised the man a meal. "Sure, I like lobster," he said. What the hell, he was on vacation. Sort of.

~

"So I say to the guy, I say, 'Suppose it was you who did it. Suppose it was you who robbed the store and shot the clerk. I'm not sayin' it *was* you, understand, but just suppose. If it was you, why might you have done a thing like that?'

"And the guy actually says, 'Man, in the first place it *wasn't* me. But if it was, it might've been on account of the dude pissed me off. You know, call me something. Piss me off.'

"So I ask, 'What might that be? What could a guy say to you might make you want to kill him?'

"'Like if the dude say something about my mama. You know.'

"'Like what?'

"'Like, he say, my mama gonna be *ashamed* of me.'

"I say, 'Well? It's true, isn't it?'

"The guy gives me this really disgusted look and says, 'Man, my mama been dead five years. That dude *deserve* to die.'

"'So, that's why you capped him?'

"The guy says, 'You damn right I did.'"

Pleasant sat back and grinned. He loved to tell that story. Pulido, still picking at his *langosta,* nodded in drunken appreciation. He probably hadn't understood most of it, but that didn't matter. They had reached that stage of inebriation where the important thing was the telling, not the listening. The story Pulido had told a few minutes earlier had emerged almost entirely in Spanish.

"You know what I think, Jorge?"

"No. What you think?"

"I think evil is a disease."

Pulido blinked, uncomprehending. Pleasant shrugged and got to his feet to go to the rest room. It proved to be a challenging journey, but on his way back to the table he had a brilliant idea.

"Hey, Jorge," he said. "You done eating?"

Pulido looked down at the scavenged carcass on his plate and nodded sadly.

"What do you say we take a drive?"

"Drive?"

"You know." Pleasant gripped an imaginary steering wheel and pretended to steer. "Go in car."

Pulido blinked unfocused eyes. "You want to go for a ride in my *cochecita?*"

Pleasant wasn't sure what a *cochecita* was, but he nodded.

Pulido thought for a moment, then shrugged. "Okay, no problem. Where you want to go?"

~

The day Paula discovered the money there had been a moment, perhaps three minutes after Mack had arrived home that night, when she had almost said, "So, I noticed you've got a few hundred thousand dollars in the garage. What's that about?"

But she had not said anything and the moment had passed, and now it stood between them: a large, hairy, invisible something. And that wasn't all. It was more than the fact that she knew about the money. Mack had been spending less time at home, leaving early in the morning and not showing up until after ten at night, too tired to talk, too tired for sex. Business had taken off in a big way. Mack was talking about adding a third shift. Money was coming in and going out at a tremendous rate. Mack had bought himself a new Mercedes and told her to buy a new car for herself, but she didn't want a new car. Her little Honda was only four years old and she liked it. Also, she would have been embarrassed to buy a new car when they still owed her folks so much money.

Every day after Mack left for work, Paula climbed up to the garage loft and opened the black nylon bag and looked at the money, the gun, and the passport, trying to puzzle it out. She imagined many scenarios—everything from Mack being an undercover agent for the CIA to Mack having robbed a bank to Mack having an affair with Rita Manbait to various combinations of the above.

Every night, she planned to confront him and, every night, she didn't. She was afraid of what she might learn. She thought about money all the time now. Not just the cash in the garage but the money they were making from the business. She had never thought of herself as a materialistic person. She could live without a new car. But being able to buy a new car if she wanted one, she liked that a lot. She did not want to risk losing it, not now.

She lifted a bundle of hundreds, about $10,000 worth, and riffled through them. The tiny packet of paper sheets was power. It could buy many things. Her parents had saved their entire lives and had come up with no more than was contained in this little nylon bag. She dropped the cash back into the bag and picked up the gun. She opened the clip, as she had done before, and looked at the rank of stubby, oily, copper-jacketed .32 caliber cartridges. Her father had taught her to shoot when she was thirteen years old, about the same time he had given up on ever siring a son. She had dutifully learned to hit clay pigeons and paper targets, but in the end she had refused to shoot at living creatures, and he had left her to her girlish pursuits. This was the first gun she had handled in twenty years. She returned the gun to the bag and zipped it closed. Maybe if she moved the bag over a few inches, Mack would notice. Maybe then he would bring it up and they would be forced to talk about it.

Paula thought for a moment, shook her head, and left the bag precisely where she had found it. She had a powerful intuition that her life had arrived at a critical juncture. One wrong move might throw it out of balance. It would all fall down.

~

The sun sagged over Cancún like a bloated orange water balloon. Pleasant drew on his *Cohiba* and watched the smoke curl up past his face. He was happy to be alive. The four-mile drive in Pulido's white VW Beetle—siren blaring, blue lights flashing—had given him a new outlook on life, mostly a desperate desire to remain in it. The beer in his belly and the powerful Cuban tobacco conspired to make the episode even more poignant. The visible universe now seemed a finite and manageable thing. He willed the sun to dip into the horizon, and a few seconds later, it did so. Orange light spilled across the ocean, filling the strait between Isla and the mainland.

He turned to Pulido. "You see that?"

Pulido was leaning against the ruins of the Mayan temple, smoking his cigar.

"Is a special place," he said. "My wife say it is a place men go to speak with dead. She will not come here." He reached down and adjusted his genitals. "You got a wife?"

"I got one."

"Is good to be marry."

Pleasant did not agree with that, but he let it slide. He said, "You want to show me where you think Teddy fell?"

Pulido pushed himself upright and walked toward the precipice. Pleasant followed. Pulido pointed at a spot about two feet from the edge. "This is where we find the golf thing."

"The golf tee?"

"*Sí.*"

Pleasant moved as close to the edge as he dared and peered down at the jagged rocks below.

"If I was going to kill myself, I don't think I'd do it here. It looks painful."

"What is in a man's secret heart?" Pulido said.

Pleasant backed away from the precipice. He looked again at the sun, now a red half disk. "I'll be goddamned if I know," he said.

30

The downside to success in business was that there was ten times as much work to do. The upside was that most of it could be delegated. Mack had always known these things, but what he had not realized was how much time and energy it took to do the delegating, especially with his number one man laid up.

For the past couple weeks, Mack had been hopping from crisis to crisis, doing both his job and Vink's, desperately trying to keep up with the new orders that had been coming in on a daily basis. He was not sure why they were getting so much new business. Maybe the NuMac story—the overnight transformation from bankrupt hulk to fiscal triumph—had caught the fancy of the business community. Everybody wanted to rub up against success. He had just delivered a new batch of P.O.'s to the factors at First Star, demanding more money to buy more fabric and hire more workers. Grudgingly, the bank had authorized a hundred-thousand-dollar increase in NuMac's credit line, but only after making it clear that cash flow would have to reverse by the end of the month. This time, Mack sensed, he would not be able to push them any further.

To make matters worse, his in-laws kept asking him for their money back. Last week it was Lady Macbeth who had called. She had talked Sally into getting him on the phone, insisting that it was a family emergency. He had listened to her whining about her damned nest egg for five minutes, then finally agreed to send her a check. It got her off the phone.

She would be calling back any day now, wanting to know why she hadn't received her check yet. He had instructed Sally to fend off her calls.

He was up against it in the factory, too. It was possible to train only so many new workers at a time. Not an hour went by without some new and costly error occurring, everything from wrong color jackets to shipping errors to—this was the worst—a zero being added to an order for one hundred embroidered golf shirts. What was he going to do with nine hundred shirts with *Litchfield G&CC* embroidered on the sleeve? The guy at the golf course had just laughed and offered him fifty cents a shirt for the overage.

And then there were the two dark clouds, Jerry Pleasant and Rita Larson. Maybe he would never hear from either of them again, but he did not think he would be so lucky. They were always there, hovering just over the horizon. All he could do was try to stay focused on the business. If NuMac failed, if he lost his momentum, nothing could save him.

Thank god Vink was back on his feet. He had shown up for work that morning walking like a kid with a full diaper, but at least he was walking.

Mack looked at his watch. Ten minutes after eleven. Thirty minutes to bring Jake up to speed on the third shift, another half hour to drive across town to look at another house, and he had to be back at NuMac by two-thirty for a conference call. He buzzed Sally on the intercom.

"Sally, where is Mr. Vink?"

"I don't—"

"Find him and tell him to get his butt in here." Lately he hadn't been bothering with the niceties. He didn't have time. He was paying them good money. His employees would just have to deal with it.

He remembered, then, something Lars had told him early in their partnership. Mack had been complaining because some of the sewers were refusing to work overtime. Lars had said, "That's because you're not a people guy, Macanudo."

"Really? I thought it was because they were lazy."

"You gotta try to see it from their point of view, pard. Take that Filipino woman—with the big mole on her chin?"

"Merlita Amurao."

"Yeah. You ever ask her about her kids?"

Mack shook his head. He didn't know she *had* kids.

"There you go!" Lars had said, as if all were explained.

"There I go where?"

"You don't give a shit about her kids, why should she work overtime for you?"

"Because it pays time and a half."

186

Lars had laughed. "Mackie, these people don't care about money. If they cared about money they wouldn't be sewing smocks for a living. You gotta learn to empathize. Smile and nod. They aren't machines, my friend. Give 'em a little sugar and watch 'em put out."

Mack walked out to Sally's desk.

"Sorry I snapped at you, Sally."

"Oh, that's okay, Mr. MacWray. I know how busy you are."

"So . . . how are you doing?" He felt awkward. He was not even sure what he was asking her.

Sally seemed equally puzzled. "I'm fine?"

Mack nodded. "Good. Great. Keep up the good work."

He fled to his office, thinking that no matter how hard he tried, he would never be a people guy. People were just too damned unreliable. Jake Vink, for instance—he was lucky Mack hadn't fired his ass after that screwup at the Radisson. Good thing Rita had disappeared instead of sticking around to press charges, or Vink would've had a lot more than a ruptured testicle to occupy his thoughts.

At least she was out of the picture—or so he hoped. There had been a few days when every time the phone rang he'd been expecting to hear her voice. But so far, nothing. Maybe Vink had actually scared her. Maybe she'd hurt her foot when she'd crunched his left nut.

Mack looked at his watch again. Eleven-fifteen. He looked up at the open doorway to his office, prepared to buzz Sally again if Vink wasn't standing right there—but there he was, bowlegged but present.

"Sorry," Vink said. "A little problem back in shipping." He waddled to the chair in front of Mack's desk and, delicately, lowered himself into it. The stitches around his eye had come out a few days ago, leaving a pink, C-shaped scar. The swelling in his jaw had receded but the yellowish discoloration remained. His story to the other NuMac employees was that he'd been hit by a Mack truck while crossing the street. He always specified the brand.

"Nothing I need to concern myself with, I hope," Mack said.

"All taken care of, boss."

The words were precisely what Mack needed to hear. He hadn't heard them often enough lately. Some of the tension left his body.

"Good job."

Vink smiled, grateful for the compliment. Mack winced internally. The altercation with Rita had taken some of the fire out of Vink. He was a dog who had been kicked once too often. Maybe it was time to start looking for a new dog.

"You feeling okay?" Mack asked.

"Better every day," Vink said with forced heartiness.

"Good, because we've got a lot of work to do. We're starting a third shift next week."

Vink's smile collapsed. "We . . . are?" His Adam's apple pulsed.

"That's right. And you're the man who's going to make it happen. I want you to hire a crew and have them sewing by next Thursday. I want you to run it."

"I, ah, what about the day crew?"

"You make the graveyard shift happen, Jake. That's where I want you."

~

The house in Bloomington was not as large as the Cottonwood Lane house, but it had a ten-acre wooded lot and an enormous stone fireplace. Mack walked over to the mantel—an eight-inch-thick, nine-foot-long slab of oak—and put his hand on it.

"Nice piece of wood," he said.

Julie stood with her hip cocked, car keys dangling from red-nailed fingers, watching him, her eyes dilated and narrowed.

"What a guy," she said. "You walk in and the first thing you do is look for the longest, thickest, stiffest structural member you can find."

Mack shrugged and looked down. "Nice rug," he said. "I don't think I've ever actually seen a polar bear rug before."

Julie walked over and gave the polar bear's nose a gentle kick with the tip of her lizard pump. "The rug doesn't come with the house. Anyway, I don't know why anybody would want a big dead animal in their living room."

"Let me show you," said Mack.

~

Julie was gasping, hanging on to the bear's two-inch-long canine teeth with both hands, when the cell phone in her purse began to ring. Her purse was only a few feet from the polar bear's black plastic nose. Mack didn't lose a beat, but the repeated ringing made Julie lose her concentration. She thought about reaching for the purse, pulling it closer, answering the phone. See how Mack liked that. She was about to go for it when Mack came, his hips slamming into her buttocks. She lost her grip on the canines and fell forward; her sternum came down hard on the bear's head. The ringing stopped. Mack lay on top of her, breathing heavily for a few seconds, then slipped out of her. Julie squirmed out from beneath his suddenly dead weight; Mack produced a guttural sound and rolled onto his back. Unsatisfied and cranky, she decided to let him know by immediately getting the phone from her purse and returning the call. Julie frowned at the display on the Nokia. Whoever had called had blocked the caller ID. She punched in her office number and held the phone to her ear as she threaded her legs into her hose, one-handed.

"Val, hi, this is Julie. Any calls for me?"

Mack, propped on his elbows and back to back with the polar bear, was watching her.

"Uh-huh. Okay, thanks." She flipped the phone shut and looked at Mack. "I hate to miss a call," she said, pulling her panty hose up over her hips.

Mack laughed. That was one of the things that appealed to her—the fact that he didn't give a shit. She didn't have to worry about insulting him. As long as she gave him what he wanted and demanded nothing in return, their relationship would remain perfect. And as soon as she was done with him, she would give him back to Paula, who would be none the wiser. She had had similar affairs in the past, but never with anyone quite like Mack.

Her phone rang again. She flipped it open.

"Hello?"

She listened, frowning, then held the phone out to Mack.

"It's for you."

~

Mack sat up; his scrotum flopped onto coarse white fur.

"You sure?" It couldn't be for him, not on her phone.

Julie's mouth twisted to the left. "See any other Macks here?"

He took the phone from her, feeling very naked. "Hello?"

"You didn't think I'd go away, did you?"

Mack's heart shuddered; he could hear the blood rushing in his ears. He closed his eyes and took a breath.

"I was hoping," he said. He wished he had his pants on.

"How is your stooge doing?"

"Much better."

"He's lucky he's not dead."

"Where are you?"

Rita laughed. "Do you want to know what I'm looking at?"

Mack did not reply.

"I'm looking at some photographs. A man is—why, it looks like he's attacking some poor woman!"

"You're wasting my time," Mack said.

"Wait, in this other photo you can see that he's not attacking her. He's, why, they're having sex."

Mack's face went rigid.

"Yes, he's clearly fucking her, and do you know where they are? They're on a kitchen counter! And do you know who this looks like? It looks like—"

Mack disconnected.

"Who was that?" Julie asked.

"I have no idea."

"Well, you must have *some* idea."

The phone rang again. Julie reached for it, but Mack answered.

"So what's it like, doing it on a polar bear rug?" Rita asked. "A little itchy?"

Mack looked around quickly. There was only one window with a view of the rug. He ran to it, pushed it open. The flower bed outside was trampled.

"I've got shots of that coming, too, only they haven't been developed yet. By the way, isn't that skinny little thing a friend of your wife's?"

Mack hurled the phone against the stone mantelpiece; it exploded into plastic shards.

Julie said, "Hey, you know what I paid for that thing?"

31

The Banamex manager greeted Pleasant with a dazzling smile and a two-handed handshake.

"Welcome to Cancún," he said in nearly perfect, lightly accented English. "I am Carlos Carillo."

"Thank you," said Pleasant.

"Señor Pulido speaks very highly of you."

"He is a good man," he said.

"Yes, very good." Carillo was dressed in a perfectly tailored charcoal-gray suit, a pale blue shirt, and a patterned gray tie. His black hair was combed straight back; his nails were manicured and polished. He appeared to be in his early thirties.

Pleasant, in his flowered shirt, Chicago Cubs baseball cap, shorts, and sandals, felt like a slob.

They were standing in the lobby between a wall of fortified teller cages and a row of patron-filled benches. Taking in the garb of the bank customers, a mixture of Mexican tourists and locals, Pleasant decided that he was not so underdressed after all. It was late summer and they were in a resort town. Carlos Carillo was the odd one.

"Please, come with me," said Carillo. Pleasant followed him through a steel door into a carpeted hallway. "Señor Pulido said you had some questions about one of our customers?"

"Yes. Theodore Larson."

"Ah, Señor Larson. Very tragic."

"You knew him?"

"Unfortunately, I do not know all of our customers. But Señor Pulido told me this Theodore Larson had died. By his own hand."

They turned into a spacious office. Several framed travel posters, all of them promoting Spanish destinations, hung on the windowless walls. Carillo closed the door and took a seat behind the glass-topped steel table that served as his desk. Pleasant made a show of examining one of the posters, a Barcelona skyline.

"I was born in Madrid," said Carillo. He crossed his legs and leaned back in his high-backed black leather chair.

"I see." That made sense. Carillo's formal attire and careful grooming were his way of distinguishing himself from the lowly denizens of this backwater New World resort town. Pleasant nodded, smiling to himself. He liked to have a handle on a guy.

"Now, you have some questions?"

"Yes." Pleasant seated himself in one of the two chairs before Carillo's desk. "Teddy and Rita Larson have a safe deposit box here, I believe?"

Carillo nodded. "That is true."

"Do you know whether either of them accessed it in the past several weeks?"

"We have records, of course. One moment." He lifted his phone, punched three buttons, and rattled off a salvo of Spanish. He hung up and said, "Señora Castro will be with us shortly."

~

Señora Castro arrived on four-inch heels, in a tight navy-blue dress, with a two-foot-long ledger wedged beneath her left arm. She was extremely tense and avoided looking at Pleasant directly. Carillo asked her some questions in Spanish, frowned, shrugged, turned his palms up, looked at each of them in turn, and crossed his wrists. Pleasant took this as permission to ask Señora Castro a few questions.

"How you doing?" he asked.

Señora Castro stared at him for a second before replying. "I am doing fine," she said.

"Good. Excellent. I just have a few questions for you . . ."

~

Referring to her ledger, Señora Castro told Pleasant that Rita Larson had visited the safe deposit box only once in the past two months, on June 26, and that Theodore Larson had visited it three days before that. Pleasant asked her if she remembered anything peculiar about either of those visits.

Señora Castro looked at Carillo, shrugged, and said, "Mrs. Larson was upset."

"Why?"

"I think she did not find what she wanted. Mr. Larson, he maybe take something."

"You mean you think he took something out of the box?"

"Yes. She was very upset."

"And you say Theodore Larson was here three days before that, on the twenty-third?"

She checked her ledger again. "That is correct."

"The day his body was discovered."

"He was here in the morning, ten o'clock."

"Actually, the police say he jumped from the cliff on the twenty-second."

Señora Castro compressed her lips and rapped a red nail on the canvas cover of her ledger. "*This* is correct."

Pleasant nodded. "I don't doubt it. Was Mr. Larson known to you?"

"*¿Perdón?*"

"Did you know Mr. Larson by sight?"

Señora Castro wrinkled her brow. "I do not think so."

"Do you remember his last visit here?"

She shook her head.

Pleasant held out a photograph of Teddy Larson, a six-year-old mug shot. "Look familiar?"

Señora Castro looked closely at the photo. She shook her head. Pleasant put the picture back in his pocket and handed her another photo, the Polaroid he had taken of Mack MacWray.

"How about that one?"

Señora Castro's pupils enlarged. For a moment she sat frozen, staring at the photo, then thrust it back at Pleasant with an exaggerated shake of her head.

"I have not seen him."

Pleasant took the photo back and smiled.

"I see," he said.

～

"Have you ever been involved in a car accident, Jeeves?"

"Sir?"

"It's a simple question."

"Yes sir."

"So you have?"

"Yes sir."

"Were you injured?"

"I believe I was slightly bruised, sir."

"It's a good feeling, isn't it?"

Jeeves raised his eyebrows.

Mack said, "I was in an accident once. I was a teenager. We were in my buddy's Chevy Nova, middle of the winter. Got broadsided by a van. My buddy lost half his teeth and broke his collarbone, and the guy in the van was trapped behind his steering wheel, hardly able to breathe. My arm was broken, but at the time I didn't know it. I remember it like it was yesterday.

"We're waiting for the paramedics. My friend is laid out on a blanket. This weird fog is hanging a couple feet above the road. Headlights pointing at strange angles, cold as hell, and I'm out there in the middle of the street, no gloves, no hat, directing traffic. People driving around us, gawking. I was like a conductor, waving my arms, controlling everything. I'm on some kind of adrenaline high. I don't feel the cold, don't feel scared, don't feel a thing. I survived. I'm okay. I'm the center of the universe."

Mack sipped his drink. "Was that how it was for you, Jeeves?"

"Not exactly, sir."

"Too bad. It's a good feeling."

Mack had loved that feeling then, and he loved it now. He'd had it in Cancún, he'd had it again when he'd forced Bob Seaman to refinance the business, and the call from Rita had put him there again. He was directing traffic in the midst of a disaster, and the ordinary rules did not apply. Without the usual constrictions, his thoughts became utterly lucid and focused. Strategies never before considered became available and obvious. He considered changing his identity and starting a new life. He considered suicide. He even considered committing murder—an option that, the more he thought about it, made a kind of sense.

32

"Last night he came home, I was standing in the kitchen cutting up some carrots, he came in through the garage door and walked right past me. I said, 'Hey!' And he looked at me and—I swear to god, Jules—he didn't see me even then. It was like he heard a noise and looked in my direction and his eyes went right through me.

"I said, 'Hello?' And he sort of blinked and said, 'Oh, hi.' Like I was the maid."

"Maybe he was just distracted." Julie used her chopsticks to stir some wasabi into a dish of soy sauce. "Doesn't he have a lot going on right now? With the business?" She began to rearrange her tuna rolls. She had been playing with her sushi assortment for fifteen minutes, but Paula had yet to see her take a bite.

"It's not just the business. He doesn't want to look at me. A few weeks ago he was jumping me like a sailor, and now I'm furniture. You want to know what I think? I think he's having an affair."

"Really?" Julie dipped a tuna roll into the wasabi-soy mixture and popped the entire thing into her mouth. Her eyes immediately widened and began to water. She chewed and swallowed, then grabbed her vodka tonic and took a large gulp. "Hot!" she said, fanning her mouth. "I think I got a little too much wasabi."

Paula, miffed that her friend was upstaging her tale of woe with a bit of Japanese horseradish, bit into a disk-shaped piece of tempura. Sweet potato. She forced herself to chew and swallow.

Julie said, "So, how are things at work? Is Ginny still seeing that peculiar little man?"

"Jake Vink? I think so. He was in some kind of accident."

"I *know!* That *hand*—"

"No, I mean he was just in a car accident. Ginny said he hurt his testicles."

Julie's face twisted into a pretty knot. "That can't be good."

"She says he's very angry about it."

"I don't blame him."

"Maybe the three of us should have a girls' night out. Three frustrated women."

Julie laughed, a little louder than her usual laugh. She hooked a finger behind the thin gold chain encircling her neck, found the tiny crucifix dangling there, pinched it between her thumb and forefinger.

Paula said, "Seriously, though. I don't know what to do about Mack. Something is going on with him. I mean, what else could it be?" Julie was staring at her sushi tray. Paula reached out and put a hand on her arm. "Jules?"

Julie let go of the crucifix and looked up. "Um, do you have some reason to think he is? Seeing somebody?"

"He sure isn't seeing *me!*"

"That happens to guys sometimes."

"This is different. I saw him with someone."

"Oh?" Julie pulled her arm back.

"In a restaurant."

Julie let her breath out in a way that was not quite a laugh. "Oh well, maybe it was just a business thing."

"It was that Rita Manbait."

"Oh. Oh! You don't think he's . . ."

"I don't know," Paula said. "I don't know, but I just can't stop thinking about it. I keep thinking about . . . if I caught them together."

"What would you do?" Julie leaned forward, the gold crucifix dragged across the top of a California roll.

"I don't know. I think about it and I just don't know."

~

196

Rita waited a week before calling Mack again.

When dealing with people, Teddy had taught her, you must decide which part of them is most likely to make the decision most beneficial to you. If you want them to think with their gut, you have to pressure them for a quick response. If you want them to reason from greed, you give them a little longer, but keep the prize in view. Fear-based decisions are usually the easiest to elicit, but certain personalities do not respond predictably to threats. Rita put the new Mack MacWray in this category.

The decision she wanted from Mack was for him to decide to pay her a large sum of money. Everything he had stolen from her safe deposit box would be nice, but a lesser amount might suffice. For him to pay her, she now believed, he would have to see it as his only option. His decision would have to be logic-based and rational. The alternative to paying her would have to be, in his mind, completely unacceptable. Rita thought that she could now produce such a scenario.

But Mack had another aspect to his personality, one that she had seen that afternoon at the Lotus. He had been about to offer her some money—she had seen that—but pride, stubbornness, or conceit had sent him off in another direction. She could not afford to let that happen again.

Teddy had once said to her, "Sometimes you want a guy to get smart. You want him to act in his own self-interest. You don't want him thinking with his nuts; you don't want him stewing about ethics; you don't want him reacting out of fear. You want him to do what's practical. Now, you might think that the key to this is to give him a persuasive accounting of the facts, and you got to do that, for sure. But that's just part of it. The most important thing is, you got to give him time to think."

She had to give him time to calm down, time to look at his life, at his newly revitalized business, at his marriage, at his standing in the community. He had to see that by not paying her, he risked losing all of that. He had to realize that if he did not pay her she would do everything in her power to destroy him.

She did not want Mack to do something stupid. She wanted him to do the right thing.

Seven days ought to be long enough.

~

At first, Mack did not understand what the man on the phone was talking about. This was not what he needed first thing in the morning.

"Lawsuit? Who did you say you are?" he asked.

"Alan Frankel. I'm an attorney with Vincent, Roberts and Josephson. I represent Mr. and Mrs. Halston Wright Byrnes," repeated the lawyer.

The names meant nothing to Mack. He moved the phone from his left ear to his right ear. "You sure you're calling the right number? I've never heard of these people."

"Well, you borrowed two hundred and eighty thousand dollars from them," the lawyer said. "And you married their daughter."

"I— Wait a minute. *Hal* Byrnes? *Hal* is suing me?"

"Not necessarily. As a courtesy, Mr. and Mrs. Byrnes asked me to call you. They would like to know what your intentions are vis-à-vis the money they loaned to you."

"You're a collection agent." Mack felt his face heating up.

"I am an attorney, and I am representing the Byrneses. And at this point all I'm trying to do is ascertain what you plan to do about this debt. I'm sure that Mr. and Mrs. Byrnes would look favorably on any reasonable payment plan."

"You listen to me, Franklin—"

"Frankel."

"My in-laws invested that money in a start-up business. It was not a 'loan,' and we never discussed a time frame for repaying the money. The money is tied up in the business, and if those people will leave me the hell alone for five goddamn minutes I'll make this sucker fly."

"Ah, according to the agreement you signed, Mr. MacWray, it *was* structured as a loan. A personal loan. And they have the right to demand payment as of, ah, a month ago last Friday."

"Oh? Well, in that case I—" He hung up on himself. Let the lawyer think he had been disconnected. Now he had to add Hal and Joyce Byrnes to the collection of alligators hanging off his ass. "Sally!" he shouted, not bothering with the intercom.

Sally appeared in the doorway.

"That guy, Alan Frankel, goes on my 'no calls' list, okay?"

"Okay. Um, you just got a call from Jerry Pleasant?"

"Isn't he on the list?"

"Yes, but he didn't want to talk to you. He just asked if you were here."

Mack's teeth came together with an audible clack.

"Also, you got a call from a woman who wouldn't leave her number, but she said to tell you that 'Lovely Rita' called."

Mack flexed his jaw so hard he could hear his teeth creak.

"If she calls back, do you want me to put her through?"

Mack touched his fingers to his temples, massaging the throbbing veins, staring at the oak surface of his desk, seeking answers in the golden whorls and umber streaks. After a moment—or was it longer?—he looked up. Sally was still standing in the doorway, her brow etched.

His mouth distorted into a smile. "Lovely Rita? Sure, she calls again, put her through."

~

The call had come while she was in the shower.

A woman's voice: "Hello? Macanudo? Come to the phone, Mackie." Breathing, made harsh by the tinny speaker of the answering machine. "Macanudo?" More breathing, then a click.

Did the voice belong to Rita Manbait? Paula replayed the message. *Macanudo? Come to the phone, Mackie.* The words—the tone—chilled her. So familiar; so demanding. *Come to the phone, Mackie.* As if she was used to getting what she wanted. But what did she want? Paula reached down to play the message again, but her finger went to the erase button and held it down, wiping the tape clean.

"Come to the phone, babe," she whispered.

The telephone rang. Paula picked it up and put it to her ear, saying nothing. After a moment a man's voice said, "Hello?"

Paula cleared her throat. "Hello?"

"Is this Paula?" The voice was vaguely familiar, but she couldn't place it.

"Yes?"

"Hi! This is Jerry Pleasant. I tried you at your office, they said you weren't in yet, so I thought I might catch you at home. Just want to say thanks for sending me to Cancún. I had a fantastic time!"

"Oh. You're welcome."

"I went parasailing, went fishing, read a couple trashy novels."

"That's great," Paula said.

"I even took care of some business. With a little luck, I'll get the department to pay for my flight."

"What did you do? Arrest somebody?"

"No, no, no!" Pleasant laughed. "Actually, I was looking into the death of your old friend Lars Larson."

"Lars? Died?" Paula's thoughts accelerated.

"Yes. Mack didn't mention it to you?"

"He . . . I don't know. Maybe I knew that."

"I told him about it a couple weeks ago. Lars died on Isla Mujeres."

"What was he doing there?"

"He was living there, it turns out. He and his wife had been living there on and off for years."

"Was he shot?" The gun in Mack's overnight bag filled her mind.

Pleasant didn't say anything for a moment. "Was he what?"

"Shot?"

"Why would you think he was shot?"

Paula fought down a panicky, lost feeling. "I don't . . . I don't know. How was he killed?"

"You think he was killed?"

"No, I . . . I don't know. I mean, how did he die?"

"The Mexican police think he committed suicide."

"Oh. What about his wife? That Rita."

"I haven't been able to locate her."

Paula nodded. She wanted desperately to get out of this conversation. "I gotta go," she said, and hung up.

~

Jerry Pleasant, suntanned and wearing a white guayabera he had purchased in Mexico, looked at his cell phone and twisted his mouth into a wry smile. He got out of his car and pocketed the phone. It was a beautiful cloudless day, but after his week in Cancún, the sun felt dilute. In another couple of months it would be low and dim. The parking lot would be slick with ice and packed snow. He had some vacation time coming. Maybe he would go back to Mexico once winter settled in.

Why would Paula MacWray imagine that Larson had been shot?

The parking stall reserved for MacWray was occupied by a new white Mercedes-Benz 600 SEL. Pleasant put his hand on the roof of the Mercedes and drummed his fingers on the lustrous ivory surface. He looked in through the driver's side window at the beige leather interior and imagined how it would smell. What did a car like this cost? Sixty, seventy thousand? He wondered how MacWray had paid for it. Something else to look into—another one of many, many questions.

He had a lot of ways to go with this investigation. He had a feeling about it, a gut-level conviction that if he kept pushing, something was bound to give. The one thing that bothered him was that he could find no worthy victim, only Teddy Larson, who may or may not have killed himself, and whose passing was regretted by no one—not even his wife, apparently. At any rate, she had seen fit to disappear from the scene. First Star Bank had certainly been hurt by Larson's activities, but they had filed no formal complaint.

Pleasant *liked* Mack MacWray, a genuinely nice guy who had been victimized by a professional con artist. The fact that he'd gotten his business back up and running excited Pleasant's admiration almost as much as it did his curiosity. He bore no ill will toward MacWray—but he wanted to know what was going on.

Professionally speaking, he shouldn't be wasting his time on this thing. His boss would certainly agree with that, especially when the expense report for the trip to Cancún hit his desk. Pleasant had other cases he should be working, cases with dangerous, violent criminals, and real victims. But now that he thought about it, there was at least one person victimized by Teddy Larson's demise: Officer Jerry Pleasant. He was the injured party. He had been denied the opportunity to bring Teddy to justice. He had lost his nemesis. He was unrequited.

Pleasant looked up at the sign over the entrance. *NuMac Unlimited.* He looked at MacWray's car. Envy stirred low in his belly. If he had that kind of money he would . . . what? Buy himself a Mercedes? He imagined himself pulling into his driveway at home. His wife would flip. Val would be screaming at him before he opened the door.

What the hell, he wasn't that into cars anyway. If he were, he'd get something like an SUV. Something huge.

What he really wanted was to start over.

He thought back to his conversation with Jack Price, MacWray's lawyer. Price had told him that a divorce would cost about three years' salary. Three years' earnings to get single, Price had said. Three years to buy himself a clean break. Pleasant did some math in his head, arrived at a number, and rounded it up to the nearest thousand.

He rapped his knuckles hard on the Mercedes roof, tugged down the front of his guayabera, and entered the building.

～

Sally was not sure about Jerry Pleasant's status. Mr. MacWray had not exactly told her what to do if he showed up.

As if reading her mind, the first thing out of Jerry Pleasant's mouth was "You don't have to tell me he's not in, Sally."

"Okay," she said, much relieved.

"I'll just walk in on him in his office. I'll tell him I sneaked in the back way."

"He's in the factory with Mr. Vink."

"I'll tell him I flashed my badge at you and ordered you to sit tight."

"Okay, Mr. Pleasant."

"Please don't call me that. You make me feel old."

"I'm sorry!"

"Don't be sorry, just call me Jerry, remember?"

"Okay. Jerry."

"Sally, do you believe in fate?"

"I don't know."

"Well, I do. I think that you were fated to work here."

"It's just a job."

"No, it's more than that. Know how I know it was fate?"

Sally shook her head.

"Remember you were telling me that somebody stole your frog?"

Sally giggled. Someone had stolen a little plastic frog from her desk, and the last time Jerry had visited NuMac, she had suggested that he find the culprit and arrest him. He had promised to do so, and had even pretended to take notes when she described the missing amphibian.

Jerry grinned and pulled a small box from his pocket. "Well, I was just in Mexico chasing after some bad guys and guess what?" He placed the box on her desk. "I found your frog sitting under a palm tree drinking a margarita."

Sally reached for the box, hesitated, then opened it. She lifted out a small ceramic frog.

"Oh!" she said. "This isn't my frog!"

Jerry, looking very serious, said, "Are you sure?"

Sally giggled. "Don't you think I know my own frog?"

"Well then, whose frog is it?"

"You're the detective." Sally laughed at the perplexed expression on his face, then he laughed, too.

"Well, maybe you should keep him," Jerry said.

"Thank you. You're nice."

"Just doing my job, ma'am."

"And funny, too."

"Let me ask you something, Sally." He paused, waiting to make sure she was looking at him and not the frog. "Do you ever go out with older guys?"

33

"You shouldn't have accepted the shipment."

"What was I supposed to do?" Vink said, his voice taking on an uncharacteristic whine. "The guy would've just dumped the whole load in front of the dock."

Mack glared at the pile of cartons—seventy-six of them—filling the left side of the bay. Five thousand red-white-and-green Pizza America smocks.

Vink opened and closed his right hand, the good one, stretching the fingers, then making a fist. "What d'you want me to do with them?"

"Ship 'em back."

"You serious? They don't want 'em. I called as soon as the truck showed up." His hands met in front of his belly, his half hand massaging the other.

"You talk to Al Krupinski?"

"I tried," Vink said. He gave Mack a sideways look. "He doesn't work there anymore. The guy I talked to said the P.O. was 'not authorized.'"

Mack scowled. Another alligator. He didn't know how he was going to shake this one off, but he was not about to eat seventy-six cartons of red-white-and-green poly-cotton twill.

"Hey there! ¿*Como está?*"

Mack spun on his heel, ready to fire whichever wiseass employee had intruded into their conversation, and found himself staring into the suntanned features of Jerry Pleasant.

"Officer Pleasant," he said. "Who let you in?"

Pleasant shrugged and turned his mouth into that irritating smile. Mack had an intense momentary fantasy of hitting the cop over the head and shipping him out in one of the Pizza America boxes. Ship him to Siberia or some goddamn place.

Pleasant said, "You got a minute?"

"No."

"Half a minute?"

Mack closed his eyes and rolled his head, willing his neck muscles to relax.

"Okay," he said. "Let's talk in my office. Come on."

"What do you want me to do here?" Vink asked.

"I told you," Mack said over his shoulder. "Ship 'em back."

∿

"You get that suntan in Cancún?" Mack asked.

"Yup." Pleasant settled into the chair in front of Mack's desk. "Stayed at the Miramar, just like your wife recommended. Nice place."

"Good for you." Mack leaned a hip against the desk and crossed his arms, looking down at Pleasant. "So, what can I do for you?"

"Oh, I just wanted to update you on your ex-partner. I did a little poking around down on Isla Mujeres. Ever been there?"

"Like I said last time you asked, no."

Pleasant took a small notebook from his pocket, flipped back a few pages, and frowned. "I did ask you that, didn't I?" He made a note. "I get confused. It was very confusing down there. I visited the place where he is supposed to have jumped. Very rocky. Not a place that I would choose for my own final exit. Did you know that he was robbed?"

Mack shook his head.

"Yes, apparently someone stole his wallet and some jewelry, or at least that's what his wife claimed."

"Is that so."

"Have you ever heard the term *key crook*?"

"No."

Pleasant nodded as if pleased with Mack's answer. "Actually, it's a term I coined. Key crook." He rolled his shoulders and wriggled his butt into the chair, making himself comfortable. "You see, we live on the planet of crooks." Pleasant smiled, nodding in approval at his own words.

Mack contained a sigh. Pleasant had the look of a man who was going to be talking for a while.

Pleasant continued, "It's the planet of crooks because we are all criminals. Some of us jaywalk, some of us cheat on our taxes, some of us steal ashtrays from hotel rooms, some of us rob banks and abuse children. We all break the law." He pointed at Mack, then at himself. "Crooks. You and me."

"What's your point?"

"My point is that criminal behavior can be viewed as a disease. In most of us, fortunately for society, the infection is mild. We've all got a dose, but the symptoms are so minor that we do not think of ourselves as crooks. Just because we all break a law from time to time doesn't make us criminals. Right?"

Mack stared impassively at the V-shaped smile. Pleasant held it for a few seconds, shrugged, and continued.

"In some individuals, however, the disease gets out of control. This can be stimulated by genetic factors, by stress, by economic circumstance, by legislation. You never know what might bring it to a head. Look at Prohibition. There's an example of legislation making criminals of tens of millions of people. Some of them developed a taste for the dark side and remained criminals for the rest of their lives. Or look at all the guys in prison now because they were in the wrong place at the wrong time. A guy hops a ride with a buddy who happens to have a kilo of weed in his trunk. Or the guy who happens to be in the vicinity of a handgun when he catches his wife with another guy. Instead of a fistfight you've got a murder. If he'd come home twenty minutes later, or if the gun hadn't been there, or if the wife hadn't hired that personal trainer to get her ass in shape . . . It's circumstance. All kinds of things can push a person over the edge." Pleasant turned up his palms, awaiting Mack's response.

Mack stared at him, waiting for whatever was coming.

Pleasant shrugged. "So, one of the biggest factors is what I call the *key crook*. Key crooks are the Typhoid Marys of bad guys. They almost seem to be in the business of creating criminals. For instance, the fence creates burglars. The drug dealer produces smugglers, and the legislator—the lawmaker—he makes all kinds of crooks. And anytime you've got a successful crook, just about everybody they rub up against starts breaking laws."

Mack said, "I guess that's why there are so many crooked cops."

"Precisely," said Pleasant, not missing a beat. "Crooks make more crooks, and *key* crooks make a *lot* of crooks. Lars Larson, for instance, was a key crook. Very key. Did you know that he had a safe deposit box at a bank in Cancún?"

"Why would I know that?"

"You were in Cancún."

"Yes I was. On vacation."

"I spoke with the people at the bank."

"Oh?" Mack raised a hand to his chin to conceal the throbbing veins in his neck.

"Do you know what I found interesting? Apparently, Lars Larson visited his safe deposit box *after* he jumped off the cliff. Isn't that remarkable?"

"He was a remarkable man." His words sounded distant and choked.

"Yes, he was."

"Why are you telling me this?"

"Do you think that you resemble Lars?"

Mack could not reply.

Pleasant said, "Did I mention that Rita Larson might be in town?"

Mack shook his head.

"She took a flight from Cancún to here, ah, a few days after her husband's death." He wrote something in his notebook. "I don't suppose you've heard from her."

"No."

"Do my questions make you uncomfortable?"

"No."

Pleasant wrote again in his book. Without looking up, he said, "Did you kill your partner?"

Mack felt the words enter his mind one at a time, followed by a warm, calming silence. At last, they had reached the core of the matter.

"You have to think about it?" Pleasant asked.

"I just can't quite believe what you're asking me," Mack said. His voice emerged strong and true. "The answer, of course, is no."

"Of course," said Pleasant, making another note. "I think I might be able to believe that."

"Good."

"What about Larson's safe deposit box? Find anything good in there?"

Mack showed his teeth. "Next you'll be asking me if I've stopped beating my wife."

"She assured me that the beatings have stopped." Pleasant grinned back. "We talked a few minutes ago."

Mack felt as if he was taking one body blow after another. "You talked to Paula?"

"I had a few questions for her, too. Fact is, I think that Lars Larson may have given us all a dose."

Mack uncrossed his arms and gripped the edge of his desk. "Look, I didn't kill anybody, I haven't stolen any hotel room ashtrays lately, and I have to get back to work. Is there anything else I can do for you?"

"Yes." Pleasant closed his notebook and looked Mack in the eye. "Think about your situation." He stood up. "Why put up with a bunch of unnecessary bullshit when you can afford not to?" He waited, his head tipped slightly to the left, his eyes on Mack's mouth.

Mack said, "What makes you think I can afford anything?"

"New Mercedes. Growing business. Empty safe deposit box."

"The Mercedes is leased. My business is strapped for cash. And I don't know anything about any safe deposit box."

"Sure you do. All that money Larson sucked out of Mac-Lar had to go someplace, and that place was in a box at the Banamex in Cancún. I think you, or someone who looked exactly like you, emptied that box. How did you get the key? Fact is, I don't much care about that aspect of it. That's a problem for the Mexican cops. Unless, of course, I decide to get interested. Right now I'm just interested in the money."

Mack looked away. Was this cop really suggesting what he seemed to be suggesting? He recalled something Lars had said to him as they stood before the temple of Ixchel: *Lemme tell you a secret, Mack. You can buy just about anybody. Even people think they're not bribable, you show them enough money and they can't stop themselves. It's human nature.*

Was Pleasant giving him an invitation? One way to find out.

"How much do you want?" he asked.

Pleasant produced a dazzling smile, the biggest and happiest one yet.

~

The money, the passport, and the gun made perfect sense now. Paula lifted the gun and flicked the safety off and on. Had this gun killed Lars? Jerry Pleasant had not actually said how Lars had died, only that the Mexican cops believed he had killed himself. But of course they were wrong. Paula knew—she *knew*—that Mack had killed Lars. There could be no other explanation. Her Mack—quiet, unassuming Mack—had somehow found Lars Larson and killed him and taken his money and his passport, because how else could these things have ended up here in their garage?

Mack had killed Lars. She was married to a killer. She remembered that night in Cancún when Mack had ravished her. She was sure he had killed Lars on that very day. She shivered. He may even have had traces of Lars's blood on his hands. The thought repelled, then aroused her. A murderer's wife. She would never see Mack's hands again in the same way. He had killed, and he might kill again, if someone got in his way. Did that have something to do with why he had suddenly become such a success? Yes, she decided, the killing had made him powerful. He had done violence. He had taken what was rightfully his from another man. It was ancient and immutable. Men kill men to protect their property, their children, their women.

But what had he been doing with Rita Manbait? She imagined his killer's hands on Rita's silicone tits, squeezing. She had to be holding something over him. Maybe she was blackmailing him and he was just trying to keep her quiet. Did that make sense? Maybe. She wasn't sure. She didn't care. It didn't matter. If Rita Manbait was stealing her man, it was up to Paula to do something about it. Mack the killer was her husband.

Paula riffled through a packet of hundred-dollar bills. She liked having this money in the garage. She liked having this secret, this thing that only she and her husband knew. The fact that Mack was capable of murder excited her. She wasn't going to give him up that easily.

The phone rang. She scrambled down the ladder, ran into the house, and answered it on the fourth ring.

"Sweetheart, this is your daddy."

"Hi, Daddy." Paula's insides froze. A phone call from her father was such a rare event that it could only mean disaster. Mom must be dead, or in the hospital, or worse—something so awful she could not begin to imagine it.

Her father said, "How are you doing? Everything okay?"

"Everything's fine. What's wrong? Is Mom okay?"

"Your mother is fine. She's out shopping right now. She went shopping."

"She's a good shopper."

"I don't know what I'd do without her. Uh-huh."

"Daddy, is something the matter?"

"Well, sweetheart, you remember your mom and I were asking about getting some of our money back from you and John?"

Paula felt some of the tension drain away. No one was dead. This was about money.

"I wish you'd call him Mack, Daddy."

"All right. Mack. Well, your mother feels very strongly about it. You know we talked to him, and, well, he wasn't very helpful."

"Daddy, Mack needs that money right now."

"But the business is doing so well . . ."

"Daddy, I thought Mack explained all this to you. When a business is growing it needs cash. We'll pay you back, and then some, but you have to be patient."

"Your mother doesn't feel that way. You know, John—I mean Mack—was very rude to her. Terribly rude. He told her he would send us a check, but that was weeks ago. And when she phoned again he wouldn't take her call. I just about drove over to the factory and had it out with him!"

"I'm sure he just forgot." But she was sure he hadn't.

"And we heard that he has bought himself a very expensive automobile."

"It's leased, Daddy."

"In any case, your mother is very upset. The fact is—and I wanted to tell you this before you heard it from John—we've hired an attorney."

Paula was not sure she had heard him correctly. "You what?"

"Sweetheart, we're hoping that we can work things out, but I don't know. The lawyer talked to John—"

"For god's sake, Daddy, call him Mack!"

"They talked and, based on that, the lawyer is recommending that we sue . . . Mack."

"No."

"Sweetheart, I'm sorry. Your mother hopes that you'll support us in this—"

"If you sue Mack, you're suing me, too, Daddy." She wanted to say, *Don't you know that my husband is a killer?*

"Yes, but you know we don't—"

"You're asking me to choose between you and Mack. I already made that choice, Daddy. On the altar. He's my husband." *A powerful man, capable of murder.*

"Your mother feels very strongly about this, sweetheart."

Paula hung up the phone.

34

One hundred twenty-six thousand dollars was a lot of money. Mack wondered how Pleasant had arrived at such an odd figure, then dismissed the thought. It didn't matter, as long as the money bought him some space. A hundred twenty-six thousand might not be a bad price. With Pleasant off his back, Rita's threat to implicate him in Lars's death would lose most of its force. Of course, she still had the photos of him and Julie. He tried to imagine how Paula would react. The pictures could destroy his marriage.

Mack took a mental step outside of himself, setting his emotions aside. Suppose Paula left him? How important was that? He still had his business. Divorce would be an inconvenience, but it would not be hard to find another woman. A younger woman. He would start over. He tried to imagine it, but to his surprise, he could not picture life without Paula by his side. He frowned and tried to think how he felt about her. She was not the girl he had married. She did not excite him the way Julie Gorman did, but as much as he liked sex with Julie, he never wanted to wake up beside her. He was used to

Paula. But could he live without her? It was something to think about.

"Mr. MacWray?"

Mack shook his head and sat forward, his forearms slapping down onto his desktop.

"What?"

"Julie Gorman is on the phone for you. Line two?"

Mack scowled. He picked up the phone and punched line two. He would have to be firm with her, lay down some guidelines.

"Yes?" He made his voice hard and cold.

"Hey, tiger, it's me."

"I know that."

Julie paused. "Uh, just thought I'd give you a buzz, see how you're doing."

"I'm doing fine."

"I was just thinking. About you."

Mack said nothing.

"I've got a new listing. Out in Minnetonka. On the lake. Interested?"

"Not really. I'd rather you didn't call me at work."

"You want me to call you at *home?*"

"Just don't call."

"I'm your real estate agent. How am I supposed to reach you?"

"I'll call you." He disconnected without waiting for her response.

Seconds later, Sally buzzed him again.

"I have that Rita on line one."

Mack closed his eyes and took a breath. He picked up the phone and said in as calm a voice as he could manage, "Yes?"

"Hey, Macanudo."

Mack waited.

"You been thinking about me?"

"Not as much as you imagine."

"Too busy banging your real estate agent?"

"Yeah, that's right."

"She's a skinny little thing. I'm looking at her right now—a photo of her. Not much there in the boob department."

"What do you want?"

"You know what I want."

"Let's talk about it. Where are you?"

Rita laughed. "You planning to send your goon after me again? I don't think so. Next time I see you, you'll be handing me a nice fat envelope. One of those big ones you get at the post office."

"What are we talking?"

"What did you get out of the box? Four hundred?"

"Not even close."

"Yes it is."

Mack made a decision. "I can get you a hundred thousand, that's it."

"That's not good enough."

"Then I guess you have to do what you have to do." He hung up.

Sixty seconds passed, during which he did not breathe, then Sally buzzed him again.

"I have that—"

He picked up. "Yeah?"

"Hang up on me again, I won't be calling back."

Mack waited.

"Okay," Rita said. "Tomorrow morning. Ten o'clock."

"Where?"

"The airport. Chili's. In the terminal."

Mack frowned. "How about we just meet at your hotel?"

"I don't think so. Last chance, Macanudo."

He squeezed his lips to white lines. "All right."

~

Mack told Sally to hold all calls. He closed the blinds, locked his office door, and lay down on the carpet. If he could clear his mind— even just for a few minutes—he would know what to do.

Assume that he paid Pleasant the one twenty-six. Lars's death would then continue to be viewed as a suicide—which, in a sense, it was—and Pleasant would quit looking into Mack's business affairs. He locked Pleasant out of his thoughts for the moment and concentrated on the Pizza America problem. Krupinski had been fired, possibly as a result of the smock order. Other, less tractable individuals would now be in charge.

Mack considered his options. He could sue them, but that would take months, the legal fees would kill him, and if they got Krupinski to testify as to Mack's sales technique, it could backfire. He was left with persuasion, blackmail, extortion, or simply liquidating the smocks and moving on to the next deal. He decided to try persuasion, even though success seemed unlikely. Later, if necessary, he would look into blackmail and extortion.

Thinking about blackmail brought him back to the biggest gator of all, Rita Larson. Paying her the $100,000 was no guarantee he'd be rid of her. In fact, she almost certainly would come back for more.

He probably couldn't scare her off—he'd tried that. Inevitably, he circled back to the ultimate solution. Ultimate for Rita. Could he do it? He had let Lars die, killing him, in effect, but that had been a passive act. Rita would probably not cooperate by throwing herself off a cliff. He would have to assist her.

Mack imagined himself throwing her from a rooftop. Watching her fall. The imagined scene left him flat—he felt no horror, no fear, no discomfort. He imagined his hands around her neck, squeezing. Aside from a faint, atavistic stirring in his groin, the thought produced no emotion. He imagined clubbing her and stabbing her; both options produced a mild discomfort in his belly, but nothing he couldn't handle. He imagined shooting her with Lars's pistol. A sharp sound, a dark hole in her chest, she falls down. Like watching a movie. Maybe he was a stone-cold killer at heart. Once fear, guilt, and repulsion were removed from the equation, murder became a straightforward proposition.

If he could get her alone, somehow. If he could avoid getting caught.

Mack sat up. He could hear voices through the walls, a faint vibration from the sewing floor, the distant *thok* of the riveter. He stood up and picked up the phone and punched in a number.

"Hi." He smiled, knowing it would make his voice warmer. "Sorry I yelled at you. I was in the middle of something."

"You were a real shit."

"I know. You still want to show me that house?"

"I don't know . . ."

"I'll bring you a present."

"Okay."

"You're easy, you know that?"

"I've been told."

"I like easy."

~

A thousand grubby hands had handled the plastic key, shoving it in and out of the lock on room 221, rubbing the Super 8 logo right off it. It looked wrong in her perfectly manicured hand, like a turd in a platinum setting. Her mouth held in a moue of distaste, Rita used the key to let herself into her thirty-seven-dollar-a-night room. She closed and double-locked the door. The bedspread, a stunningly ugly mishmash of dull brown and dirty gold, filled her eyes. She grabbed it by the corner and threw it off and sat down on the blanket, a fuzzy beige material probably manufactured from recycled soda bottles. Rita sat with her back straight, her feet on the floor, her hands crossed on her lap. The framed print screwed onto the wall opposite the bed showed boats, water, a bronze sunset, birds. She closed her eyes. It was demeaning. Embarrassing. It was like going back ten, fifteen years to a life of cheap motel rooms, disgusting bedspreads, and carpeting that had endured the most loathsome feet imaginable.

A lake of self-pity welled up within her. Her mouth quivered; her eyes stung. Tears streaked her face while her hands clutched each other in her lap. After a few minutes the tears stopped. She went to the bathroom and dried her eyes, leaving smears of mascara on the thin white towel. She looked around the tiny bathroom. Little soaplets wrapped in paper. Plastic glasses in shrink-wrap. A small card reminding guests that toothpaste, disposable razors, and other essentials were for sale in the lobby. To stay here overnight would be intolerable, but it was all she could afford now. She had burned through the last of her cash, hiring that weasel of a photographer to catch MacWray humping his skinny little girlfriend. She had only a few dollars left, and she was four days overdue to return her rental car.

The Visa she had used to rent the car was maxed out. When she'd tried to use it to rent this room, the card had been rejected.

Ten years ago, Teddy had saved her from this motel life, and now he was gone. It was up to her to take care of herself. She could do it. Teddy had taught her a few things. One thing he had often repeated: *Nobody will give you money if they think you need it.* Even in their leaner times he had insisted on wearing the best suits, driving a new car, and staying in good hotels. *First, you gotta look sharp.*

The airport was safe. She would wear her turquoise silk dress. She would get there early and be waiting with the photo of Mack humping away on that polar bear rug, just in case he wasn't convinced.

She had him by the balls and he knew it. He would pay. She was sure he would pay. He *had* to pay.

～

Paula showed up for work three hours late. She walked past Ginny's office—she was on the phone—went straight to her desk, and started going through her messages and e-mail. Nothing looked terribly urgent or interesting. She spent a few minutes fussing, moving things around on her desk and making a to-do list, doing her best to keep her mind occupied. She wished she had somebody to talk to, but who? Julie Gorman was a good friend but not so good a friend that she could say, "My husband killed a man and we have a bag full of money in the garage." That was something she could share with no one—maybe not even Mack.

After twenty minutes of nonproductive shuffling and rearranging, she walked down the short hall to Ginny's office. She might not be able to talk about Mack, but she could at least *talk.* Ginny was still on the phone, but she motioned Paula to come in and sit down. When Ginny hung up the phone a few moments later, Paula saw that she had a cut on her lower lip, and a bruised jaw.

Paula raised a hand to her own jaw. "What happened?"

～

Jake Vink had spoken to a man named Salvatore Green, the Pizza America vice president who had taken over Al Krupinski's responsibilities. Mack considered calling him but decided that an unannounced personal visit might be more effective. It was too easy to say no over the phone. He would show up in person and do his best to sweet-talk Salvatore Green. He was prepared to do almost anything to get them to accept the smocks, up to and including letting them go at below cost. He would be a people guy. Salvatore Green would see that he was a reasonable man, willing to compromise, and they would strike a deal. As he pulled into the parking lot, Mack felt utterly confident in his ability to resolve the situation.

He checked his face and his tie in the rearview mirror. He looked good. He got out of the Mercedes and strode confidently up the wide, shallow concrete steps, through the swinging glass doors, and into the spacious lobby. The receptionist, a gray-haired woman with red-rimmed eyeglasses, smiled at him, then her head jerked back and her eyes widened. She grabbed her phone and spoke into it in a low voice, and Mack knew that things would not go as smoothly as he hoped.

He said, making his voice light and friendly, "Hi. My name's Mack MacWray. Is Mr. Green available?"

The receptionist's eyes moved toward the hallway to the left of her desk. Two men, one in his fifties, the other twenty years younger, both well over two hundred pounds, both with their chins lowered and their hands curled into near fists, emerged from the hallway and approached him. Mack gave them his best smile and held out his hand toward the older man.

"Mr. Green?"

The man clasped Mack's hand and, with a sudden, brutal motion, twisted it up behind his back and propelled him rapidly toward the glass doors.

Mack said, "Hey, I—" He was driven into the doors, hitting the glass with his chest and face, pushing through. The man gave him a powerful shove, sending him down the steps. Mack's legs worked frantically, trying to keep him upright, but his momentum was too great. He fell headlong, landing hard at the bottom of the stairs. Points of pain detonated at his right hip and shoulder.

He lay still for a few seconds, wondering if his clavicle had shattered. He rolled to his hands and knees. His shoulder hurt, but it worked. He raised his head and looked up at the two men standing in front of the glass doors.

The older man said, "You got the message?"

Mack nodded. He climbed to his feet, ignoring the grinding pain in his hip, and tottered painfully back to his car.

35

It took him more than an hour to find the house on Stubb's Bay. The tangle of streets surrounding Lake Minnetonka had the complexity of a nervous system. He had to ask directions of three joggers and a road repair crew before finally locating Adam's Field Lane. Julie's Lexus was parked in front of the small, cedar-shingled cottage. The front door stood open. He walked in, favoring his right hip. The cottage was comprised of a single large bedroom, a kitchenette, a tiny bathroom, and a screened, three-season porch. Julie was standing outside, on the other side of the cottage, looking out over the lake. She wore a black linen dress, tight at the hips, flaring just below the knees. It made her calves look thin.

"Do you know what they're asking for this place?" she asked. She kept her face turned toward the lake.

Mack stopped a few feet behind her. "How much?"

"Four hundred."

Mack looked back at the tiny cottage. "Must be the lot."

"Half acre with two hundred feet of shoreline." She turned toward him. She was wearing sunglasses. Her mouth turned down. "Your jacket is ripped."

"I had a fall."

"Are you all right?"

"I'm fine."

"I'm still mad at you."

He shrugged his good shoulder. He didn't really care.

Julie lowered her glasses, peeking over the rims and grinning in a way that was supposed to be cute and seductive.

"Did you bring me a present?"

Mack stared at her, feeling as if he were looking at a life-size poster of a very thin, very narcissistic woman—Holly Golightly, without Hepburn's self-possession.

"I forgot," he said.

Her smile became a pout. She pushed her sunglasses back up her nose. "You're no fun," she said.

"You want to do it out here, or should we go inside?"

"I thought the Irish were supposed to know how to sweet-talk a girl."

"That's a nice dress."

Julie waited a few seconds, then said, "I guess that'll have to do." She followed him into the house.

Two minutes later Mack said, "You have to get on top. I'm too beat up."

Dutifully—if petulantly—Julie mounted him. Mack lay back, closed his eyes, and tried to lose himself in sensation, with only partial success. He did not want to be here with this hungry little woman, and the image of his wife kept appearing, projected onto the insides of his eyelids.

Ten minutes later Julie rolled off him, unsatisfied. "You must've had quite a fall," she said.

"I've got a lot on my mind."

"I might as well give Comb-over Harold a call."

A wave of revulsion rolled over Mack, taking him by surprise. He sat up and started dressing.

Julie laughed and said, "Hey, I'm just kidding, tiger. You don't have to go getting all huffy."

Mack stood up and pulled on his pants. "Look, let's not do this anymore. Let's call it quits, okay? We've had some fun, but I really have to get back to my marriage."

Julie's eyes widened and her mouth fell open. Her tongue seemed grotesquely pink, and her ivory incisors were shiny with spit. Mack looked away, his gut writhing. He had a powerful urge to strike out at her. To save them both, he went into the bathroom, closed the door, and sat on the toilet. He would sit there for a few minutes, and then he would finish dressing and leave this place. He would end this thing here and now.

~

Julie stared at the bathroom door, a hellish fury building within her. After a few moments of grotesque imaginings, she opened her purse. She applied a stripe of lipstick to each lip and picked up Mack's white shirt from the floor and planted a smeary kiss on the underside of his shirt collar, where he might not notice it. She opened her bottle of Opium, applied a drop to her wrists, then rubbed her perfumed wrists on his shirttail. Dressing quickly, she straightened the bed, took the condom wrapper from the bedstand, and waited. A few seconds later Mack emerged from the bathroom.

Julie said, "I'm sorry, Mack, but I understand."

Mack nodded; she could sense his relief. She stepped toward him. "One last kiss."

She could see the distaste on his face—the arrogant prick—but he did not resist as she slipped her arms around his naked waist and pressed her body to his and kissed him hard, slipping the condom wrapper into his right hip pocket as she did so. It was only with great effort that she refrained from leaving a set of claw marks down his faithless back.

~

Mack's car was in the driveway. Paula drove on by, not ready to face her husband. She did not trust herself to act normally. She was afraid she would do or say something to make him defensive, or that might force him to lie to her. Why was he home so early? Lately he had been working until seven or eight. She had planned to make him a nice dinner and maybe down a few drinks before he got home. She drove around the block twice, girding herself for her new role as the murderer's wife, before pulling in beside Mack's new Mercedes.

She gathered her purse and the bag of groceries she'd picked up on the way home. She went in through the front door. No Mack on the sofa. She dropped her purse and carried the groceries into the kitchen. Mack was sitting at the table drinking a beer.

"You okay?" she asked.

He looked up. "Me?"

"You're just sitting there."

"I'm thinking." He appeared to be calm enough.

She set the grocery bag on the counter. "I bought some shrimp for dinner. Those big ones you like? Thought we could grill them, have them with a pasta salad?"

"That sounds good."

"I got some artichokes, too."

"Sure, that'd be fine."

Paula took a careful look at her husband. He was sounding an awful lot like the old Mack. She decided to zing him, see if she could get a rise.

"I talked to my father today."

"Oh?"

"They've hired a lawyer."

"I know. He called."

"My dad?"

"No. The lawyer."

"What are you going to do?"

Mack's expression became tight and guarded. "What do you *think* I'm going to do?"

"I know what I *want* you to do."

"What is that?"

"Tell 'em to take a flying fuck."

Mack blinked. "Where'd you learn to talk like that?"

"Oh, I don't know—from my husband?"

"No wonder your parents don't approve of him."

"You know what it says in the Bible."

"No, I don't. What does it say?"

"Something about once you get married, your parents can take a flying fuck."

Mack laughed. "I don't remember that part."

"Maybe I'm thinking of some other book."

"I'm gonna have to read that one." Mack felt a warmth deep in his chest, radiating from his solar plexus. When was the last time he and Paula had bantered like this? Not since before Mac-Lar had folded. Ever since that day, he had been alone, out there on the point, nothing but sea and sky and alligators.

"As for your parents," he said, "a flying fuck is pretty much what I had in mind. I wasn't sure how you'd feel about it, though."·

"I've been wanting to say that to my mother for twenty-five years." She picked up Mack's beer and drank the last two inches. "You ready for a real drink?"

"Absolutely." He watched Paula open the liquor cabinet and bring out the martini shaker, the vermouth, a bottle of Stoli. He liked the way she moved, confident and economical, her strong peasant fingers grasping and releasing objects. He watched her take two stemmed glasses from the cabinet above the refrigerator. She opened the freezer and scooped ice cubes into the shaker, then added a few cubes to each glass to cool them. He watched her measure the vodka—two jiggers, and a splash of vermouth. She inserted a glass rod into the shaker and stirred. He watched the muscles move beneath her pale skin as dew beaded on the outside of the steel shaker. Paula dumped the ice cubes from the glasses and strained the chilled martini mixture into the glasses. Jeeves had nothing on her.

He noticed her forearms. There was solidity there, a genetic holdover from her Irish ancestors. He imagined harvesting potatoes with her, side by side, sweating in the sun, taking a break for a roll in the hay.

"We don't have any olives," she said as she handed him a glass.

"That's fine by me."

She sat down across from him and they sipped their martinis.

"Did you see Jake Vink today?"

"I see Jake every day."

"How was he?"

"I don't know. Why?"

"He beat up Ginny last night."

Mack put down his glass, suddenly suspicious. "That why you're being so nice?"

He regretted his words instantly. Paula's eyes went dark; she sat back. For a few seconds neither of them spoke.

"What happened?" Mack asked.

"I'm just telling you something you might need to know, Mack."

"Okay. So he beat up his girlfriend. What do you want me to do? You want me to talk to him?"

Paula shook her head. "Ginny can take care of herself. The reason I'm telling you is so you know that Jake might have some problems."

"He beats up a woman, he's got a problem."

"I mean, problems as a result of what he did."

"Oh. Ginny's going to press charges?"

"I don't know what she's going to do." Paula dipped her forefinger into her martini, looked at the drop hanging there, put her finger in her mouth, and sucked it dry. "But she's going to do something."

She wanted to ask him about the money. Bring it up casually, the way she might mention that she had found a twenty-dollar-bill in the laundry. *By the way, I* . . . She brought the words up and into her mouth, tasted them, let them lay on her tongue as she watched Mack sip his drink.

No, she decided, it would be too much of a risk. He might think that she was hinting about paying her parents back. Right now they were good together. She would wait for another time. Maybe he would bring it up himself. The money wasn't going anywhere.

"Have you looked at any more houses?" she asked.

"What?" He seemed startled.

"I had lunch with Julie the other day. She said she had some new houses coming on the market. Didn't she get in touch with you?"

"Oh. She might've called. I don't remember."

"She's a lot happier lately."

"Why's that?"

"I don't know. She's got this cat-ate-the-canary grin on her. It can't be a boyfriend or she'd have told me about him." Paula laughed. "Maybe she got herself a new vibrator."

Mack smiled, shaking his head.

"We're going to be okay, Mack."

Mack nodded.

"Whatever you do. Whatever happens. Whatever you've done. Whatever you become, I want you to know I'm with you, Mack."

~

Jukes, Mack's bassett hound, had died twelve years ago, shortly before Mack met Paula. It had been a difficult parting. Jukes had been Mack's oldest and closest friend. The best times were when Mack came home from work. Maybe he had done his job well that day or maybe he hadn't. Maybe he had said something cruel to someone, or broken a traffic law on the way home, or dropped a cigarette butt on the sidewalk. Jukes didn't care. Jukes loved him unconditionally. Mack could have committed any sin, failed in any endeavor, and Jukes would have seen nothing but godliness.

Early in their marriage, Mack had gotten that same feeling of unconditional love from Paula, but as their relationship matured, he found that love had become part of an ongoing negotiation. If he failed to mow the lawn, he risked her loving him less. To be fair, it worked both ways. They were constantly dickering, using love as currency.

Nevertheless, he had always taken it on faith that there was a bottom, a foundation of shared love that was powerful enough to carry them through the worst of times, but he had never tested it, and he would not test it now. He would not tell her about Julie, or Lars, or the things he had done to build his business. But it was good to know that the base was there, that she was with him no matter what.

"I'm with you, too," he said, seeing the girl he had married in her earth-colored irises, knowing that he could not risk this thing, this marriage. He would protect it from Rita Larson, no matter what he had to do.

36

Paula sat up in bed, her heart pounding. Bad dream. Bugs, insects, crawling things invading her body. She turned on the light and threw back the covers. Nothing there but her legs. Where was Mack? She slid a hand to his side of the bed. The mattress was still warm from his body. Five-forty-eight. He was probably in the kitchen making coffee, getting an early start. She went to the window and opened the blinds. The sky was light in the east. Her heart was still hammering. Bugs burrowing from the mattress into her flesh. She stepped into her slippers and donned her bathrobe. She did not want to get back into bed.

Mack was not in the kitchen, but the coffeemaker was gurgling. Paula, still trying to shake the memory of her dream, poured herself a cup, added a shot of tap water to cool it, and drank half of it.

She heard a series of thumps from the garage, then the sound of a car door slamming. Seconds later, the door to the garage opened and Mack stepped into the kitchen. He was wearing blue jeans, a yellow polo shirt, and the huaraches he'd bought in Cancún.

"Hey!" he said, surprised to see her. "What are you doing up?"

"Bad dream," Paula said. "What about you?"

"Busy day. I figured I'd get an early start." Mack poured himself coffee. "I've got a meeting out at the airport at ten, and I thought I'd squeeze in a few hours at the office first."

Paula felt a tingle; something in Mack's voice sounded off-key. "Why at the airport?"

"The client's got a two-hour layover. It'll be my only chance to talk to him in person."

"Who's the client?"

Mack hesitated. His eyes narrowed. "Olde Towne Cafeterias," he said. He sipped his coffee, watching her.

"I thought . . ." Paula caught herself. She'd been about to remind him that Olde Towne Cafeterias had recently filed bankruptcy. "Oh, never mind." She didn't want to catch him in an overt lie. Not after last night, when they'd made some real progress. He hadn't actually confided in her, but they'd moved so far in the right direction . . . He had to learn to trust her as completely as she trusted him. She said, "Would you like me to fix you some breakfast?"

Mack shook his head. "I'd better get going."

Paula couldn't restrain herself. "You're wearing that to meet a client?"

225

Mack looked down at his jeans and huaraches. He shrugged. "I'm sick of wearing suits. He'll just have to deal with it." He gulped the rest of his coffee, gave her a peck on the cheek, and left her with her thoughts.

~

The mirror was thin and greasy looking, with tiny gold flecks scattered across its surface, but the reflected image, the goddess in the turquoise dress, was a thing of beauty. Rita caressed the fabric, textured silk, almost a brocade but not so heavy. It was a simple dress—sleeveless, with a modestly scooped neckline, fitting her closely, sexy but not provocative. She had purchased the dress in Cancún. She had been saving it for Teddy's birthday. This was not Teddy's birthday but it would have to do. She would be meeting MacWray at the airport where, a lifetime ago, she had met Teddy.

Rita smiled, remembering that afternoon. She had been working the terminal with her girlfriend Patsy, stealing bags and, when the situation was right, turning the occasional trick. They called themselves Tits and Ass.

Rita had spotted him drinking a rum and Coke at a table in the cocktail lounge on the Gold Concourse. He was wearing a nice suit and a Rolex. His leather Mark Cross overnight bag was deposited carelessly behind his chair. It looked as if it might have some interesting contents. Rita pointed him out to Patsy, and they went into their routine.

It was Rita's turn to be Tits. She put her own watch in her purse, then took a seat at the table directly in front of the mark and ordered a glass of red wine. Women who drank red wine were more interesting to men, she had found. Being a pragmatic woman, Rita had never troubled to wonder why, but it was a fact. She sipped her wine and let her eyes drift about the room until, by happenstance, they fell upon the ruddy gentleman with the Rolex watch. She was forced to repeat this performance several times before catching his eye. She smiled and gave him a slight but definite nod, which he returned. She sipped a little more wine, then looked at her wrist and frowned. She leaned across her small table, displaying maximum cleavage, and said, "Excuse me, sir?" She tapped her empty wrist. "Do you have the time?"

She watched his eyes explore the tops of her breasts. This was back in her pre-implant days, but even then they'd been pretty damn good. After a second he indicated a large clock behind the bar. "I believe it's two-thirty-eight," he said. He had a great voice.

Rita smiled as if he had just paid her a compliment. "My name's Bonnie," she said. She used a different name every time to confuse the airport cops. So far, she had escaped their notice.

He raised his eyebrows. "Really!" He gave her a smile that matched hers in intensity. "Then I must be Clyde." He gestured toward the other chair at his table. "Won't you join me?"

"Love to!" She changed seats, bending over as she sat to give him a close-up shot. At that moment, Patsy walked behind his chair, snatched his overnight bag, and made for the rest room.

"Where are you headed, Clyde?" Rita asked.

Clyde was smiling at her, his eyes cold and bright. He let his hand fall on her wrist, a move that startled her. "You want to know where I'm headed?" His voice had taken on an edge. She tried to pull her hand back, but his fingers closed around her wrist with shocking force.

"I'll tell you where I'm going, Bonnie. I'm going straight to the airport cops unless your friend has my bag back here in about sixty seconds." His lips were tight against his teeth in an unpleasant grimace.

"You're hurting me!"

He squeezed harder. "I will do more than that, darling. I will break your wrist."

Rita saw that he meant it. "Okay!" she said. "I'll get it for you."

"We'll get it together."

"We can't. Ow! She's in the ladies' room."

"Let's go," he said. Without another word he walked her down the concourse to the nearest women's rest room and pushed through the door. He forced Rita down on the tile floor so that she could see under the stalls. Rita pointed out Patsy's burgundy pumps, too scared to do anything else. Without releasing his grip on Rita's wrist, Teddy kicked in the stall door and snatched his overnight bag from Patsy's lap.

"Everything here?" he asked.

Patsy, openmouthed, holding her knee where the door had smashed into it, could only nod her head.

"It had better be." He laughed, then astonished Rita one more time by handing her his business card. "You want to make some real money, honey, you give me a call. My name's Teddy."

He walked out of the rest room with his bag. Rita looked at the card: *Theodore Larson, Marketing Consultant.*

A few weeks later, after a tiff with Patsy that effectively dissolved their partnership, Rita had given Teddy a call.

Rita stared intently at the woman in the mirror, ten years older now, and better looking than ever. Maybe she didn't have that same juicy eighteen-year-old bloom, but she had more of what really counted. She thrust out her chest and treated herself to a smile.

"You're the best," she said, turning this way and that. The dress needed something—a brooch or a necklace. There was a lot of unadorned turquoise fabric between her throat and her breasts. She sorted through the modest collection of baubles in her jewelry case. Something in coral and silver would be nice, but of course she had left the perfect coral pin back on Isla. She tried on several items but found nothing suitable. Oh well, it would have to do. She wasn't out to seduce the guy. Polar bear rugs weren't her style.

❧

After Mack left, Paula sat quietly drinking her coffee and sorting out the turbulence in her head. They had come so far. The business. The money. She had turned her back on her parents. She had allied herself with her husband in a way that superseded their marriage—nowhere in their vows had she said, "I will take thee in depravity and in sin, in evil and in greed . . ." But now she had. She had loved him above and beyond anything he had done or would do. In a way, they were like outlaws. She wished he would trust her more—but maybe it was not a matter of trust. Maybe he was protecting her.

That had to be it. So long as she remained ignorant of the money and of what he had done to Lars, she was safe from the law. Also, he might fear that she would love him less if she knew . . . but that brought her back to the trust issue.

Frustrated, she pushed her coffee aside and went back to the bedroom. Mack's black wool trousers, the pair he had worn yesterday, were draped over the back of a chair. His shirt lay on the floor. She picked it up and held it to her face, inhaling his scent—but it wasn't his scent. She shook the shirt open and sniffed again. A woman's perfume. Her stomach knotted. "No," she said aloud. It meant nothing—he might have brushed up against an overscented woman in an elevator, or given an employee an encouraging hug—there were dozens of explanations. She held the shirt up, frowning. The scent was quite strong, more than might be left by a glancing encounter. And what was that hint of pink? She turned up the collar. Lipstick. An anguished shudder ran up her body. Lipstick on the underside of his collar could only have gotten there while he was dressing—or undressing. Paula dropped the shirt to the carpet, stepped on it, grabbed a sleeve, and tore it. Her arms flailed, her nails digging into the fabric, ripping, shredding. She heard herself gasping over the sound of tortured fabric. She separated the shirt into four pieces, ran them into the bathroom, stuffed them into the toilet, and flushed. Water rose swirling in the bowl, mounted the lip, spilled over onto the tile floor. Paula screamed in fury, slammed down the lid, and walked stiff-legged back to the bedroom. She grabbed his pants from the chair and pulled the pockets inside out; a gold plastic wrapper fluttered to the floor. She scooped it up. Trojan, lubricated, reservoir tip. She crumpled the wrapper and flung it away. She and Mack didn't use condoms. She threw herself onto the bed and curled into a ball and let the rage corrode her guts. Images came and went, anger shot out in all directions—at Mack, at her parents, at Lars Larson, at Bob Seaman, at every face that drifted in and out of her thoughts. Even innocents like Ginny Bettendorf and Julie Gorman and Sally Grayson seemed somehow responsible, but most often it was the same hateful face smiling and taunting her: Rita Manbait.

I won't let her, Paula thought, he's mine. A terrifying idea struck her; she uncoiled and was off the bed in an instant. She ran down the hall through the kitchen and out the door into the garage. She dragged the stepladder to the loft and climbed.

The bag was gone. For several seconds Paula stared at the place where it had been, willing it to reappear. Then she began to go through the rest of the luggage, throwing each piece off the loft onto the garage floor when it proved to be empty, empty, empty. Panting, she knelt on the plywood floor of the loft, her jaw twitching in unrelieved fury. Jeans and huaraches. He had been wearing travel clothes. Clarity descended upon her. He wasn't going to the airport to meet a client, he was going to meet Rita Manbait. Her eyes blurred; she wiped them with the sleeve of her bathrobe and looked around, her head jerking this way and that like a ferret in a trap.

37

The graveyard shift was just leaving when Mack pulled into his parking spot. He sat in his car and watched them filing out of the factory. Nearly all of them were Asian. He did not know one of them by name. A few months ago he had known the first and last names of every person who worked for him. Today he saw nothing but strangers. A twinge of regret came and went. He wished that his life had not become so complex. The thrill of building his castle from hopes and fears and promises now palled; he craved simplicity.

Today he would take steps. He would figure out a way to cut back his business to accommodate the loss of the Pizza America account. He would start to learn the names of his employees. He would deal with Jerry Pleasant and Rita Larson.

The past few months seemed like a dream. Everything he had done since the day he had been forced to lock the doors of Mac-Lar had taken on a monochromatic cast. Julie Gorman was a black-and-white dream. Other memories were preserved in sepia, like gunfight scenes from old Westerns.

He had done what he had to do. He had done some other things, too, but now he was losing momentum. Thinking too much. Feeling too much. *Just sew it and ship it, Macanudo.* He wished he could get back to that. Keep it simple. How had Lars dealt with Jerry Pleasant and Rita Larson? He had avoided one and married the other. What would Jeeves recommend? Mack smiled and shook his head. Jeeves would venture no opinion on the matter. He would have to find his own answers.

～

Mr. MacWray's car was parked out front and his office door was closed when Sally Grayson showed up for work. The clock read 7:49. She was eleven minutes early. She took her seat and did a silent inventory of the items on her desktop. Ever since she had lost her lucky plastic frog she had been suspicious of the cleaning service. Today nothing appeared to be missing. She adjusted the photograph of her cat, moved her pencil caddy two inches to the left, rotated her miniature cactus, and straightened the gold plastic nameplate. Why did they always have to move everything?

Seven-fifty. She wished a phone call would come in, or that Mr. MacWray would pop his head out so that he would see her sitting at her desk ten minutes early. She tried to think of a reason to buzz him, but she couldn't come up with anything. Oh well. She unlocked her top desk drawer and took out the ceramic frog. She set the frog beside the cactus. She hadn't heard from Jerry since he had given it to her. Maybe he'd just been kidding about going out. He was kind of old, but he was funny and she liked him. If he called she'd probably go out with him. She imagined sitting in a nice restaurant, very romantic. She crossed her hands on her lap and waited for her workday to begin.

At five minutes after eight, Mr. Vink hobbled in through the lobby door. He had two black eyes and his nose was covered by a big white bandage. The white of one eye had turned cherry red, the other eye was swollen nearly shut.

"He in there?" he asked, pointing toward Mr. MacWray's office.

Sally nodded, unable to look away.

She asked, "Did you—"

Vink cut her off with a chopping motion and limped directly to Mr. MacWray's office.

～

Mack did not smile when he saw Vink, but it wasn't easy.

"Thanks for coming in early, Jake."

"No problem. I couldn't sleep anyways. I'd been awake two hours when you called."

"You look like hell."

"Thank you."

Mack stared at him for a few seconds, then said, "I'm afraid the Pizza America account is unsalvageable. We'll have to liquidate those smocks. We'll have some layoffs."

Vink nodded.

"You up to it?" Mack asked.

"I'm okay."

"Is Ginny okay?"

Vink hesitated, then said, "I didn't lay a hand on her."

"Lately, you mean."

"That's what I mean."

"Tell me what happened."

"Which time?"

"I know you knocked her around two nights ago. I want to hear about last night."

Vink looked away. "I called her up to, you know, apologize. Went over to her place with a dozen roses, long stems, baby's breath, cost me sixty bucks. I mean, I was really sorry I'd popped her. Don't know what came over me. But I figured I could make it right. So I show up with the flowers and she invites me in and gives me a gin and tonic. Next thing I know she lays into me with a pool cue. What's a broad doing with a pool cue? Broke my nose, hit me a couple good ones on the back while I was making for the door. If I hadn't got away I coulda been killed. Plus I tore the stitches in my left nut while I was trying to get away. I was four hours at emergency."

Mack let his smile spread across his face.

Vink managed to look offended. "It's not funny."

"Yeah, it is. Remember what you said to me the first time you saw her? You said, 'I'd probably just fuck it up.' You were right."

Vink's face changed shape but it was impossible to read his expression. "Just because we had a couple disagreements doesn't mean we don't like each other."

Mack shook his head. "Let's talk about who we have to let go."

Vink shrugged and straightened as if an invisible backpack had been lifted away. "Whatever you say, boss."

～

Just before eight-thirty, Jerry Pleasant walked through the doors. Sally almost didn't recognize him in his dark suit and sunglasses.

"Hi, Jerry," she said quickly.

"Hi, Sally. How's that frog doing?"

"He's pretty happy." She touched the smooth glaze. "I like him. He sort of reminds me of you."

"Really?"

"Yeah. He's funny and cute and he never calls." Sally clapped both hands to her mouth and felt her face turn instantly red. She hadn't meant to say anything like *that*.

Jerry Pleasant gaped at her, then grinned.

"Hey, it's okay," he said. "I've been meaning to call but I've been busy lately."

"That's okay . . . I was just, I mean you don't—"

"How about dinner on Friday. Okay?"

Sally nodded, her embarrassment still raging. She was glad she had worn her hair down—her ears must be glowing.

"Okay, then, it's a date. Now I have to talk to your boss."

Sally swallowed and moved her chin up and down.

Pleasant waited a few heartbeats, then said, "You want to let him know I'm here?"

～

A familiar sensation bloomed in Jerry Pleasant's chest as he walked into MacWray's office. It was the same special feeling he got when he was about to arrest a suspect: a surge of energy fluttering his heart and swelling his arteries. In an arrest, often following a long investigation, the excitement came from the fact that he was about to make a huge change in someone's life. He was about to tell someone that tonight they would not be going home, they would be going to jail. Life as they had known it was over.

He wondered whether murderers felt something similar—the power to make a real difference. If so, he could understand why they killed.

But he was not there to make an arrest. He had come to accept a bribe, his first, and the feeling came not from his anticipation of redirecting MacWray's life but from the change he was about to make in his own.

MacWray sat behind his desk, his face impassive. A brown paper grocery bag sat on the corner of his desk next to a box of tissues. The top of the bag was folded over several times and was secured with a piece of strapping tape. He directed Pleasant to a chair.

"You want some coffee?" he asked.

"No thanks," said Pleasant.

"Good. I don't have any."

The two men regarded each other wearing similar half smiles.

MacWray indicated the bag. "One hundred twenty-six thousand dollars."

Pleasant nodded, his heartbeat speeding up.

MacWray said, "Before you take it, I think we should get a few things straight."

"Like what?"

"Like what I'm getting for my money."

Pleasant frowned.

"I'm serious," MacWray said. "I've never been extorted by a cop before. I want to make sure we have an understanding."

Pleasant wanted to laugh, but he held his features rigid. "The first thing you need to understand is the difference between extortion and bribery."

"A matter of perspective, I imagine."

"Not really. As I recall, you have offered me a gift, in exchange for which I agree to discontinue my investigation of both your business practices and your, ah, vacation activities. That is what we call offering a bribe."

"And when you take the money?"

"That would be called accepting a bribe. Now, if I had threatened to harm you in some way—which I have not done—unless you paid me a certain amount of money, that might be called extortion. This"—he reached out and lifted the bag—"is bribery. I am accepting your bribe." Pleasant grinned. "Now we're both in trouble."

"Why a hundred twenty-six thousand?" MacWray asked.

"Not your concern."

"I didn't kill him, you know."

Pleasant lifted one eyebrow at the classic criminal response. Even when they were off the hook, most crooks continued to assert their innocence. MacWray's statement meant absolutely nothing. Not that it mattered.

MacWray said, "He fell. We were talking and he just . . . fell."

"Just like that?"

"I watched him fall."

Pleasant stood up and tucked the bag under his arm.

MacWray said, "Something else you should know." He lifted the tissue box to reveal a small tape recorder.

Pleasant stared at the red blinking light on the face of the recorder. He stood with a smirk frozen on his face. His first instinct was to confiscate the tape. Take out his firearm and put it in the guy's face and pocket the tape and that would be that. But Jerry Pleasant had drawn his gun only twice in his nineteen years as a cop, and only when he felt his life was in danger. This was not one of those times.

MacWray shrugged in mock apology. "Just a precaution," he said.

"I understand." Pleasant moved toward the doorway. "See you around."

"I hope not."

Pleasant ducked his head. "You're right, of course."

He headed out through the lobby.

"Friday," he said to Sally, who was on the phone. "I'll call you."

~

Mack followed Pleasant out to the lobby and watched until he got into his car and drove off. He turned to Sally, who had just hung up the phone, and asked, "What did he just say to you?"

"I was on the phone," said Sally. "I didn't hear." She looked away.

Mack compressed his lips. She's lying, he thought. For a moment he felt the terrifying thrill of finding oneself in the midst of a conspiracy, but the feeling left as quickly as it had arrived. Pleasant was paid off, and there was no point in wasting any more mental energy on him.

The phone rang.

"No more calls," he said. "I'm not here. For anybody."

He returned to his office, where he sat quietly for a time, thinking.

～

As soon as he was out of the parking lot, Pleasant loosened the microphone under his shirt, wincing as the adhesive tape tore loose several chest hairs. He pulled out his shirttail and disconnected the wire from the small recorder in his pants pocket and pressed the rewind button. He drove slowly, putting all his thoughts on hold. When the tape had completely rewound, he hit the play button and listened to the conversation he had just had with Mack MacWray.

He came off rather well, he thought. The question now was, which way should he go? It was not every day that life presented one with such a definite and irrevocable choice.

Driving aimlessly, he let his mind explore alternate futures. After a few minutes he could contain his curiosity no longer. He pulled into a McDonald's, untaped the paper bag, and looked inside. It was filled with money. It looked like $126,000. He took out a twenty-dollar bill, retaped the bag, and bought fries and a Coke from the drive-up window.

He could still turn in the money. He imagined himself walking into his boss's office, handing over the tape and the bag full of money. Would it get him anything? Probably not. On the other hand, $126,000 was $126,000. And the fact that MacWray had also taped their conversation was a good sign. There was balance—both sides had gotten what they wanted.

As he ate his fries one by one, he phoned home. Val picked up on the fourth ring.

"Hi honey," he said.

"Is that you, Jerry? Did you know you left the coffeepot on the burner this morning?"

"I did?" Pleasant was surprised. He was usually careful about such things.

"You could have burned the house down, with me in it."

"Sorry." Maybe his subconscious had made him do it.

"All I ask is that you *think*. Just *think*."

"I'm thinking right now, honey."

"Don't forget tonight," she said.

"What's tonight?"

"Don't tell me you forgot!"

"I forgot."

"It's my mother's birthday."

"Oh yeah. I knew that."

"I want us to be there no later than six. I made her a cake."

"A cake? She can't eat." Val's mother had a feeding tube and could no longer talk. Secretly, Pleasant had thought the old harridan's loss of speech a blessing. She'd always hated him, but now she could only scowl and make mewling sounds. It made their frequent visits to the Shady Lake Elder Care slightly less excruciating.

"She appreciates the gesture. I know *you'll* eat it."

"What kind of cake?"

"Poppyseed. It's Mom's favorite."

Pleasant grimaced. He hated poppyseed. All those little black things caught in his teeth.

"Jerry?"

"Yeah."

"What did you want?"

"Want?"

"Yes. You called, remember?"

"Oh. Just checking in, I guess. You know. Checking on my life."

~

"I'm sorry, but Mr. MacWray is not available."

"Sally, this is Paula—Mrs. MacWray."

"Yes, Mrs. MacWray."

"Well? Is he there, or not?"

Sally felt her insides twisting. She hated this. She shrunk her immediate universe to include only the lobby area and said, "He's not here." Her voice sounded wrong.

"Do you know where he is?"

"I'm sorry, Mrs. MacWray."

"Where is he, Sally?"

Sally drew a shaky breath. "I'm sorry. I don't know."

"I know you're lying to me, Sally."

"I'm sorry!"

"Well, did he show up this morning?"

"Yes."

"Is his car there?"

"Yes."

"Has he left the building?"

"No."

"Sally, I want you to listen to me. I am getting in my car and driving over there. You will not tell Mr. MacWray I am coming, and if he leaves, you will find out where he is going. Do you understand?"

Sally felt herself shrinking along with her universe. Another job gone bad.

"Sally? Do you understand?"

"Yes, Mrs. MacWray."

"*Thank* you."

Sally hung up the phone and began to think about two questions: Where might she find a new job? And if Mr. MacWray left the building, how would she ask him where he was going?

38

On her way out the door, Paula grabbed Mack's extra set of car keys. She imagined his car parked in its usual stall. She imagined the bag in the trunk or on the backseat. She would get the money and then she would get Mack, and if she didn't get Mack, then she would have the money. The money was the thing. Even as these thoughts coursed through her mind, she understood them to be twisted, but deep down, gut level, she knew she was right. She had to take care of herself. If he was leaving her she would not let him leave her broke.

She pulled out onto the street and drove too fast through the neighborhood. Every few seconds, with each realization of Mack's infidelity, a new wormhole would open inside her, sucking in bits of Paula MacWray, sending them spiraling away into some hellish dimension. Feeling as though she was being emptied from the inside out, she tried to focus on the physical: her palms on the smooth steering wheel, cars and trees and other physical objects to avoid, the way her lips numbed as she sucked them hard against her teeth.

Scorned. Worse than that. Scorned and betrayed.

She fought the hollowness inside, and a warm shell of self-righteous fury formed around her. There was power in that, and comfort.

~

At 9:22, Mack slung the overnight bag over his shoulder and headed out through the front lobby.

"I'm not sure how long I'll be gone, Sally. I'll call in for my messages."

"Mr. MacWray?"

He stopped and turned back toward her.

"They, ah, when I drove in this morning they were starting work on the freeway. I mean, you don't want to go that way. Depending on where you're going."

"Which freeway?"

She looked away. "The Crosstown?"

Mack nodded. "I'll take 494 instead."

"But I think Crosstown is okay, um, until you get to 35W."

"I'm going to the airport, Sally. But thank you."

He walked out to his car feeling uneasy. Something was going on with Sally. She had seemed stiff and uncomfortable, as if she had been lying to him. But why would she lie about road construction? He wondered whether it had something to do with Jerry Pleasant. Maybe Sally was an undercover cop and he was about to become the victim of a sting operation. No, that was absurd. He wasn't that important. He wasn't even a criminal, not really. Except for bribing a cop. Plus a few minor things, like raiding that safe deposit box in Cancún—but it was his own money he had stolen. No, he decided, Sally was exactly what she appeared to be: a nice kid who answered phones for a living. He got into his car, smelled the leather, started it, and turned on the CD player. He began to drive. By the time he pulled out onto the freeway he had set Sally Grayson aside and was thinking, again, about Rita Larson.

~

Rita walked from the parking lot into the terminal, pretending that she was on a movie set being filmed by a tracking camera. She kept her back straight, her strides crisp and regular, her chin high. Teddy had taught her that if you want to be noticed, you should act as if you know you are being watched. As a rule, Rita was more comfortable when men were looking at her. It gave her a sense of control.

She had never been good at the other end of the formula: that to become invisible you must act invisible. That had never been one of her skills. So she strutted and she was watched, and that was fine with her.

Chili's was in the main part of the terminal, past the security checkpoint. Rita passed through the metal detector without incident. She walked directly to Chili's. It had just opened; they were still taking the chairs off the tables. She chose a table outside, where they would be visible to a maximum number of people. She ordered a Virgin Mary.

~

Paula MacWray looked awful. Her denim shirt was misbuttoned and her hair was tied roughly back in a misaligned ponytail. Her eyes were red and puffy. Her palms hit the edge of the desk and she leaned deep into Sally's space. "Is he here?"

Sally's only coherent thought was to offer the woman some lipstick and a shot of Listerine, but she kept her lips together and shook her head.

Paula pushed herself off the desk and headed into Mr. MacWray's office. Sally noticed that her sneakers were untied. A few seconds later she reappeared.

"Tell me where he went."

"I'm not sure," Sally said. "Maybe the airport?"

"He went to the airport?"

"He said he was going toward the airport, but I don't know."

~

The dreamlike state began as he parked his car on level three. Nine-fifty on a bright, sunny morning, already seventy-five degrees. Airplane and car sounds echoed through the massive ramp. A bearded man wearing nylon warm-ups passed the front of the Mercedes, rolling a large suitcase toward the terminal. The suitcase began to wobble, and a few steps later it tipped over onto its side. The man righted the suitcase and started off again, only to have it tip again a few steps later.

Mack sat in his Mercedes and watched the man, circus music playing faintly in his head, running his hand over the leather bolster of his seat. He felt as if something in his belly was trying to get out. Would he still be driving this car tomorrow, or would he be sitting in a jail cell wearing orange coveralls?

The thing writhing in his gut was fear, but it was not fear of imprisonment. Was it fear of losing his things—his car, his money, his business? His pride? His wife? Or was he simply afraid of losing? His shoulder ached where he had fallen on it outside the Pizza America building. No, not losing. A guy who never loses isn't taking enough chances. Taking chances had made him a success. He had been pushing himself, raising the stakes and the pace at every opportunity. The risk energized him, kept him going. What, then, frightened him?

Weariness settled upon him—a great, soft, smothering hand pressing down, dulling his anxiety. If this was a dream he could sink deeper, slip into an interdream fissure, sleep the sleep of the dead. Or he could wake up. He thought about what Paula had said to him last night: *Whatever you do. Whatever happens. Whatever you've done. Whatever you become, I want you to know I'm with you.*

Whatever you become. That was what really scared him—not evolving into someone new but going back to what he had been. He did not want to lose his momentum, his power, his sense of purpose. The old Mack had possessed none of that. Mack shook his head, throwing off such disturbing thoughts. The man with the suitcases had disappeared; the circus music faded.

He looked at his watch. Rita would be waiting. Maybe he would just give her the cash. She would go away. He could liquidate NuMac. Just close it down. Sell the house. Let the car go. Give Hal and Joyce back their money. Go back to Cancún with Paula. Lie in the sun. Bake together. Get clear again. Or move to Idaho. Get a regular job. Start over. The concept was seductive. Was this how Lars felt when he had fallen? A simple relaxing of the finger muscles, and the burden evaporates. Mack tried to remember Lars's eyes in those final moments. Had there been an act of will involved, or gravity and nothing more?

39

According to the receptionist, Mack had about a ten-minute head start on her. Paula hit the freeway with her foot on the floor and kept the speedometer needle above eighty all the way to the airport exit. There was no way—*no way*—he was going to walk out on her, not with that bag full of money, not with that top-heavy succubus Rita. No way.

Mack had driven his car. He would have to park it. She hoped that would give her time to get into the terminal and intercept him. She entered the airport road and immediately had to choose from arrivals, departures, and parking. She chose departures, drove up the ramp to the passenger drop-off area, pulled up to the first vacant section of curb, and parked, got out, and walked quickly into the terminal. The ticketing and baggage check area was immense, with hundreds of travelers moving in every direction. Where would be the best place to wait for him? There were two ways to get from the parking ramp to the terminal. He would probably take the skyway, which led directly to the ticketing area and baggage check. Paula positioned herself near the escalator from the skyway. He would have to come this way. Unless she'd missed him. Could she have missed him? She started toward the security gates and almost immediately saw him standing a few feet from the end of the line, his overnight bag slung over his shoulder. She stopped. All her thoughts and energy had gone into finding him—her plans from this point forward were clouded. She stepped back behind an information kiosk.

Mack wore a puzzled expression. He stood very still, apparently trying to make a decision or waiting for something to happen. Even over the airport din, Paula could hear herself breathing. Suddenly, Mack turned and headed back toward the exit. Paula watched him get on the escalator. She waited until he reached the top and disappeared into the skyway, then she followed.

～

Mack forced calm upon himself as he walked through the skyway back into the parking ramp. What was wrong with him? What had happened to that razor-sharp mind, that talented and brazen fellow he had become? He had completely misremembered the layout at the terminal. The shops and restaurants were all on the other side of the security gates. At least he'd had the brains not to send his bag through the scanner. Security personnel were notoriously unfriendly to people with handguns in their carry-on bags. The cash inside would not have made matters any easier. Stupid, stupid, stupid.

He walked faster. Rita would wait, but he didn't want to alarm her. He would have to go to her empty-handed and, somehow, get her to accompany him back to his car. And then . . . they would have to see what happened. He would know what to do. He would do something. He would watch himself make a decision and act upon it.

He popped open the trunk of the Mercedes and tossed his bag inside.

～

Paula watched Mack walking back toward the terminal, empty-handed. What was he doing? Why would he carry the bag into the terminal, then walk all the way back and dump it in his car? Was the money still in the bag? And where was Rita Manbait? Her mind flailed at the question but found no purchase. She started after him, then stopped. The bag. She walked back to Mack's Mercedes, opened her purse, took out the extra set of car keys, and opened the trunk. She unzipped the bag, prepared for anything. She opened the top and looked inside. Money. Bundles of bills. There were fewer bundles than she remembered. She reached in and stirred, using her hand like a slow whisk. Her hand struck something hard and cold. The gun. She looked back toward the terminal, motionless, one hand on the edge of the trunk, the other buried in cash, gripping steel. He would not go far without the money. The money would be her leash.

She zipped the bag shut and lifted it out of the trunk.

~

"You're late," said Rita. She looked at his hands. "You're light."

"I'm not walking through security with a hundred grand cash."

"Nothing illegal about cash."

"There is if you're taking it out of the country."

"You're not. I am."

Mack was staring at the photos on the table. "I wish you'd put those away."

"You know which one's my favorite?"

"I don't really care."

"You just can't beat a polar bear rug for dramatic setting."

"You want the money, or not?"

Rita smiled.

"It's in my car," Mack said.

She looked at her watch. "I've got time. Go get it."

He pulled out the chair across from her and sat down.

"I don't have *that* much time," she said.

"I want you to know something," Mack said. "I did not kill Lars."

Rita stared at him; the skin around her eyes tightened.

"I really didn't. He fell."

"He fell," Rita repeated, her voice dead flat.

Mack nodded. "I didn't touch him."

Rita spat out a bitter laugh. "You're even more of an asshole than I thought."

"I know you don't believe me, but it's the truth."

"Is that why you came here? To tell me this?"

"No." Mack gave his head a weary shake. "I came to give you some money."

"Then do it."

"Assuming that I do, what kind of guarantee do I have that I'll be rid of you?"

"If you don't, I guarantee that you won't be. Not ever."

～

Walk with her to his car. Open the trunk. Take out the gun, shoot her in the head, several quick shots, drop the gun, drive off. As clear and quick and decisive as moves in a video game. Easy to imagine, but could he do it? Would it change him as much as Lars's death had changed him? Would he grow colder, smarter, and more competent?

He examined Rita's face, noting several flaws—a wrinkle beginning to appear between her eyebrows, a lack of symmetry in her lips, a tiny red vein threatening to breach the surface of her left nostril. He wondered what she had looked like as a little girl. Before she had met Lars. He wondered whether she had really loved Lars, and he wondered why she had chosen to wear this turquoise dress. The heavy fabric and high collar reminded him of a bridesmaid's dress, only much closer fitting. The slanted shelf of turquoise fabric between her collarbone and the tips of her breasts needed a necklace, or a cutout, or a brooch.

"It's your choice," she said.

Mack nodded. It was his choice, but then it wasn't. The chain of events led to a future both immutable and obscure. He would kill this woman and it would be no more than another stitch in the seam. Or he would pay her and be sewing a different garment altogether. He did not know which way things would go.

He stood up, a bland expression on his face. "Okay. Let's go get your money."

"I'm comfortable right where I am."

"I told you, I'm not walking through security with a bag full of cash. You want it, you're going to have to come with me."

"Not likely."

"What are you worried about?"

Rita shook her head.

Mack said, "Tell you what. Walk out to the front of the terminal with me. You wait there. The money is in a bag in my car. I'll bring it around to the curb, hand over the money, and that'll be that. Okay?"

The corners of Rita's mouth drew in.

"You'll be back on Isla by tonight," he said. If he could get her out of the terminal, keep waving the promise of money before her, maybe he could lure her to his car. One step at a time.

"I'm not going to Isla," she said.

"Then you'll be wherever you want to be."

~

It was gone.

Paula stood by the curb staring at the place where she had left her car. Instead of her little blue Toyota, the space was occupied by a white limousine. She looked down the unloading area and saw her car, attached to the back of a tow truck, heading out the exit. She ran after it, but stopped after a few paces. No way she could catch him. She stood with the weight of the bag cutting into her shoulder and wished pain and horror and death upon the tow truck driver. She would have to take a cab.

She started into the terminal to take the escalators down to the cab stand when she saw Mack coming toward her, a woman in a bright blue dress beside him—*Rita Manbait!*

Paula turned away, her heart thudding, her throat dry, her face white. It was really true. He was going away with Rita Manbait. Things were rolling and twisting inside; she wanted to throw up and shrivel up and beat her head on a rock and explode all at once. From behind the escalators she watched him talking and smiling. She knew that body language—he was trying to convince Rita of something. Rita, her eyes hidden behind oversize sunglasses, stopped near the doors. Mack pointed outside toward the parking ramp—toward the *money.* Or where he *thought* the money was.

She saw Rita laugh and shake her head. He was making her *laugh.*

Paula's mind locked as Mack's hand touched Rita's arm and he guided her out through the sliding glass doors. She could see them— *see* them on a beach, in a restaurant, at a show, in bed, together.

~

Rita said she would wait at the curb. He could not coax her into the ramp. Heart pounding, he formulated a new plan on the spot: he would pull up to the curb, shoot her, and drive off. Once he got clear of the airport, he'd be safe . . . But no, it would not be that simple. There were the photos. She had probably stashed the rest of them in an airport locker. He would have to grab her purse, find the key, and recover the photos later.

"Why are you looking at me like that?" Rita asked, taking a step back. She stared at him, her body tense. For the first time, he sensed how scared she was, and how alone. She had lost everything. He knew how that felt. She had lost her husband, too. At least he still had Paula.

"Don't be afraid," he said. He meant it. There was no point in being afraid. What would happen would happen. He was not in control of events. He had stepped too far out of himself. He recalled Lars's words: *You can't change who you are, Mackie. That's the one thing you don't want to do.*

He wished he knew who he was.

He said, "I—"

A sound sharp and low, like a truck backfiring or a firecracker in a steel drum, slapped his eardrums. Mack's nervous system bucked, but he did not look back to see what had happened. His eyes were on Rita. Somehow she had added a beautiful ruby or garnet brooch to her ensemble. It looked like a flower—perhaps a rosebud—blooming high on her right breast. She took a step back, and he shifted his eyes to her face. Her mouth had fallen open and her eyes were aimed at something above and beyond him. He turned and looked up, expecting to see some sort of flying thing, but he saw nothing. When he returned his eyes to Rita, the rose above her breast had enlarged and sagged. He realized that he was looking at a dark red liquid stain.

The sharp sound came again. Rita jerked and took another step back. A second rose bloomed; her hands came up and clasped the new stain on her belly. She bowed like an actor acknowledging applause, and then she dropped to her knees. He heard the sound of patella striking concrete, and faintly, the circus music started up in his head.

Mack's mind struggled, frantic but sluggish, trying to organize what he was seeing. Irrational theories came rapidly, tumbling over one another: someone had thrown a glass of red wine at her; a small blood vessel had burst in her breast; it was all an act—a thing Rita had cooked up to bewilder him; she had a nosebleed . . . He liked the nose-bleed theory for a fraction of a second, then she pitched forward toward his feet. He danced back; her face struck the curb.

Shouts and a scream, as if from a great distance, then the sharp sound again, three more times, and something hot tugged at his side. He saw people running, and for the first time, the idea that he was hearing gunshots came to him. He turned toward the sounds and saw a jumble of images—cars, abandoned luggage, people moving rapidly, steel girders, glass, the sky—and then his eyes found a woman, forty feet away, denim shirt, crazed eyes, a gun in her hand.

"Paula?" he said. His voice was swallowed by the air.

She held the pistol in both hands, sighting down the short barrel. Mack blinked and saw her father, Hal, just for an instant, in the way her blunt fingers wrapped the grip. He started toward her, pushing through thickening air, memories and connections buzzing and sputtering and snapping inside. He perceived a sequence of events, a collapsed row of dominoes, that had begun at the edge of a cliff on the Island of Women and ended here, now. He had done this to her.

She fired again when he was only ten paces from her; the bullet struck his thigh but he felt only the feeble blow of a child's fist. He kept moving, and as his arms surrounded her, she dropped the gun. He hugged her.

"It's okay," he said.

She said nothing, but he felt her hands flutter on his back, and the shouting and screaming and commotion surrounding them faded as if an invisible shell had formed around them. He looked into her eyes, seeing constricted pupils and bright red spots high on her white cheeks and two puzzled furrows set hard between her eyes, and he knew that she had followed him to wherever he had been.

"I am so sorry," he whispered.

The voices returned. Gruff, shouted orders. But he would not let go.

Rough hands grasped and tore them apart.

40

Ever since the American police officer, Jerry Pleasant, had visited Isla, Jorge Pulido had made it a part of his daily routine, on those days when the breezes were slack and the air mild, to drive his *cochecita* out to the temple and sit upon the crumbling rocks and smoke one of the *puros cubanos* he had found in Teddy Larson's apartment. Often, he would make a dedication. He would dedicate the smoke to a friend's new baby boy, or to surviving the ravages of the latest hurricane, or to fourteen years of marriage. There were many reasons to smoke. On this day, he would be enjoying the last of the *Cohibas*. He would dedicate it to the memory of the wife of Teddy Larson.

He had spoken with police officer Jerry Pleasant that morning and he had learned that Rita Larson had died two weeks ago, killed by gunshot in the city of Minneapolis in the state of Minnesota. Such a beautiful woman. She would be missed. She would be remembered, mostly by men, mostly while they were making love to their less-statuesque wives, but in time even such erotic memories would fade and be replaced. Like the goddess sentinels that had once stood upon the point, they would crumble to rubble and dust.

Jerry had also told him that he would be coming to visit again, soon, and this time he would bringing his new *amiguita*. Pulido looked forward to meeting this woman, who he expected would be very beautiful, though perhaps not as beautiful as the late Señora Larson.

He parked his *cochecita* at the head of the walkway. He carefully lifted the last cigar from the box on the passenger seat, bit the tip off, and placed it gently between his teeth. He got out of the car and hiked up his trousers. The air was still and warm and moist with the ocean, perfect for enjoying a fine cigar. Walking easily, no hurry, he followed the stone path toward the point.

He thought often about the day he had spent with Jerry. So little happened on Isla, Jerry Pleasant's visit had been the highlight of his year. He had never before spent an entire day with a real policeman, a cop from a big city in the United States, just like *NYPD Blue*. And to work on an actual case, that had been exciting, even if it was just a *suicidio,* a man with death in his soul. And the *puros,* a tremendous find, better even than coming across a stash of pesos. Pulido smiled and listened to the crunch of his shoes on crushed rock. That had been quite a day.

His smile remained in place as he neared the lighthouse, then faded as his thoughts turned again to the woman, Señora Larson. To be shot dead, in daylight, people all around. Only in America could such a thing happen. And by a woman, no less, the wife of Señora Larson's lover, who was also shot but lived to cheat again. Pulido doubted that Isla would ever have another like Señora Larson.

It was a good story, and a very old one. Pulido tried to imagine a woman with a gun, shooting. He imagined his wife. Yes, perhaps, if she were jealous enough. If he were bold enough to find an *amiguita* of his own. A faint shiver scampered up his spine. A woman might do anything. This was why handguns were *prohibidos.*

He continued along the path, now flanked by low stone walls. The sun hovered over the mainland, casting an orange glow upon the lighthouse. Pulido wondered, as he wondered each time he visited this place, whether the ancient Mayan gods were still alive, if they were looking down upon him, and if they saw him, whether they cared. Had they seen Teddy Larson jump? Had they smiled or wept as the rocks had shredded his guayabera and crushed his skull?

A tourist couple approached from the point, heading back toward the parking area. The man's shorts rode low on his hips, and a small silver camera bounced off his chest as he walked. The woman was sunburned and tired looking. Pulido exchanged nods with the man as they passed. Perhaps he would have the point to himself this evening. There was a special place on the ruins of Ixchel's temple where he liked to sit, a break in the wall that fit his rear end like an easy chair.

Once, he had come here to smoke and found a young American sitting in his spot. Pulido made the young man leave and took his place. Then his cigar had gone sour and he had felt bad. The man had flown thousands of miles to be there. Pulido knew that he had been unfair. But he would do it again.

As he approached the temple, Pulido saw that he would not be alone after all. A lone man was standing between the temple and the precipice, leaning on a cane and staring into the bloated sun. Pulido took his place on the temple wall and lit the *puro* and observed the man, who stood less than ten meters away.

The man wore a white dress shirt, the kind of shirt you would see on a banker or a lawyer, the sleeves rolled up to just below his elbows. His hands were in the pockets of his dark and heavy-looking trousers. Black dress shoes. His tousled hair was also black, or nearly so, with hints of red. Pulido could not see the man's face, but something in his dress, his posture, and the texture of the hair told him that the man was not Mexican. He was American, but not a tourist. His cane was aluminum. He looked entirely out of place.

Pulido drew a mouthful of rich tobacco smoke. There was not a breath of wind. He let the smoke curl from his mouth up into his nose and past his eyes, blurring the shape of the figure before him. If the man was aware of his presence, he gave no sign. Pulido leaned back and crossed his legs, wishing that the man would leave. How could he find peace in his mind with this motionless stranger blocking his view?

Just then, the man moved. He took three steps toward the brink, then stopped and looked down over the edge. His shoulders rose and fell. Pulido frowned, suddenly intrigued. Was the man intending to leap? Was this how it had been for Teddy Larson? Had he stood at the precipice and considered his action? Had he made one or more false starts before finally flinging himself to his death? Or had he simply shrugged and let himself tip into oblivion?

It occurred to Pulido that he should, perhaps, attempt to stop the man from harming himself. *El suicidio* was a crime, and a mortal sin. But he was curious—would this man actually do it? If he interceded now he would never know. And he might startle the man, accidentally send him to his death when, left to his own will, the man might turn away and walk back to the north end, drink a few margaritas, find some reason to live for a while longer.

The man was very close to the edge now. His shoulders were shaking as if he were crying, but Pulido heard no sobbing. He took in another mouthful of smoke, but neglected to taste it. What right did he have to make this decision for another man? Who knows what lies within a man's secret heart? It was not impossible to imagine a situation when even he, Jorge Pulido, might find it necessary to take his own life.

No, he decided, he would not interfere.

The man inched closer to the edge, to where a tiny gust of wind, or a sudden noise, might send him over. Pulido watched with his mouth open, the forgotten cigar smoldering between his fingers. It was remarkable how long this man could stand without moving. Pulido waited, breathing shallowly. Minutes passed, and then something changed in the man's posture: a slight sagging of the shoulders, a lowering of the chin, a relaxing of the fingers. Pulido swallowed. He knew what he was seeing, and it embarrassed him. The man had come to this place to speak to the dead, but he had not the courage to join them. In a moment he would turn away from the sea and he would see Pulido sitting there and he would be ashamed. Perhaps he would say something. Perhaps the man would want to say what was in his heart, but Pulido would refuse to listen because there are too many unhappy men, and his cigar was burning, and he did not have all the time in the world.

I see his fingers slip and for a heartbeat he is balanced on the narrow rock shelf, arms wheeling, eyes immense with fear, jaw hard with effort, then he is falling backward and hope crosses his face, only for an instant, as if he expects a raft of hands to catch him and gently set him upright once again. The half smile comes and goes in less than a blink; the hands are not there for him. His mouth opens wide and his body eclipses his face and I see the bottoms of his huaraches as he does a sprawling backward midair flip and his head strikes the sharp lava shelf twenty feet below. There must be a sound, but the wind and surf are all I hear as his body twists and continues toward the sea. I lose sight of him. But I am still there, because I am falling, too.

Acknowledgments

Thank you to these daughters of Ixchel: Becky Bohan and Nancy Manahan, for unlocking the secrets of Isla; Marianne Mitchell, for the *español;* Amanda Murray, for showing me a kinder, gentler point of view; and Mary Logue, for everything else.